In Search of Yannelli

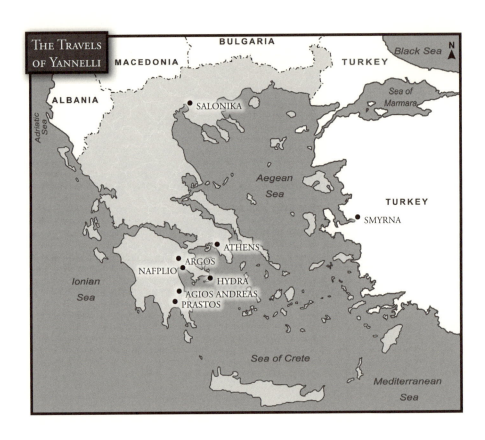

THE TRAVELS OF YANNELLI

BULGARIA

MACEDONIA

TURKEY

Black Sea

ALBANIA

Adriatic Sea

SALONIKA

Sea of Marmara

Aegean Sea

TURKEY

SMYRNA

Ionian Sea

ATHENS

ARGOS

NAFPLIO

HYDRA

AGIOS ANDREAS

PRASTOS

Sea of Crete

Mediterranean Sea

IN SEARCH OF YANNELLI

A SON'S JOURNEY TO KNOW HIS FATHER

MICHAEL J. BAKALIS

HARBRIDGE PRESS

Harbridge Press
Woodridge, Illinois

FOR MY FAMILY.

Table of Contents

Author's Note

I t is probably a rare individual who knows everything about his or her parent's life. We grow from children to adults, go to college or start a job, marry and have children, and suddenly all aspects of our own lives take center stage, and the questions we may have had or wondered about regarding our parents recede into the background. And then, one day, our parents are gone, and the opportunity to ask those questions is also gone.

It was that experience that prompted me to attempt to write a book about my father. *In Search of Yannelli* is a work of historical fiction, and those two key words, *historical* and *fiction* are important to emphasize. It is historical in the sense that many, but not all, of the events chronicled actually did happen, and the references to Greek history and culture are true to the extent that my research could verify them.

But it is also a work of fiction. Bits and pieces and fragments of my father's life that I heard about in passing were just that—bits, pieces, and fragments. His early life was like finding a jigsaw puzzle of 1000 pieces, except that 700 of those pieces were missing. So I have filled in those missing pieces with my imagination of what might have or should have happened, and the resulting book is not a biography but rather a novel. Some of the characters depicted were real, some I have invented. However, even this creative journey into exploring my dad's early life has provided an important sense of comfort, and I feel I know this man I so loved and admired just a little bit better.

MICHAEL J. BAKALIS

Chicago, 1980

In the first pew of the large church Michael sat silently, seated next to his mother, his wife, and his two daughters. He was troubled. Dozens of unanswered questions were swirling in his mind, questions that only now had come to the forefront of his consciousness. But he tried now to not confront them, to clear his head, so that he could listen to the priest and respectfully absorb the solemn liturgy being performed at this, the funeral of his father.

Across the center aisle in the first pew Michael's brother George sat with his wife and his two small children. Everyone was dressed appropriately, the men in dark suits with white shirts and black ties, the women in stylish clothes with dark colors. Within moments of their having arrived at the church and finding their assigned seats, they watched the pallbearers slowly walking down the center isle of the church accompanying the casket that had been placed on a support structure with wheels to allow it to be wheeled into the church. The church was crowded with friends and family, but there were empty pews as well.

This church, the Assumption Greek Orthodox Church in Chicago, was large, and it would take an especially large number of people to fill it to capacity. It was a beautiful structure with stunning stained glass windows depicting various saints and colorful Byzantine style icons surrounding the altar. Gold trimmings accented the columns of the church

1

as well as the round dome that formed the high roof. The dome, as was characteristic of many Orthodox churches, was painted with images of the Twelve Apostles of Jesus who had followed him during his brief three-year ministry. Looking into the altar, the congregation could see the large cross with the representation of Christ, sentenced to death but, as every parishioner knew, soon to rise from the dead after three days and through His sacrifice offer the hope of everlasting life to every believing Christian.

The church had been completed forty-three years before in 1937 in what was known as Chicago's Austin neighborhood. It had, at one time, a church membership of more than two thousand people until the late 1960s and 1970s when the Austin community began to change dramatically. It had once been a completely white residential area with many Greek-Americans and other white ethnic groups living there, but the 1960s and 70s witnessed the area undergoing panic selling. Blocks of homes changed from white to black in a matter of weeks.

Now, in 1980, Austin had become an almost completely black community, and the church became the only Greek Orthodox parish in Chicago remaining in a poor, crime-ridden, minority community. But, for some strange reason, there seemed to be an unwritten agreement or understanding between the church and the people who now lived in the neighborhood. While crime and violence ran rampant in the community, the church itself was never a victim. It had never been broken into or vandalized or had its valuable stained glass windows shattered as were so many other windows in the surrounding homes. If the gangbangers of the neighborhood knew of the valuable metal and gold trimmings that adorned the interior of the church, they never sought to secure those valuable items. Few parishioners now lived in the area, but some still came every Sunday out of loyalty or nostalgia even though for most there were other, safer churches closer to their homes. But for many, and Michael was one of them, this church, the one that on this day would conduct the funeral service for his father John, was a special place that held many memories of his own life.

It was at this church where Michael as a child had attended Sunday school, often times coming by himself on public transportation because the family had only one car that his father used when working on Sundays. As he sat in the church on this day, he thought back to that time, asking himself who today would send their eight-year-old child alone on a Chicago bus to travel a considerable distance to attend Sunday school by himself? He knew he would not allow his own daughters to make such a journey. Times had changed, he thought, and it was not all for the good.

It was in this same church where he had served as an altar boy, wearing the shiny robes given to all who served while they carried the candles in the holy processions and while they attempted to tactfully hold back old women who never understood the concept of standing in line or waiting their turn for anything. This church, too, was where, when he was nineteen years old, he attended mass one Sunday and saw a girl across the aisle with fair complexion and reddish hair and made the decision that he wanted to meet her. When they finally did meet, they both taught Sunday school together at the church and looked forward to the Wednesday evenings when the Sunday school teachers came to the church to receive religious training themselves. Michael and the young girl both knew that they looked forward to the meetings not so much because of their religious devotion but rather because it was an opportunity to see each other. And three years later Michael and his teaching partner were married in this same church, and later their first daughter was baptized here. So there were many happy memories associated with the Assumption Church, but this day was not one of them.

For Michael this was a day he, like every child, knew would come, but he had never really wanted to think about it. But it had come. His father was dead, and this funeral service was for him. His father was not young—he had celebrated his eighty-second birthday this past January—but it really didn't matter how old your father was when he died; it was always a life-changing experience. Michael loved his father, in fact, his father was his hero. He had often said his father was the most important person he had ever known. But as he sat in the church half-listening to the priest conducting the service in Greek, a language he barely understood, his mind raced again through thoughts he had never really had. What did he know about his own father? As he thought about that question, he realized that he knew only a general sketch of his father's life. His father had been born in Greece in a rural village, one of eight children who lived a life of poverty. He had served in the Greek army and then in the 1920s came to America, settling in Chicago because his older brother had emigrated there many years earlier. He was only in his twenties when he came to Chicago and did not marry until he was almost forty. Michael's thoughts were interrupted as the priests voice increased in volume chanting:

> With the Saints give rest, O Christ, to
> The soul of your servant where there is
> No pain, nor sorrow. Nor suffering,
> But life everlasting.

Recovering his thoughts, Michael realized that those few facts were all he really knew. Why hadn't he asked questions of his father? Why hadn't he talked more with him? What had his father wanted out of life? What had he aspired to do or to be as a child or as a young man? What was his family in Greece like? What was their story? What had shaped his thinking, formed his character, and directed his life's

4

journey? Had he loved anyone before my mother? If so, who was she or who were they? Suddenly a rush of new questions entered his mind only to once again be interrupted by the chant of the priest:

Have mercy on us, O God, According to your
Great mercy: listen and have mercy.
Again we pray for the repose of the soul
Of the servant of God, Yiannis, departed this life:
And for the forgiveness of his every transgression,
Voluntary and involuntary
Let the Lord establish his soul where the just repose:
The mercies of God, and the Kingdom of Heaven,
And the remission of his sins: let us ask Christ our
Immortal King and our God.
Let us pray to the Lord. Lord have mercy.

Michael pondered the few words he had understood. What transgressions had his father been guilty of? From the perspective of his son, there had been none. But, then again, what did he really know about his father? Michael turned his head to look at his mother. She was still a beautiful woman, her full thick hair that had been pitch black when he was a child had now turned silver gray. She was not sobbing, but tears were rolling down her cheeks as she wiped them dry with the small tissue in her hand. Michael wondered, what did even his own mother know about her husband? Had he told her anything about his family, his life, his hopes, his aspirations?

As the priest continued the funeral service Michael reached for the small book that was placed in the pocket section of the pew. It was an explanation, in English, of what the funeral service was all about. The service, the book explained, attempts to discuss the event of death to allow us to develop a deeper understanding of life and life's purpose.

The priest's words, the book continued, helps us to deal with the emotions and grief that accompany the loss of a loved one. The prayers and hymns that are put forth speak to the frailty of humans and the misplacement of our concerns for worldly and material things. Our minds were to be redirected to God, His Kingdom, and the blessings He has bestowed upon us. And, most importantly, the explanation in the book reminded the reader that for Christians death does not represent the end but rather offers hope of salvation and eternal life. Again Michael focused on the words of the priest as he spoke:

> *For you are the Resurrection, the*
> *Life, and the repose of your servant Yiannis O Christ our*
> *God: and to You do we send our glory, with You Eternal*
> *Father, and You all Holy, Good, and Life creating*
> *Spirit, both now and ever, and to the ages of ages,*
> *Amen.*

Michael dutifully followed the example of others in the church, making the sign of the cross three times and sitting in the pew again, thinking about the words he had read and heard. If there were such a thing as salvation, would his father be saved? Saved from what, he wondered—eternal damnation in Hell? All these readings and rituals had come to mean little to him. Who made all these things up anyway, he asked himself? Who were these priests or ancient church fathers to say if his father, this good and decent man, would go to Heaven or Hell? Ritual without meaning—that's how Michael had come to view the church. Greeks had been in America for more than one hundred years, and here he was, at his father's funeral, understanding virtually nothing that was being said. When Paul went to convert the Greeks, did he speak to them in Aramaic? Hebrew? No, he spoke to them in the language of those he wanted to influence. This was America, Michael thought, and this church was still somewhere back in the tenth or eleventh century.

Only still half-listening to the chants he barely understood, Michael's eyes focused on the open casket that was placed at the front of the church, just before the altar. The cold and motionless body was the man who had carried him in his arms and driven his old second-hand cars on their family trips to Wisconsin. And it was his now still hands that had worked fifteen and sixteen hours each day at the wholesale bakery at his job and later at the small sandwich shop he had opened. The vision of seeing his father with his head buried in his two hands, totally exhausted from work, would be an image etched in Michael's mind forever. This was how he had allowed his sons to succeed—Michael with his PhD and a career as a university professor and as an elected government official and George with his law degree and his position as a distinguished judge. Maybe that was what his father's life purpose had been. But what talents did his father have that were never realized? At a different time and in a different place, what might his father have become and accomplished in his own right? The questions now seemed to rush at him at a dizzying speed and began to totally consume his thoughts. He now became oblivious to the priest's ongoing chants:

> Blessed are You, O Lord: teach me your statutes
> Give rest, O God, unto Your servant, and appoint
> For him a place in Paradise: where the choir of the Saints,
> O Lord, and the just will shine forth like stars: to your
> Servant that is sleeping now do You give rest,
> Overlooking all his offenses.

Eventually the long service ended. The guest mourners who had come to the church slowly made their way to the front of the church, approached the casket, kissed the icon that was stationed to the side, looked upon the lifeless John for the final time, made the sign of the cross, and slowly exited the church to await the coffin and begin the procession of funeral cars that would methodically make their way to the cemetery in Elmwood Park. Finally, Michael, his mother, his family, and the family of his brother George made their way to the front of the casket. Suddenly a rush of emotion, which he had been able to control thus far, overtook him. Michael stood before his father's body and unleashed a sobbing cry. "I love you Dad," he whispered. "Thank you," and he bent over and kissed the cold forehead of his father. At that very moment he knew that all the questions that had surfaced in his mind on this day had to be answered. The realization came to him that he had to find answers to those questions not only to discover his father but also to discover what made him, Michael, who he was as well. But how could he do it? Where could he start? At this moment of profound grief he had no answers, only the absolute certainty that somehow he had to begin.

• • •

In the weeks that followed their father's funeral, Michael and George spent time with their mother, hoping to help in the transition from having lived with their father for more than forty years to now having to live alone. Their mother had always been organized, and every important document, every insurance policy, and every piece of paper relating to the ownership of their small Chicago house had been carefully labeled, sorted, and filed in folders. While her sons offered to help deal with any of the aspects of what needed to be done following their father's death, their mother really needed no such assistance. However, there was the need to sort through their father's belongings, his clothes, his tools in the basement, his small instruments he used to tend to the garden he so loved. It was a necessary, but inevitably sad, chore.

Every item identified, every shirt, tie, suit, pair of shoes immediately triggered thoughts and memories of the man his wife and his sons had loved so much—but these tasks had to be done.

Michael and his brother arrived at their parents' house early on a Saturday morning a few weeks after their father's funeral. The house was the one in which they had been raised and held good memories for them. Theirs had been a happy childhood. Their father John had worked long hours, and their mother Blanche had done all that a good mother should do—she taught them values, made sure the church was in their lives, showed them love and discipline and respect. She had gone back to work when the boys were in high school because the family needed the money for college. The family was not poor, but neither were they wealthy. They typified the middle- or lower middle-class ethnic working class population that lived in the Austin community on the west side of Chicago. As an adult when he returned to visit his parents, Michael often wondered what those who lived in the rich North Shore suburbs of Chicago thought of his neighborhood as they drove through it. Did they think this is where the poor people lived? Or is this the Greek, Italian, Polish, or Irish neighborhood?

Their house was a typical small Chicago bungalow-style residence. It had a small living room, dining room, kitchen, two bedrooms, and one bath. Their parents had added an enclosed back porch that served as the television room. They had purchased the house for about $14,000. Michael and his brother had shared one of the two bedrooms until the day Michael was married. The one bathroom—with only a bath and no shower—was shared by everyone in the family, and Michael now recalled every time he entered the house how, as he grew up, he had washed his hair in the kitchen sink. The house itself stood on a small lot with an apartment building close on one side and another bungalow-style house close on the other side. The front lawn and the backyard were so small that both lawns could be mowed in ten or fifteen minutes, and a separate one-car garage off the backyard led to the alley. This was the house and the neighborhood in which the two sons had grown from boys to men. And now they had come to take away and discard, in some way, some of their history and cherished memories.

Michael and George sat with their mother at the small kitchen table. Their mother had made coffee and put some cookies on a plate. "How are you doing Mom?" Michael asked as he reached for one of the cookies.

"Oh, I guess I'm okay," his mother answered. "It's just hard getting up every morning and realizing I'm the only one here. The days are long, and time seems to drag. I miss your Dad a lot."

"I think you've got to get active in some clubs or organizations, Mom," George said. Their mother was silent, lowered her head, and finally answered.

"I'm really not good at that sort of thing, and even so I'm really not ready yet. Let's just do what we have to do and go through Dad's things."

"Sure Mom," George replied, "let's do that."

The mother and her sons spent the next few hours sorting through John's belongings, his clothes, shirts, and shoes. In the top drawer of his bedroom dresser was a small pistol.

" I didn't know Dad had a gun," said Michael. "What was it for?"

"Well, you know your father knew all about guns. He has a few hunting rifles in the basement, too."

"I know about the rifles," said Michael, "but what was the pistol for?"

"He just kept it for protection," his mother replied, "and he kept it in the store just in case."

After working first for a pie company, then a wholesale bakery, John had opened a small snack shop and apparently felt the need to keep the gun for protection. The store on Chicago Avenue was located in an area that had undergone rapid demographic changes. It had been a heavily Polish and Ukranian community but had become one increasingly populated by Hispanics and African-Americans. He had never really had any trouble because the community and the customers had come to like and respect him personally. He often gave those who had no money a free hamburger or coffee, and when the neighborhood was ravaged in the aftermath of the assassination of Martin Luther King, Jr., his store had been untouched since he had posted a picture of Dr. King in the store window and his one employee was an African-American woman. Even so, he felt he needed the pistol just in case, and he was a person who knew exactly how to use it.

After going through their father's possessions in the rooms of the house, Michael, George, and their mother went to the basement to go through his tools and other things he had stored there. There was a picture on the wall. It was of John as a young man dressed in the uniform of the Greek army. From the style of the dress it appeared to be of the kind worn by many nations in the era of World War I.

"You know, Mom," Michael said, "I've seen that picture a million times as I grew up here, but I never really asked Dad why that particular one was hanging on the wall. Why did he do that?"

"Your father loved his time in the military. I always thought he would have liked to have made it his career, but too many things happened and he never could do that."

"Mom," George interrupted, "Dad didn't talk very much. He really didn't tell us much about his life, his family, himself. And unfortunately, we never asked. Did he talk to you much about all those things?"

"We talked, we talked about everything, but Dad didn't like to dwell on his childhood or what his life was like before he came to America. I'm not sure why, but I think there were memories that he didn't want to relive. Your dad was a man of few words. He used to say it was a heritage from the Spartan influence. It was the 'laconic' way of communicating—say everything with as few words as possible. I remember your father telling me a few stories he had learned as a child in school. One was that when a Spartan king was asked why the list of Spartan laws was so short, he replied that men of few words require few laws. The other one I remember his bringing up was that at the famous battle of Thermopylae, the Persian King Xerxes offered to spare the Greeks if they would simply surrender their arms. The Spartan leader Leonidas's laconic reply was, 'Come and get them.' So I guess that's the heritage and the history of why Dad didn't talk so much."

"I really wish we had had the time to sit down with Dad and interview him on tape and ask the questions we're now thinking about," said George as he wandered through the small unfinished basement where he and Michael had played as children. As he walked through the basement, he finally came upon a small chest on the floor, almost hidden behind the boxes that had accumulated for more than forty years, "Mom, what is this thing?" he asked, "and why does it have a padlock on it?" Michael and his mother walked toward the old dark brown chest.

"I'm not sure," their mother said as she looked down at the chest with a quizzical look on her face. "I don't think I've ever seen that, or if I have I just didn't pay any attention to it. I guess I just must have assumed Dad just kept some junk in there. Open it, George."

"That lock is pretty thick, Mom," George answered. "I think I'll have to saw through it, because I don't want to break the top of the chest."

For the next two hours the two brothers took turns at sawing at the lock with the less than state-of-the-art tools their father had kept in the basement. Slowly the saw ate away at the lock until finally it snapped open. George opened the cover of the dusty chest. In the chest were a few old photographs of their Dad, his brother Mike, and some people with whom he had become friends in Chicago. There were also photos of him once again in a military uniform as a young man alongside others also in uniforms with whom he had obviously served. One individual appeared to be slightly older, perhaps a commanding officer. Under the photographs in the chest were some other, more bulky things. They looked like books with covers that were scraped and discolored. There were five of these books.

"What are these things?" Michael asked as he slowly lifted the volumes from the chest and carefully placed them on the nearby folding table.

"I have never seen these things," said their mother with a look of amazement revealing that after more than forty years of marriage she had never known about these books and her husband had never even spoken about them. "Open them, Michael, see what's inside."

Michael slowly opened the cover of the book closest to him, careful not to tear or damage the pages, which were dry, fragile, and turning yellow. "I don't know, Mom, it's all in Greek, and the only thing I can read is the date on the top of the page. It's 1908." As Michael then proceeded to look at the other books, the results were the same. Everything was written in Greek, and the only thing he could read were the dates, 1908, 1913, 1915, 1917, 1919, and 1922. From 1913 on, the passages seemed to be longer, and the handwriting evolved from the script of a child to that of an adult.

George then picked up one of the books and slowly turned the pages, looking carefully as though he could actually read what was on those pages, when in fact he could not. But that, thought his older brother, was typically George, careful, thoughtful, methodical, and analytical as he signaled no emotion through his facial expression or his body language. He was a judge, and a very good one, and he was examining the book as though it was a brief with numerous citations of case law. As usual he said little as he looked at the old dusty notebooks. Both brothers had inherited that sparse laconic speech trait of their father, but George even more so. As a child sitting at the dinner table he often said little or nothing at all. As he watched his brother inspecting the new discovery, Michael smiled as he remembered the time their father had looked at George sitting at the dinner table and simply said, "George, say something." George, probably eight or nine at the time, simply looked at his father and quietly and deliberately replied, "I have nothing to say." Michael always recalled that incident with amusement, and he knew that with his brother's intellect and temperament, he would probably someday become a judge. George carefully put down the volumes he had investigated and sat on the old folding chair that had been in the basement for twenty or twenty-five years.

"Mom," he said, "I think these may be a diary or something. Maybe it was Dad's, but maybe it wasn't. Maybe he just kept it, and it was written by his mother or father. Or maybe it's correspondence between Dad and someone else. I think we need to get someone who knows Greek to translate it for us."

"George is right, Mom," Michael said as he again picked up one of the books and looked at the pages that were showing signs of deterioration. "We need to do it now before all these books crack, fade, or simply disintegrate. And we need to do it because maybe these will answer some questions about Dad, his family, and his life that we never asked but I really feel I need to know."

Before they left their Mother's house that afternoon, the brothers decided to have someone translate the entire body of material they had discovered. They contacted the Greek consulate in Chicago, discussed the task with the education attaché who worked there, and made an agreement with her to translate all of the notebooks. The translation of all the books and the typing of the volumes in English was expensive—about $5,000—and Michael and George agreed to split the cost. The project, the attaché said, would take a number of weeks because she would have to do it in addition to her daily work and probably work on it at night and on weekends. It wasn't quite clear to Michael and George what the woman really did all day long, but they accepted her word that she actually did have a schedule to follow.

After two full months the brothers were contacted by the woman doing the translation. She had finished the job and wanted to return the original manuscript and the translated version to the family. Blanche invited the woman to come to her home for dinner. The boys' mother had prepared Greek-style meatballs, salad, vegetables, and potatoes for dinner. For dessert she had baked a devil's-food cake with chocolate on the inside and topped with vanilla frosting on top. She didn't know if the guest would like it, but she knew her sons would. Michael and George knew their mother was an average cook, but not a great one. Her mother, the sons' grandmother, Venetta, was an excellent cook but never let her daughters or sons in the kitchen to learn how to make the various dishes. There were no recipes, of course; Venetta had it all in her head, probably having learned everything herself from whomever she lived with when she came to Chicago from Greece at age sixteen or seventeen. She had come alone, and it always amazed Michael to think about his grandmother's leaving Greece and coming thousands of miles on an immigrant ship by herself. He tried to imagine what that was like and how she did it. She had been an orphan, and someone from her village must have known someone in Chicago who would care for her and raise her to adulthood, so they put her on one of the many immigrant boats coming from southern Europe in the first decade of the twentieth century and shipped her to America. It was all so incredible when Michael thought about it. What must that have been like? Did anyone watch over her during that long voyage? How did she make it through Ellis Island? How did she get to Chicago? Whom did she live with and what did she do when she got here? From the pictures the family had it was clear that she had grown into a beautiful woman, so it really wasn't surprising that she had married his grandfather when she was nineteen. As he thought about all of these questions as well, he again realized how little he knew about his own family—there were so many questions and so very few sketchy answers. Maybe those questions and answers about his grandmother and grandfather could be answered at another time, but right now the woman from the Greek consulate might have some clues and answers to questions he had asked about his father.

The woman from the consulate who had done the translation was named Sofia Economou. She was a woman of average height, probably somewhere between forty and fifty years old. She was dressed stylishly and professionally, and her makeup was carefully done as was her very blond and very colored hair. She had made a career in the Greek diplomatic service and in that capacity had served in Greek consulates not only in the United States but in England, Australia, and South America. She was clearly a highly educated woman and spoke perfect English since she had done her college work in London. The dinner conversation deliberately avoided the translated books, and the discussion centered on her career and how she viewed America and particularly Chicago in comparison to all those many other locations in which she had worked. As coffee and the dessert of devil's-food cake was served, she seemed to enjoy the cake very much and complimented Blanche about it.

"Mrs. Bakalis," she asked, "may I ask you something? I see you go by the name of Blanche, but I am curious, is that your real name? I'm not sure I have ever met anyone of Greek origin named Blanche. I associate the name with something more French."

"Well," Blanche responded, "it is my name, but it is unusual and there is a small story behind it. I was born in Chicago and, as you might guess, grew up from birth to the time I was to enter school in a home where only Greek was spoken. So when I entered kindergarten, which is the first grade children in America enter at age five, I spoke only Greek and knew only a few English words. My baptized name is Panayiota. When I arrived at school and they asked my mother my name, she told them, and they attempted to spell it and pronounce it. Somebody at the school, I'm not sure I really know who, decided it was too difficult a name to deal with, so whoever it was simply gave me the name Blanche and put it on all my official school documents. As I progressed through grade school and high school, I became Blanche. I don't think what happened to me is particularly unique; I believe it happened to many children of immigrants from every nationality."

"I wasn't aware that those kinds of things happened," Sofia said, "and, in some ways it's unfortunate, because Panayiota is such a beautiful name."

"I guess so," Blanche replied, "but I've come to accept it and I really don't think about it."

As everyone completed their coffee and dessert, Michael took the initiative to open the conversation about why Sofia was really present. "Miss Economou," Michael began, "let's talk about the notebooks and what the contents are." The translator finished her coffee, carefully wiped the napkin across her mouth, and began to speak,

"First, Mrs. Bakalis, the dinner and the dessert were wonderful. Everything was excellent, and thank you for inviting me to your home. These notebooks," she continued, "are a journal kept by your husband over many years. If, as you have told me, he was born in 1898, the first entry is dated 1908 when he was a small boy of ten years old. The journals continue, not daily, monthly, or even yearly but rather stop and then resume at a particular year. So the books do not represent a day-to-day diary or journal but rather reflections on some key events in his life that happened in a particular year and that he felt he had to capture in writing."

As she spoke, the family, the mother and two sons, said nothing, almost transfixed upon her every word. Michael leaned forward, his hands resting on his knees and supporting his head, absorbing every word of what the woman was saying.

"Because it is not a daily diary or journal there seem to be many things that are not connected or explained. Your husband and your father was a careful observer and a man of deep emotions and feelings that he was not hesitant to put into words. Was he that kind of person?" she asked.

"He seldom verbally expressed his feelings," Blanche answered, "but it was clear to me that he felt deeply about many things. I could see it in his eyes and hear it in his voice." The identification of their father as a man who felt deeply was no surprise to his sons either. Both had witnessed many occasions when a song, a word, a photograph, would trigger something in his past memory and tears would quickly fill his eyes.

Sofia then continued her report regarding the contents of the notebooks. "The passages," continued Sofia, "cover episodes in his life from about 1908 to 1922, and then they stop. There is nothing, at least in these books, after that date. The only clue I found is that in the final notebook he speaks of preparing to come to New York and then to Chicago to meet his brother Mihali. But there is nothing after that. What your husband and your father describes are periods of joy, happiness, love, but also heartbreak, tragedy, violence, hatred, and the experiences he had in the army and in war. You may not know this, but until he left Greece for America he was known by his family and friends as 'Yannelli'."

"What was that?" asked George, "say that again."

"Yannelli," she replied, and then spelled it out. "Y-A-N-N-E-L-L-I. It is the Greek equivalent of how you Americans call someone named John, Johnny. Yannelli is to Johnny as the formal name Yiannis is to John."

"I never heard that," said Michael as if he had discovered some secret code to his father's life. "But Mrs. Economou, you said he wrote of hatred, violence, and tragedy. What was that all about?"

"I have decided," she said, "not to go into details about those things with you. I don't think it is appropriate for me, and I really don't know all the facts and details. As I said before, there are gaps in the story, and there are not always answers in what your father chose to write. These things are the business of your family and your family alone."

Sofia rose from the table, walked slowly over to her hostess, gently took her hand, and kissed her on both cheeks. She then went to each of her sons and shook their hands. "Thank you for your hospitality," she said. "The originals and the translations are yours, do with them what you will. Your family's story is certainly an interesting one."

When their guest had left, Michael and George sat with the translated copy and began to absorb the contents of the material as men who could not control some insatiable appetite. After two hours of skimming portions of each notebook, they put the volumes down and sat silently looking at each other.

"Can this all be true?" asked George, as his face betrayed a look that combined surprise, shock, and disbelief.

"I don't know," said Michael, "some things are so sketchy, so many statements are made with no explanation. All I know is that I have to find out. I've got to find the truth. I need to know our father."

Greece, 1980

FROM THE JOURNAL, 1908

MY NAME IS YANNELLI. I AM TEN YEARS OLD. I LIVE IN TWO
VILLAGES. AGIOS ANDREAS IS A VILLAGE IN KYNOURIA, ARCA-
DIA. MY OTHER VILLAGE IS PRASTOS, WHICH IS HIGH IN THE
MOUNTAINS. MY GRANDFATHER TOLD ME THAT A LOT OF AN-
CIENT THINGS HAPPENED IN BOTH PLACES. MY FATHER'S NAME
IS CONSTANTINOS, AND MY MOTHER'S NAME IS DESPINA. I HAVE
TWO BROTHERS AND TWO SISTERS.

Michael had taken the translated journals to his house to read them and re-read them more carefully. He had spent hours trying to understand things his father had written that still seemed to make no sense, because he had no context for understanding why the words had been written. The only thing he knew for sure was that he had to put the pieces together and fill in the blanks where his father had written something or felt something and had offered no details and no explanation.

As he read the first page where his ten-year-old father had, in ef-fect, introduced himself and his family up to that time, Michael tried to picture his father as a small boy writing words, probably sitting some-where alone, sharing his words with no one. Why had he decided to keep such a record? Was this unusual for a small boy in a rural village? Had his father ever hoped to be a writer? These and countless other questions kept springing forward in his mind.

He told his mother, his brother, and his wife that he would go to Greece and try to assemble the pieces of what now had become a family puzzle. He phoned his cousin Jenny who lived in Athens to tell her he was coming and to ask her if she would help him in his quest to find answers to the many questions he had following his father's death. And even more questions he now had with the discovery of his father's journal.

Jenny was really a second cousin. Her father, Tassos, was the son of Michael's dad's sister—so Tassos was Michael's first cousin. Tassos was almost twenty years older than Michael as were most of his cousins in Greece, since Michael had been born when his father was forty years old, and his cousins in Greece had been born much earlier when their parents were in their twenties. Tassos was now in his sixties. He had been a general in the Greek army, fought against the Italians and the Nazis in World War II, and was now retired and living with his wife Penelope on a military pension. Years earlier, when Michael was about fifteen, Tassos had come to the United States for some special military training and had visited his parents at their home in Chicago.

Tassos's daughter called herself Jenny because she was a certified tour guide in Greece and wanted a name that could be easily pronounced by the many Americans, Britons, Canadians, and Australians who came to Greece to tour the classical sites or to visit the Greek Islands. She thought that her real name "Evgenia" would just be too difficult for her English-speaking guests. Jenny spoke perfect English and had a deep knowledge of the history of her country, as well as its myths, legends, customs, and superstitions. She also had a keen understanding of the Greek character and "mentality" as she always liked to characterize it. She was now in her thirties, an attractive woman, but certainly not one who would be considered beautiful. She was now divorced and had a young son, Alexander, and the entire family lived in one house in a section of Athens populated mostly by military families and those of retired military men. Michael knew that Jenny, with a complete knowledge of both English and Greek and her vast knowledge of Greece and its history, would be a valuable and indispensable partner in his quest for information and answers.

Michael was teaching at Northwestern University, and since he taught no classes in the summer session, it was the perfect time to make his trip to Greece. Jenny had agreed to accompany him for at least two weeks. Her availability to stay longer with him depended on how good the tourist season turned out to be. If it was a good year, she would have a great deal of work as a guide; if not, she have more time available. Michael and Jenny and her family were not strangers. He had been to Greece a number of times before but virtually always in some business capacity. He had given management seminars in Athens over the past few years and had visited Jenny, Tassos, and Penelope often. But those visits had been different. The first time he came he was almost a tourist himself, and he traveled with Tassos and Jenny to all the classical sights in Athens and the Peloponnese. In the trip he was about to begin, he was not seeking tourist sites but answers and a hope to link Greek history to his father, his family, and ultimately to himself.

The flight from Chicago's O'Hare Field to Athens was a long and tiring one. Michael never liked flying, even within the short distances in the United States. The planes were crowded, the seats were small, and the food he found disgusting. He always prayed he would not be seated next to someone who wanted to be his friend and talk and talk and talk. His usual plan was to get situated in his seat and immediately open a book or take out some papers and appear to be doing work. That usually sent the message immediately to his seatmate that this was a man who was busy and wasn't interested in conversation. It didn't always work, but most of the time it was effective and did the job. Some twelve or thirteen hours later, including layover time in Rome, the plane arrived at the Athens airport, and the passengers disembarked to waiting busses that drove the short distance to the main terminal where Michael, with the rest of the passengers, awaited the arrival of their baggage. The Athens airport in 1980 was a sorry sight. For a country that depended so heavily on tourism as the backbone of its economy, Michael could never understand why Greece had not built a modern, decent airport. It was old, falling apart, and basically an ugly structure. It seemed to belong more properly to some third world country in underdeveloped Africa or Asia. As soon as Michael approached the area for baggage pickup, he once again realized why he had such mixed feelings about the land of his ancestors. He loved coming to Greece but only for a short time. He was an organized individual who like planning, structure, and order, and all three of those ingredients seemed to him to be totally missing in Greece. Few people at the baggage pickup showed any signs of civility, pushing ahead, bumping into people to retrieve their luggage. None offered words such as "excuse me" or "I'm sorry." From the airport the cab drove into Athens to his hotel on Ermou Street. The hotel, where Michael had stayed on previous trips, while small, was modern, clean, and located near Syntagma, the center of the city near the Greek Parliament building.

The drive to the hotel was always, to Michael, a fascinating experience. The traffic congestion was terrible, the motor scooter riders dangerous as they weaved in and out of cars in traffic lanes. It was always amazing to him that in a city of some seven million people, the presence of police was so absent. It explained why drivers could be so bold, drive so fast, and at their convenience park on curbs, sidewalks, or anywhere else that might be available. But he recalled that Greece had one of the lowest crime rates in all of Europe. The cab ride also, however, passed sites that revived memories of this ancient land. Seeing the large Arch of Hadrian reminded one of the role of Greece in the expansive Roman Empire while the drive past the Grand Bretagne Hotel conjured up images of Nazi storm troopers marching in front of that structure that had been taken over by the Germans as their headquarters during the occupation of Athens during World War II.

No site, however, could ever equal the view of the Parthenon, still standing at the top of the Acropolis, a physical reminder of the incredible civilization and accomplishments of these people who had laid the foundations of all of western civilization. The Parthenon, thought Michael, was a symbol of both a blessing and a curse to the nation. The blessing was that the nation could take great pride in the achievements of its ancient past. The past was also a curse as well. For Michael, as an American, the focus was not so much on the past but rather on the future. For the land of his father, the ancient past was a constant factor. It was the glory that was Greece, not the miracle of modern Greece. And one could not be faulted if occasionally one thought that this country had an incredible past, but what had happened to it? Even the work ethic that his father had displayed and his sons had inherited seemed to be absent here. It seemed to Michael that Greece in 1980 was a promise unfulfilled—the Greeks were very intelligent people, but the energy, creativity, and entrepreneurship of the past seemed to have disappeared. Maybe it was the millions who had left the country for America, Canada, and Australia who were the true heirs of the past heritage since they had created a remarkable record of success in a variety of fields in a very short time. Or maybe it was just the beautiful weather, the kind that made you rather not work if you had the choice. Or maybe it was the Turks who had enslaved the Greeks for more than four hundred years who had snuffed out that ancient genius. But as the taxi had approached his hotel, all Michael knew for certain was that he loved visiting the country but could never live here.

After he had checked into the hotel, Michael knew that he needed some rest before he contacted his cousin Jenny. The long flight from the United States to Greece was exhausting, and he never could sleep on planes. So his plan was to shower first and sleep for an hour or two before he met Jenny in the evening. By six o'clock in the evening he was rested and ready to have dinner, although he knew that only foreigners like Americans ever ate dinner at that hour. For Greeks, dinner time was closer to nine or ten o'clock in the evening, even though he could never understand how people could eat that late. By eight-thirty Jenny had come to meet Michael, and they walked a few blocks from the hotel to a small restaurant to have their dinner and to talk about Michael's visit.

"You're looking good, Michael," said Jenny as she reached for the menu on the table.

"Thanks, Jenny, you look good, too. How're your mom and dad?"

"They're good. They both seem to keep busy although neither one really has any set schedule of things to do. I guess that's okay when you're retired." Michael looked at the menu thinking of what to order and wondering if the local population ever tired of Greek food and cooking.

"So, Michael," asked Jenny, "what is this trip all about? What are you looking for?"

"As I told you on the phone, Jenny, when my father died, I realized how little I knew about him, and I felt this great need to know more. And when we found those journals and I read them, I knew I had to come here. There were so many mysterious passages, clues that were never developed and things that seemed like family secrets that I just have to find out more about."

"I've heard some things, too," Jenny said, "but I never really thought too much about them. Maybe we will get answers for both of us. Where do we start?" Michael told Jenny that he wanted to go to his father's village, Agios Andreas, first. He said he wanted to see if anyone there who knew his father could unravel some of the things he had read in the journal.

"My father," said Jenny, "said there were at least two or three old people in the village who would be somewhere around your father's age, who might be helpful. One was a woman named Angeliki who he thought had been a friend of your father's sister. Another was a man named Phillipos who had served with your father in the army. My father wasn't sure, but he thought a woman named Alexandra might still be alive and lives on the island of Hydra."

"So what's her significance?" asked Michael. "Why would I want to speak with her?"

"My father thinks she is the woman that your father loved and probably would have married if he hadn't gone to America."

Michael said nothing, but continued to think about what Jenny had said. The woman my father was in love with? The thought was a strange and difficult one for him to comprehend. He knew his father had loved his mother and that they had had a happy marriage. He had heard once or twice, his mother kidding his father about an old girlfriend in Greece, but he never took it seriously or gave it much thought. Finally he said, "Do you think she is still alive? Did she marry someone? Do you think we can get her last name and try to see if she's alive and track her down? She would probably have to be in her late seventies or nearly eighty now."

"I really don't know," answered Jenny. My father wasn't sure of any of this, but he had heard about it from his mother who probably knew something, being your dad's sister. I assume they must have talked. I guess there's only one way to find out. When do we leave?"

The next morning Jenny drove to the hotel to pick up Michael and begin their drive to Agios Andreas. The ride took about three hours and moved across the Corinth Canal into the Peloponnese. As they drove through the various towns and villages, Michael realized how valuable his cousin would be in his quest for answers. A trained tour guide licensed by the National Organization of Tourism, Jenny was a living encyclopedia of Greek history and geography. The licensed tour guides underwent extensive preparation and training before they were allowed to lead groups throughout the country. The training amounted to the equivalent of a university degree in Greek history, drama, art, philosophy, geography, and mythology. It was a comprehensive education in the history of classical Greece. As they drove through the rugged, rock-strewn countryside of rural Greece, Jenny began to offer to Michael her knowledge of what they were seeing and where they were going.

"Greece," she started, "is divided into regions, prefectures, provinces, and municipalities. I guess these might be the equivalent of speaking of the Midwest, Illinois, Cook County, and Chicago. So where we are headed is the Peloponnese region, the prefecture of Arcadia, in the province of Kynouria, but I think calling the villages of Agios Andreas and Prastos municipalities would be a bit of a stretch."

"You mentioned Prastos," Michael said, "I heard my father mention it many times, but I never quite understood that village's connection to his home village of Agios Andreas."

"I think the answer," Jenny responded, "is that Prastos and Agios Andreas are both your father's villages."

"Both?" Michael asked as he looked at Jenny with a look of confusion.

"Yes, both. Prastos is the village very very high in the mountains, and Agios Andreas is situated in one of the few lowland plains areas of this mountainous region. Virtually everyone would reside in Prastos during the hot summer months and in the lowland village during the winter. But from what I know, the major family house was in the village of Prastos."

The drive from Athens to the villages turned out to be a condensed seminar on Greek history and of the particular region to which they were headed. Jenny had obviously researched the region both for personal reasons as well as part of her training as a tour guide. Michael listened intently as Jenny conveyed her knowledge of their destination.

"As you can see from the window," Jenny began, "Greece is a very mountainous country. Only about twenty-five percent of the land is arable, and about forty percent serves as pasture. So a booming farming economy is very hard to create and sustain here. So our family, like most others, lived by harvesting olives for oil and raising sheep. And you can see why from ancient times the Greeks became a colonizing seafaring people and were commercial traders. They really had little choice if they were to survive."

As they drove by a roadside gas station displaying a large Greek flag, Michael looked at the sign written in Greek. "I really wish I knew the language," he lamented, "but I'm glad so many things here are also written in English."

"The English," Jenny responded," is because of the importance of tourism here. With our alphabet, no one would be able to get around if everything were in Greek."

"What do we know about the language, Jenny?"

"We know it's Indo-European in origin, and it has been used since around 2,000 B.C. but, of course, it has evolved and there have been some changes. And by the way, just for your information on Greek society, the huge flag that we just passed is symbolic of the importance of the sea I just mentioned. The blue and white stripes represent the sunlit waves of the sea that surrounds three-fourths of the country. And I guess you can figure out that the cross is representative of the fact that this is a Christian nation of Greek Orthodox faith. You know the Greeks became Christians early after St. Paul did his missionary work here, and then the Roman Emperor Constantine became a Christian himself and moved the capitol to Constantinople in 330 A.D. I guess you could never have something like that cross in your flag."

"Hardly," Michael responded. "First of all, the idea of the separation of church and state is a key American idea and value, and we are such a multicultural country that no specific religion can take preeminence, although we are still a predominantly Christian nation."

"We would never admit it," Jenny said, "but Greece is a multicultural nation, too. The fantasy is that we are all direct descendents of Herodotus, Socrates, Plato, and Aristotle, but anyone who studies history knows differently. No one in Europe is pure anything."

"Do we know much about the ethnic origins or mix of peoples in Arcadia?" Michael asked as he continued to be struck by the beauty of the huge mountains and the pockets of deep blue sea water they passed on the highway.

Jenny answered with an almost scholarly lecture on the area of Arcadia. She spoke of archaeological finds of ancient tribes that had inhabited the area and of the Arcadians who were the founders of the Mycenaen civilization who had come to the area sometime around 1600 B.C. Evidence of this group had been identified at Agios Andreas and surrounding villages. "It's interesting," she said, "that the physical characteristics of the current inhabitants of the region have been analyzed, and the conclusion was that the people there constitute a group going back thousands and thousands of years. Actually, archaeologists now believe that Greek tribes have been living in this area since Neolithic times."

"It's amazing," said Michael. "You know, the first time I ever visited my dad's village a few years ago, what immediately struck me was that the people there didn't fit the standard view of what Greek people look like. My Dad himself was very fair-skinned with light brown hair and slate gray eyes, the village was filled with many blue-eyed, fair-skinned, blond people. I even saw, for the first time in my life, a young boy with flaming red hair, the kind I usually associate with the Irish."

"Well, even that isn't totally impossible," smiled Jenny, "but I'll tell you about the Celtic invasion of Greece later. You know the entire Balkan Peninsula has been invaded by a variety of peoples. In the third to first century B.C. the Celts were there, Germanic tribes in the third century A.D., and the Slavs in the fifth and sixth centuries A.D. Some historians believe that the original homeland for these Slav invaders was even north of the Danube, and then, of course, during the Ottoman Empire Greece was occupied by Turks for more than four hundred years."

"I know about the Turks, of course," said Michael, "but I have also read some things about the Dorians in Greece."

"There's a lot of controversy about them," said Jenny. "Some people call it the 'Dorian Invasion,' others the 'Dorian Migration.' We believe these people moved into Greece from the north, from the Epirus and Thessaly areas of the Balkans at about 1200 B.C., but some historians think they originally came from even farther north. As they moved into central and southern Greece, they intermingled with the indigenous people and left a major stamp on Sparta and the entire area where our family is from. In fact, the Dorian impact was so strong that a different dialect was spoken by the Dorians and is still spoken by some today."

"You know," said Michael, "that is probably the dialect my father knew. He told me it was different and was called 'Tsakonika.'"

"That's exactly what it's called, and your father and my grandmother did speak it. We will probably meet some people who speak it when we get to the village," said Jenny. Jenny sensed that Michael had heard enough of ancient history and archaeology for a while, and they continued their drive through the mountains, both silently observing the incredibly beautiful landscape. Michael stared out the window thinking about all that Jenny had said. He thought about how distant and unclear not only his origins but also those of everybody were. Maybe, he thought, he should do one of those DNA tests that National Geographic and others do for about $100.00 and see if they could determine some different strains in his genetic background. But what if it turned up some surprises, he thought. Well, everyone would have some surprises, he guessed. After driving another hour, Jenny said that they were approaching his father's village.

"We're coming to the great metropolis of Agios Andreas, St Andrews, to you Americans, population about 1100 people," she said smiling. "I have called ahead and we are going to speak with Mrs. Angeliki Soukis, a lady about eighty-eight years old who knew your family and was a very good friend of your father's sister, Katerina. She'll probably be able to tell you a lot, but when I talked with her, she said that she would be happy to talk but said there were some things she didn't want to talk about. I'm not sure what she meant. But, before we meet her, I also want to take you to your father's mountain village, Prastos. I think you'll find some answers you are seeking there, but also you will discover some new questions."

Michael was only half listening to Jenny. His mind was on what she had said a moment before, that the old woman they were to meet had things she didn't want to talk about. What did that mean? Why would she not want to talk about whatever those things were? And then he remembered another thing that puzzled and troubled him. When he had looked through the pages of his father's journal, it ended in 1922, and the final paragraph read:

This is only part of the story. Some things
we should forget. Every family has secrets.
We are no exception.

Jenny drove the French-made car past the sign signifying that she and Michael were entering the village of Agios Andreas. It was an attractive village with white houses and rooftops painted mostly in blue. The streets took on a somewhat winding path, which all eventually led to the central area of a large open space in front of the village church. Directly opposite the church was the small office of the village mayor. The Greek national flag waved briskly from the pole that stood in front of the mayor's office.

"This is the center of the village, Michael. Every evening, in good weather, the residents come here for coffee, games, and mostly conversation. That, of course, is the church. The priest these days often goes among two or three villages because of the shortage of priests but mostly because so many villages have lost population but still have a few hundred or so people living there. There is always a church in each village, mostly standing virtually empty."

Michael had visited the village once before but had never been with anyone with whom he could discuss various aspects of village life and ask questions about village life and customs. "Are these priests full-time clergy?" he asked.

"Some are, but many do other things to supplement their incomes so that they can provide for their families."

Michael had always believed the Greek Orthodox Church had many problems, mostly because it had never left the Middle Ages and was obsessed with ritual but short on relevance and meaning for twentieth century Americans. However, he did at least commend the Church for having married clergy, who could raise children and in some way relate to the lives and issues of their parishioners, even though a married priest could never advance in the hierarchy to be a bishop or archbishop since those men were theoretically celibate. It was at those higher levels, he always suspected, where many of the gay ones were probably situated.

"But when your father and my grandmother were growing up here," Jenny said, "the village was larger, and there was a full-time married priest here. I think, even then, though, he had some pastureland where he raised sheep to be able to support his family."

"And what about the mayor? That can't be a full-time job," Michael said, "What does he do all day?"

"Probably not much, but I'm not sure. I met him once, and he is a very nice man."

"Jenny, it's only mid-afternoon, and the place seems deserted. I still have seen only one young child in the streets, riding his bike."

"Well, it's a pretty hot day, and this is what the Mexicans call siesta time. It's really too hot to do anything, so you might as well sleep now and stay up later when it cools off."

"So why are we out?"

"Basically, because we have nowhere to go to sleep. That's why we're driving around now, and later we'll come back to the village when it gets more lively. First, we'll drive past some archaeological sites. Remember this village has very ancient roots and, as I mentioned before, is identified by ancient writers as the community of Anthene, so its history goes back thousands of years. After that, we will head up the mountain to your father's other village, Prastos."

Jenny drove past some of the sites that archaeologists had dated back to the time of Agamemnon and the Mycene period. Mostly they were remains of walls that had been parts of houses. Michael had always been fascinated and impressed by the way archaeologists could come upon sites like these, minutely and painstakingly sift through dirt and rubble, and identify artifacts that had value and meaning. He was sure that his untrained eye would probably throw away things that professionals would view as amazing finds and treasures.

"What we don't know," said Jenny, "is when our family ancestors first came to this region. There is a man, a cousin I think, who has traced the family history back to the eighteenth century. I don't know how he did it, but he makes a convincing case that it is accurate. Before that time, he says, the trail runs dry."

"The eighteenth century!" Michael exclaimed, surprised that the family tree could be identified even that far back. "That's the 1700s, that's amazing. I'd like to meet him if we have the chance."

"I'm sure we can look him up. He would be glad to meet you and share his findings."

The drive up the mountain to reach the village of Prastos was treacherous. The road seemed to be wide enough for only one vehicle, and Michael wondered what would happen if another car was making its way down from the village at the same time—as they were driving up! The road had no barriers or fences protecting the driver from the edges, and a fall would result in sure death if the car slipped or struck a rock or in some other way go out of control. Michael looked out the window and stared down, then quickly and deliberately did not look out and down again. He became visibly nervous, as they drove up a never-ending road which took them higher and higher away from safe ground.

"Jenny," he finally said, "is there some monastery around here or something? I see a number of crosses at the side of the road."

"There is no monastery," she answered deliberately looking straight ahead as she drove, not daring for even one second to take her eyes away from the narrow road. "Those crosses are put there by families of those who have had accidents at that particular spot and have gone off the road."

"Oh," said Michael softly as he slowly felt his stomach turn. He didn't speak again until they finally reached the entrance to the remote village. Entering the village, he felt that such a ride would make every atheist a devote believer in God. He took a deep breath and finally felt as if he could relax.

The village was different from Agios Andreas with many multi-storied homes with white stucco exteriors. The walk through the village created a strange and eerie feeling. No one seemed to live there. It seemed to be a ghost town. "Where is everybody?" Michael asked. "Does anybody live here?"

"It's almost a ghost town," Jenny answered. "Actually there are only a few dozen people living in the entire village. Back when you father was a boy, there were about nine or ten thousand people living here. About fifteen years ago there were about five hundred people who lived here, but now it's down to twenty-five or thirty people. Things change; it's just too remote, and the jobs for people are in the surrounding areas of the villages below. At one time, however, this was an important place. It had been the capital of Tsakonia, the region where descendents of invaders from the north had settled in Greece and spread their particular dialect called Tsakonika. At one time, in this village, in Agios Andreas, and in a number of nearby villages, this was the language everyone spoke. It is one of the most ancient languages in Greek history and is still spoken by a diminishing number of people, some of whom you'll probably meet."

"Do we know its origin?" Michael asked.

"Well, there is a great deal of controversy about this and no one has yet given a convincing definitive answer. As I told you earlier, sometime around 1200 B.C., Greece became populated by people from the north, called Dorians. Most scholars believe they came from the Balkans, particularly from Epirus in the west and Thessaly in the east. There is some thought that their origins are from even farther north in Europe before they inhabited the Balkans. It's interesting to me that they inhabited the same geographic area that the Celts later did in the Balkans. And remember that the Celts also invaded Greece and the Peloponnese. Whether the Dorians and the Celts are related, no one knows, but I think there are some logical historical explanations for why you saw so many blue-eyed blonds and even real redheads in your father's village."

"But what do these Dorians have to do with the unique dialect we just talked about?" asked Michael, with an expression in this face that conveyed both confusion and fascination.

"Most scholars are pretty certain that the Tsakonika language and dialect was the language of the Dorians and has survived even until today. But here's where it really gets interesting to you and me. The area of Arcadia occupied by the Dorians was called Tsakonia, and the most important center was the village we are standing in right now, Prastos. It also included Sparta, and the Spartan-Dorian influence is strong and evident in Tsakonia. And Prastos had a special role in this area. During the time the Turks occupied Greece, this community was one of the richest in the entire Peloponnese. The merchants here had acquired special trading rights from the Ottoman Empire and did a brisk and lucrative trade with Constantinople. What the Turks didn't know was that in the late eighteenth and early nineteenth centuries the money the inhabitants were making off the Turks was used to finance the Greek Revolution against the Ottoman Empire, which eventually led to Greece's liberation and independence."

Michael thought for a moment, rubbed his hand across his forehead, and seemed as though he had made some connection in his brain. "You know my dad's family sent him to Constantinople to go to school for a number of years. He never really said much about it, but I know some branch of the family had moved there many years before. I always wondered how his family, who were poor, could afford to send him there. Maybe at some earlier time they weren't that poor or at least their relatives in Constantinople weren't poor."

"That could be," replied Jenny. "It could be that the family in Prastos became poor after one key event happened during the time of the revolution. Being high in the mountains, most Greek villages located there were relatively safe from Turkish invasion, but Prastos was different. Apparently when the Turks found out about the role of the town in financing the Greek revolt, they took their revenge, and Abrahim Pasha, who was actually from Egypt, led his troops into Prastos, sacked the city, and left it virtually uninhabitable for decades. That's when most of the families fled down to other villages like Agios Andreas, Leonidion, and elsewhere. Whatever wealth was being generated by Prastos was now gone, but at one time in the past, this community played an important revolutionary role. In fact, there is an old song with lyrics that reflect this history. Part of the lyrics are, 'In Constantinople they make money and in Prastos they turn it into warships.'"

Michael and Jenny continued their inspection of the town by walking up and down the deserted streets. The town square was empty, the only presence being an old deteriorating statue of a hero of the Greek Revolution. The church remained in decent shape, but it was closed since no priest is available for the few dozen who still inhabited the community. Eventually they did come across a solitary figure, sitting on a bench and smoking a cigarette. Jenny greeted him. "Hello, mister, the gentleman and I are just visiting. Our family comes from here, and we are looking for the house in which his father and my grandmother lived. Can you help us?"

The man, dressed in a pair of brown pants, a white shirt, and wearing a Greek fisherman's cap, drew heavily on his cigarette, slowly exhaled a cloud of smoke, and looked the visitors squarely in the eye. "Hello," he said softly, "my name is Pavlos Michalopoulos, and who are you?"

"I'm Jenny Berdalis, and this is my cousin, Michael Bakalis. He is from America and is here to find out more about his father."

"Bakalis? Bakalis?" said the man, "I do know that name, and I know Bakalis from Agios Andreas sometimes come here. Come with me, I will show you and your American friend the family house."

As the three walked through the empty streets, Michael carefully observed every aspect of the surroundings. This, he thought, is where my father grew up and where he lived with his family, where he played as a child. It was a strange emotion he felt but a satisfying one as well. He was beginning to feel a sense of connection to his history that he had never felt before. Looking at each house he passed, he observed some houses had a similar image over the entrance to the house—a cross with what seemed to be a faded image of a blooming red flower, perhaps a rose. The local man, happy to have some visitors with whom he could talk, gave the two strangers a detailed tour of the village, describing the few people who still lived there as well as offering information about which family had occupied a particular house in past years according to the official town records, written histories, and oral traditions. Finally they came upon a grayish, stucco two-story structure. The man stopped, turned to Michael and Jenny, and said. "Here, here is the old Bakalis family house."

Michael said nothing; he simply stood and stared at the building. Emotion overcame him, and tears came to his eyes, as thoughts of his father and his father's family raced through his head. He continued to remain silent and began a slow walk around every inch of the house and property. Seeing a carving on the wooden railing that led to the front door, he suddenly stopped. The carving read, "Mihali—1898." "That carving," he said, "that's my Uncle Mike, my father's brother! He must have been only six or seven years old when he or somebody, did that. That's amazing." And as he continued his inspection of the house, he again saw over the front door the same faded image he had seen on three or four other homes in the village—a cross with blooming red roses placed on the location where the horizontal and vertical arms of the cross met. "There it is again, that cross with the roses. Why is it on our family house, on some other houses, but not on others? What does it mean?"

Their local guide said he didn't know what, if anything, the image signified, and Jenny, for once at a loss for historical knowledge and words, could offer no help either. "I don't know, Michael. I have never come across anything like that in my studies and training," Jenny replied. But the image, for some reason, stuck in Michael's mind.

As dusk began to envelop the town, Jenny thought it wise that they head down the narrow road from the mountain community before darkness set in. They thanked the local man and headed in the car toward the city of Nafplio, where they would spend the night before going to Agios Andreas to meet the elderly woman who hopefully could supply more pieces to what Michael increasingly viewed as a puzzle with still many missing pieces. He was, as yet, not even close to seeing the totality of the picture. The stay in Nafplio was necessary because there were no hotels in Agios Andreas, and Nafplio was a beautiful and lively place. It served as the first Greek capital of the Greek nation after the revolt against the Ottomans, and it was beautifully situated next to the sea. The architecture of the community clearly showed the influence of yet another foreign invasion, that of the Venetians. Michael and Jenny had dinner at an outside restaurant surrounding the main square, and each then went to their rooms to rest for the next day's adventure. Michael could not sleep, his mind was racing through what he had seen and heard, and he tried to imagine the life of this father in every place they had been.

In the morning they drove to the village of Agios Andreas to meet with the elderly lady Jenny had said knew the Bakalis family. Her name was Mrs. Angeliki Soukis. The old woman lived alone in small house with the barest of necessary furniture. She had invited Jenny and Michael for coffee and had baked some sweets that had been placed on the table along with some bread and feta cheese. Mrs. Soukis was dressed all in black except for a white sash she wore around her waist. Her face and its lines displayed all of her eighty-eight years. Her hair was a white-gray and pulled back to form a bun that rested on the back of her head. She spoke no English so Jenny provided the translation between the woman and Michael.

"Thank you for seeing us," Michael said. "I know Jenny told you I am in Greece to find out as much as I can about my family and particularly about my father, John Bakalis. I hope you can help. Yesterday, we visited Prastos, and it was very enlightening. Did you live there as a child?"

"I did," the old woman answered, "and our home was very close to that of your family. I knew the whole family well. Your grandfather raised olives but also had the local grocery store, an occupation the family was engaged in for generations. I don't know if you know this, but your name, Bakalis, simply means grocer, so that line of work seems to go back many, many generations in your family."

"My father did tell me about the name," Michael said, "but I never thought of it as being an occupation that went back generations."

"Yes, that's how many Greek surnames originated. Your grandfather was often gone from the village for long periods of time, sometimes months doing business and trading to stock his small store. Your uncle,

Mihali, left for American at a very young age, maybe fourteen or fifteen years old. He did come back a few times, but I rarely saw him and didn't know him at all. Your father's brother Christos at one time left the village to become a career soldier but gave up that idea and returned. The other brother, Manoli, was very religious, and I remember when he was a young boy he was always at church with the priest. But he never did become a priest himself, and he lived in the village with his family when he was grown. Your father's sisters, Katerina, Stamatina, Erini, and Maria I knew well when I was young. Stamatina married and had children, but her husband died in an accident on the mountain road up to Prastos. Erini and Maria were much younger than me, so I really didn't know them well. Both eventually, through your father's help in providing a dowry, did marry and settled in nearby villages with their husband's families." The woman paused for a second and then slowly and softly said, "Unfortunately, your father's sister Katerina died very young. She was only nineteen."

"How did she die, Mrs. Soukis," asked Michael, "and why so young?"

Mrs. Soukis paused again. "I really would rather not talk about it. She was my closest friend, and I become very emotional about her."

Jenny then interrupted. "Michael, she says you must have other questions, and she would like to be of help on those if she can." Michael saw that the subject needed to be changed, so he took the opportunity to see if the woman might know about the rose and cross images on some of the houses in Prastos.

"Mrs. Soukis, when we saw my father's home in Prastos, there was a image over the door. It was badly faded, but I could tell it was that of a cross with blooming red roses at the center. It was not on all the houses, but it was on some. Do you know the significance of these images?"

"I know a bit about it, but I have a book written by one of our residents here that explains more. Jenny, could you please get the old book with the green cover over there and see if it helps answer Mihali's question." Jenny looked through the book and scanned the pages to see if any of it was relevant to the question Michael had asked. She noticed the book had been written by the same individual who had traced the Bakalis family tree back to the eighteenth century. Finally she found some pages that discussed the issue, and she took a few moments to read what was written.

"It says that when the symbol appeared on a house it signified that the family was a member of some secret fraternity or society."

"Secret society? What kind of secret society?" Michael asked as he moved closer to look at the book that was written in Greek and that he could not read. Jenny continued reading.

"It says the historic symbolism of the rose has meant 'silence.' The phrase 'sub-rosa,' which means 'under the rose,' means to keep a secret. In ancient Rome, a rose would be placed on the door of a room where secret matters were discussed. Some believe it's associated with the Rosicrucian brotherhood founded sometime in the thirteenth and fourteenth centuries. They were a secret order that had an invisible college of mystics who were preparing for a new age of Christianity. The group seems to have had some early connections to the Freemasons."

Michael listened intently to Jenny's summary of what she was reading. It still made little sense. What did all this secret stuff have to do with families in Prastos and particularly his family?

"Others, this book says," continued Jenny, "believe the rose represents silence and the cross represents salvation, or that the rose represents the blood of Christ who died on the cross for our salvation. It also says here that the homes that displayed the symbol were families that were helping to fund the Greek revolts of the nineteenth century and used this symbol to signify that they were part of a secret group that was raising money for the revolt against the Turks. If the symbol does have religious meaning, it might mean that these were Christian families doing what they could to overthrow the Muslim enslavers."

"So our family members were revolutionary conspirators?" Michael asked.

"It's very possible," Jenny replied. "I do know from my studies that there was a secret organization of Greeks living in Russia and Constantinople called the *Filiki Eteria*, which you can translate as the Friendly Society or the Company of Friends. Their purpose was to raise money to eventually incite revolution against the Turks. They started out in Odessa, which was an important center of Greek merchants who lived in Russia. They had an elaborate system of secrets and codes and also seem to have had connections to the Freemasons. I guess we will never know for sure, but it could be that the homes that had the symbol over their doorway could have been affiliated with the revolutionary group, the *Filiki Eteria*." Jenny put the book back on the shelf. "I'm not sure what all this means, Michael, but the evidence seems to point to some kind of family affiliation with a movement to overthrow the Turks."

"Sort of like the Committees of Correspondence in the American Revolution," offered Michael with a smile, then quickly recognized that Jenny had no idea what he was talking about. Maybe one of the family was the Sam Adams of Greece, Michael thought. When he and Jenny had finished their examination of the book and the mystery of the rose symbol, Michael again turned to Mrs. Soukis.

"Mrs. Soukis, I have come a long way to do something that is very important to me. I loved my father, he was my hero in many ways, and I need to know him and about those things that made him who he was. I truly respect you and your feelings and memories, but I am asking you to please help me. Tell me what you know about my family. Tell me the good and the bad, I need to know."

The woman put her head down and slowly lifted it until her eyes set on Michael's. "There are some things about you, Mihali, that remind me of your father. You don't look like him, but something, something about the way you stand, the way you speak reminds me of Yannelli. You know, even though he left here as a young man, he was not forgotten. People always spoke highly of him and respected the kind of man he had become. He went through much in his younger years, saw things and heard things I'm sure he would have rather not seen and heard. But all those things developed his character and made him the good man that he was. He was eight or nine years younger than his sister Katerina, but they were very close. She had always looked after him, and he loved to go with her to hunt rabbits in the open fields." The woman now hesitated, thinking carefully if she should say more. Michael said nothing, waiting to see if the woman would continue. Wiping from her eyes what appeared to be a single tear, she finally began speaking again.

"All right," she began, "I will tell you what I know, Mihali, I will tell you everything. But first I must explain to you some things that you may not be familiar with. Your grandparents had eight children, and while they were not destitute, they like most of us were poor. There was little money to send their sons to adequate schools, so only your father was able to go to Constantinople to be schooled and even then for only a short period of time. But to have four daughters was a serious problem for a family. The goal was to have them married and raising a family, but it wasn't quite that simple. The girl's family had to provide a dowry to the prospective groom and his family. Let me first explain some things as they were years ago, particularly about the institution of the 'proika.'"

"The 'proika,'" said Michael, "what is that?"

"It's the dowry," answered Jenny, speaking quickly so the woman could resume her story.

Mrs. Soukis went on to explain the importance of the dowry. She said that it was part of a male-dominated society that had been so strongly prevalent generations ago and whose legacy could still be seen today. The dowry was an economic resource a girl could bring to a prospective husband and to a new union. It was not simply an arrangement between individuals but rather between two families. For many young men and women, but certainly not all, this was a key element in whether a marriage could be arranged or even take place. The dowry could consist of money, land, a home, or even things such as blankets, rugs, and cooking utensils. Custom had it that the eldest daughter was supposed to be the first to marry, followed by the next eldest. Mrs. Soukis explained that brothers who were near the age of the marriageable sisters were expected to wait until the sisters had found an acceptable husband.

"Mrs. Soukis," Michael interrupted, "it sounds like a strict business deal. Were there feelings involved between the two people?"

"Nothing like the love stories of your American movies," she replied. "The family reputation was important as was the reputation of the respective bride and groom. Looks sometimes mattered but not often. The idea was that the prospective couple would learn to be compatible, respect one another, and possibly even learn to love each other. It's how your grandfather and grandmother were brought together, as were your ancestors for many generations before them. And finally what is really important for you to understand is that for a poor family who had many children, especially daughters, to not be able to provide a dowry probably meant a daughter would never marry. Now let me tell you about your family and about your beautiful Aunt Katerina, whom I loved as a sister...."

Katerina, 1908

FROM THE JOURNAL, 1913

I AM VERY SAD. THIS YEAR WAS NOT GOOD.

SOMETHING BAD HAPPENED TO MY SISTER, AND I CANNOT TALK
ABOUT IT. I AM GLAD I AM GOING TO SCHOOL IN CONSTANTINOPLE.
MAYBE THERE I CAN FORGET.

Evangelos Adamidis, like most of the residents of Prastos, was
a man who earned a modest living raising sheep and tending
to his olive trees. He was known in the village as Vangeli. He
was a tall and heavyset man, his round face partially covered by a
beard and mustache that now bore traces of graying hair. He had
lived in the village for all of his fifty-five years, married there and
had one child, a son now aged twelve. A year and a half earlier
his wife had died of tuberculosis, a disease that was widespread in
many villages partly because of the lack of care given to the sanitary
conditions of the water supply. His aging mother lived with him
and now had the responsibility of caring for both her son and
grandson, although she was in poor health and had just reached her
eightieth birthday. Vangeli did his best to provide and care for both
his mother and son, but he found it increasingly hard to do so. His
mother suffered from a severe case of arthritis and the mere task of
walking through the house became more and more arduous. His

son was also becoming more difficult to discipline and control since his wife had died. As a father, he tried his best, but there was only so much he could do, since his work kept him out of the home for too many hours each day.

He was friends with Costandinos Bakalis, and before his wife had died, Vangeli met Costandinos at the coffeehouse at the village center two or three times a week to talk about their families and friends and to inform each other about things one might know that the other didn't. It was at one such coffeehouse meeting on a hot summer night in July that the two friends met to catch up with each other's lives.

"Vangeli," said Costandinos, who was known as Costa by those who knew him well, "you don't look so happy. I know the past year since you lost your wife has been hard for you. How are your mother and the boy?"

Vangeli raised the small glass of thick Greek coffee, slowly sipped a tiny portion, and gently placed the cup back in its saucer. "Costa, I need to talk to you about something important and confidential. I am speaking to you as someone who has been my friend since we were boys, And as someone who needs your help."

"What is it, Vangeli? You know I am your friend, and we can speak about anything."

"I can't do it anymore," Vangeli said as he thrust is head into the palms of his two hands. "I just can't do it anymore. My mother is virtually an invalid, and I can't seem to raise my own son. I need a wife, Costa, and that's what I need to speak to you about."

Costa leaned forward in the chair as Vangeli fought to hold back the tears that were filling his eyes "What can I do for you?" Costa said softly, careful to keep his voice down so that the others in the coffeehouse could not overhear the conversation.

"There is something we both need and that can solve problems we both have." Vangeli hesitated before he could respond to the quizzical look on Costa's face. "I need a wife, and you have a daughter. You need to find a suitable husband for her, but I know you do not have an adequate dowry for any prospective bridegroom. And besides, you have three other daughters yet to be married. I am asking you for permission to marry your daughter, Katerina. I know there are many years between us, but, Costa, you know me, I am a good man, and I will respect her and provide for her. Importantly for you, I seek no dowry. I want nothing except Katerina for a wife."

Costa did not respond immediately. He was, in fact, at a loss for words. He had not expected this, particularly from his lifelong friend whom he had known since childhood. Finally, he rubbed his hand across his forehead and beard and spoke.

"Vangeli, I'm not sure what to say. I just don't know what to say. You are a good man, and I know you would provide for my daughter—but..." Costa did not finish his sentence, conveying to Vangeli that he was unsure or troubled by the prospect of his nineteen-year-old daughter marrying a man only one year younger than himself. "Vangeli," he finally continued, "this request has come as such a surprise that I need a day or two to think it over. Let's meet again, just you and me, in two days."

For the following days Costa thought of little except of his conversation with Vangeli. He loved his children and worried about their future. He knew Vangeli well and knew he would provide a good home for his daughter. Yes, there was a large age difference, but such unions were not that unusual, and besides, he thought, Vangeli had been right about the dowry—he really had nothing to offer someone who expected or demanded such an economic gift from the family of the bride. And how would he ever provide a dowry for yet three remaining daughters? For two nights he slept little, turning over in his mind the decision he needed to make. His daughter would not only have to take on the duties of a wife to Vangeli but also raise his child, perhaps have more children, and care for his ailing mother. On the other hand, Costa knew full well that in his village, if his daughter never married, it would cause her and his family serious problems. Women who did not have a husband found themselves as individuals with no status in the village, and they were actually looked upon suspiciously by other villagers because of their innate sexuality that had no outlet. Men, the value system held, could indulge in premarital, or extramarital sex, but neither of these was permitted a woman. Two days later he and Vangeli met again at the coffeehouse.

"Vangeli," said Costa, "I have given much thought to what we spoke about, about your desire to have Katrina as your wife. And I have also thought about what you said in regard to the dowry. Unfortunately, you are correct. I have no means to provide a dowry for Katerina, and you ask for none. And I know and trust that you will care and provide for my daughter. So Vangeli, through the bond of our friendship and as a man of honor, I grant you permission to take Katerina as your wife."

Vangeli listened, a broad smile slowly enveloped his face. His eyes became alive, and he rose from the chair and embraced Costa. "Thank you my friend, thank you. I will care for your daughter, and when the time comes for God to take me, I promise you, she will not be left wanting. Thank you." Finishing their coffee, both men rose to go to their homes, Vangeli to plan for a new future and Costa to meet with his wife and daughter.

After their evening meal together, Costa asked his other children to go outdoors and enjoy the warm summer evening, telling them he needed to speak with their mother and Katerina about something private and important. As the other children filed out the old wooden door of their home in Prastos, the head of the family beckoned his wife and oldest daughter to sit with him. Katerina was nervous, and her usually smiling face was serious. What was this about, she thought? Had she done something wrong? Something to dishonor the family? Her mother was puzzled as well. Her husband had never before asked all the other children to leave the house so that a private matter could be discussed. This must be, she thought, very important. Costa sat at the old table with his wife and daughter sitting opposite him, and he began slowly to speak.

"Katerina," he started, "you are now nineteen years old, and it's time for us to look to your future. It's time for you to be married and have a husband." Katerina sat silently, displaying no emotion, her face betraying no expression. She seemed frozen, in shock. This was not what she had expected, but she really hadn't known what to expect. She continued to listen as her father spoke on, and her mother listened, with equal surprise, silently looking on. Her husband had said nothing of this beforehand. He had not consulted her or asked her opinion; as usual he was acting alone.

"I have made a decision and have reached an agreement. Katerina, I have chosen for you as your husband Vangeli Adamidis." Katerina and her mother froze. An expression of pain and disbelief came over their faces.

"Costa, Costa," his wife erupted, "What are you saying? What are you saying?"

"No father, no!" screamed Katerina, "I can't do it! I won't do it! He is an old man. I don't want him! You are destroying my life!" Katerina arose from the chair, her fists clenched, as she pounded furiously on the table. "Father, don't do this to me, please, please!"

Costa stood to hold and comfort his daughter. "You are my eldest daughter, and I love you as I love your brothers and sisters, but you must hear me. We have no means to provide a dowry to anyone, do you understand? We have no dowry! This will be your only chance to marry, because Vangeli has asked for no dowry of any kind. He is a good man, and he will provide for you."

Katerina interrupted her father's explanation, "But I will care for a child who is not mine and an old woman who is ready to die and a husband who will someday die while I'm still young! What life is that father? What life is that?"

"Katerina," her father said in tone of voice that left little more to be said, "enough! It is done. The word is given." Costa stood, looked at his daughter now consumed by tears, opened the door, and walked to meet Vangeli and relate to him the news.

In the days that followed Katerina spoke as little as possible, though that was difficult in a household of nine other people. In the few times she could find some privacy, she sought out her mother for support and guidance. "Mother, do I have to do this?" Her mother sat beside her and held her daughter close as she wrapped her arm around the young girl's shoulder. At first she said nothing, merely trying to comfort the young woman whom Despina still viewed as her little girl.

"Katerina," she finally said, "in our life, I'm sure you know by now, we as women must play a special role. Our world centers on the man. Without men, we have no role, no place in the eyes of society. No existence at all. Is this right? Do I believe God made these rules? No! No! I have never believed that, but our society has over years created these so-called rules. I don't know where they come from. Maybe this is part of the price we have paid for being enslaved for four hundred years by the barbarian Muslim Turks who treat their women as cattle. I don't know, but it is a fact we must live with."

"But mother," said Katerina, trying with all the control she could muster to not begin crying again, "it's wrong, it's stupid! All we have done is substitute one kind of slavery for another. Men do what they want. Men go out, out to coffeehouses, or wherever, while we must stay in the house, that's ridiculous! Men treat us as inferior, and then we begin to believe it ourselves. What happened to love?"

"Love," her mother said softly, "sometimes does come later. Your father is a good man. I hardly knew him before our families agreed that we would marry. My own dowry was very small, but that did not concern him, and over the years together we have been blessed with you and your brothers and sisters. I guess, in the only way I understand it, I have come to love him."

Katerina seemed to become more calm as her mother spoke. She had never really thought about her mother's life. Like every child, she had taken for granted that she had a mother, father, sisters, and brothers, without ever thinking as to what her parents felt toward one another. It had never entered her mind to think about whether there was any true love between them. "Mother," she calmly said, "I'm glad you feel love for my father. I've never heard you speak of that before, but I'm glad. But I must tell you something, Mother, something you must swear in the name of Jesus not to tell father."

Despina looked at her daughter, always dreading to hear some terrible news when anyone opened a conversation by requesting an oath that whatever was to be revealed be kept secret. "What, Katerina, what? I am your mother. I love you. You can tell me anything, and it will remain between us alone."

Her daughter began by saying that over the past year when she and her mother and father had gone to church, she had noticed a young man from the village often glancing at her and smiling. It was the son of Nikos Petropoulos. His name was Haralambros. Within the last five months she had periodically spoken to him when he came to find her while she was out alone harvesting olives. Her mother said nothing as she spoke, but the look on her face revealed everything. It was clear that she was thinking that she prayed her husband would not find out. Of these encounters nothing had happened, Katerina assured her mother; they had merely spoken. But Despina knew that in the code and culture of the village, even that was enough, if seen by the wrong people, to start gossip, and possibly bring dishonor to the family. "I like him very much, Mother, and he has told me he feels the same for me. He will be leaving for the army soon, but he told me that when he returns he will speak to Father about having me for his wife."

54

"That cannot be," her mother said. "That cannot be! Your father has made the agreement with Vangeli; he has given his word, and it cannot be changed or broken. It cannot!"

Katerina ran her fingers through her light brown hair and began pulling at it and began a quiet crying that quickly became a hysterical outburst. "Mother, I cannot do it! I cannot do it! I will not do it! Do you hear me?" she asked as she turned and opened the door, running out to find a place where she could be alone.

In the following days Despina acted as though she had heard nothing of her daughter's meetings and desires for the young man, Haralambros. Katerina did not attempt to discuss the matter with her mother again, assuming that it was a discussion that would result in nothing but more tears. The days were filled with plans for the engagement of Katerina and Vangeli. In many villages, including the one in which they lived, the engagement was an important event of major significance. It was planned as a festive occasion hosted by the family of the prospective bride. Local village musicians were asked to perform so that dancing could be part of the celebration. Special foods were prepared. The engagement was, in fact, not merely a celebration of the future uniting of two families but an occasion in which the entire village participated. The engagement involved special ceremonial aspects in which the couple pledged themselves to one another, exchanged glasses of a sweet liqueur from which they both drank. A key element of the event was the exchange of rings, by the prospective bride and groom. The bride's mother first gave the rings to the couple, and the father of the bride repeated the act. The local priest had no role in the engagement ceremony. The engagement was an important step because it was viewed as something that could not be broken; the engaged couple was expected to marry. In the tradition of the village the engagement ceremony was as serious as the wedding itself, since the couple would have announced to the entire village that they intended to marry. Engagements lasted for a period of weeks to sometimes as long as a year. After the engagement, the prospective groom was allowed to visit with the prospective bride, usually in the home of the bride with her other family members present.

On the day designated for the formal engagement and celebration, Yannelli approached his sister Katerina who sat in the chair staring out the small window that had been opened to allow fresh air into the house. It was one of those rare occasions when everyone in this large family, except the young boy and his older sister, were out somewhere in the village or in the fields. "Katerina," Yannelli said, interrupting her thoughts and her faraway look, "I know you are sad. I've been watching you since the day you found out what father had done. I want you to know that I am sad for you, too, but maybe things will turn out well for you. I hear Vangeli is a good man, he will take care of you, and you will have a good house. That isn't so bad, is it?"

Katerina brought Yannelli close to her and wrapped her arms around him. "Yannelli, I love you, but you are too young to understand. You're ten years old, but what will you think when you are twenty or twenty-five? Will you want father to pick the person you may not even know to spend the rest of your life with? Will you? My life is over, Yannelli. I will be among the living dead, married to an old man I do not want, do not love, and will never love. And today I must go through the charade of pretending to be happy on the day of my engagement and smile and dance, while inside my heart and soul have died. Someday, someday, Yannelli, you will understand."

Katerina spent the remainder of her day of engagement dutifully acting out her assigned role. The villagers congratulated her and Vangeli, observed the traditional ceremony, ate the food that Costa and Despina had prepared, and danced to the music of the three-piece local band that had arrived with a bouzouki, a clarinet, and drums and played traditional Greek folk songs into the late hours of the night. The prospective bride had smiled when she felt she had to but only then. A number of times she had sought out her little brother Yannelli, held his hand, and brought him into the traditional circle folk dances. She had always been especially fond of Yannelli and had been assigned to care for him soon after he had been born because their mother could not devote her time to any one child and still fulfill all her other duties, chores, and responsibilities. And Yannelli had reciprocated in this special bond and love for his older sister, helping her when she needed help, telling her how beautiful she was, and admiring her for her ability to speak her mind. He loved to go walking with her, or follow her into the olive groves as she worked. Of all his sisters she was the one who asked him to come along when she went hunting for rabbits or birds. She was an excellent hunter, and they had spent many hours together laughing, joking, and hunting. He was only ten, but already he had learned how to handle his rifle and had become very proficient for his age.

Because Vangeli was older and a widower, it was decided that there was no need for a long engagement. Normally, longer engagements were for the brides who needed additional time to assemble whatever would be the total of their dowry. But this engagement was different since there would be no dowry. Vangeli already had a home. What would be the purpose of waiting to have the actual wedding? The wedding date was set for three months after the day of the engagement. For Katerina it was as if she had been handed a death sentence and was awaiting the day of execution. She did her chores, spoke little, and declined as much as possible to participate in the family plans and discussions regarding the forthcoming wedding. The boy she had wanted had been drafted into the army, and she had heard that he was stationed somewhere near Thessaloniki on the border between Greece and Bulgaria. She was nineteen years old, and what continuously entered her mind, which she mentioned to no one, was a feeling of dread that made her physically ill. The dread was that within a short time, she would have to sleep with Vangeli, this old, old man, the same age as her father. The pain she felt in her stomach seemed at times to be unbearable. Often when alone in the fields she could not bear the thought, and she began to cry uncontrollably until she was on her knees, her mouth open, and the contents of her last meal spilled out onto the ground. Her mother knew of Katerina's pain but could offer little help or comfort. She, too, had had no choice in picking the man with whom she had spent her life. It had, fortunately, turned out better than she had expected, but others she knew about had not been as fortunate. At least Costa had not been an old widower when their families had come to an agreement. As Despina observed her daughter's mental agony, she wanted desperately to help her but could not. This was our way, she thought to herself, our life, our customs, and traditions, and they could not be changed or broken. Costa seemed relieved in some way. He would be able to marry one daughter, not provide a dowry, and give her to a man he knew and respected. He could sense that his daughter continued to be unhappy, although she had really said nothing to him after that initial outburst when he had announced his decision to her. But he felt that once the wedding was over and Katerina settled into her new home and new role as a wife, she would come to see the good and decent qualities of Vangeli and live a satisfying life. He was confident that in the long run his decision would be in the best interest of his daughter,

Two weeks prior to the wedding Katerina seemed to take on a different attitude, She continued speak little about the wedding, but she generally spoke more often, laughed more frequently, and spent time with her siblings, joking and gossiping about others in the village. Her entire family noticed the change, and it pleased and comforted them. Perhaps, they all thought, Katerina had seen things differently now. Perhaps she had accepted what her life would be and had come to terms with it, seeing that there were some positives in the arrangement as well as the negatives that had obsessed her in the previous weeks. She joked with Yannelli and challenged him to a contest. "Yannelli," she said with a smile to her brother, "let's see how good a hunter you have become. Let's see which of us can bring home the most rabbits in a two-hour period. I know I'll beat you. I know I'll win this one. Are you ready, Yannelli? You know, once I am married, we won't be able to do this very often, perhaps not at all."

"When do we start?" asked her younger brother. "You may be good, but you're not that good, and it will be embarrassing if a ten-year-old can out-hunt someone who's almost twenty, even if you are a girl!"

Katerina and Yannelli decided their contest would be held on the following Wednesday. On the designated day they both rose early at five o'clock in the morning. After they had some cheese, bread, and goat's milk for breakfast, they headed out to the fields, starting out together but eventually separating so that each could pursue small game alone. Within a half-hour they met up again, Yannelli carrying in his bag two rabbits. Katerina smiled, because thus far she had shot only one.

"I guess the ten-year-old is going to win," boasted Yannelli, "but don't worry. I won't tell anybody and embarrass you at your wedding."

"Not so fast, little boy, we still have over an hour left. Let's see who the winner is when the time is up. Why don't you go that way and I'll go this way, and let's meet back here in exactly one hour. Yannelli laughed, kissed his sister on the cheek, and headed off to add to his winnings.

As Yannelli disappeared from view, Katerina's smile left her face, and a strange calm overtook her entire being. No matter what customs and traditions dictated, she was different. Perhaps others could be content with a life of unhappiness, a life without love, a life sleeping with and being a servant to a man she barely knew, but not her. Slowly and deliberately Katerina took the hunting rifle, held it directly under her chin and, with the strength of her bare toe, pressed on the trigger. Within seconds it was over. Katerina would not be a bride ever, to anyone. She had made the final decision.

Ten minutes later, Yannelli returned to where he was to reunite with his sister. As he approached the area, he saw Katerina's body on the ground, her clothes splattered with blood, her face almost unrecognizable. Screaming, he ran to her side, bent over her lifeless body, and began to cry hysterically.

Michael and Jenny, 1980

Michael and Jenny listened intently as Mrs. Soukis finished her story. Jenny said her father had made some reference to the incident long ago, but she had never followed up with any questions or details, and her father was not eager to talk about it. "It must have devastated the whole family," Jenny said. "What did happen after Katerina died?"

"My father," said Michael, "mentioned it once or twice but never stayed on the subject very long. I know that once, when I was very young, he showed me a photograph of Katerina, which he kept in his top dresser drawer, and my brother and I found it when we were going through his things after he died. It must have had a terrible effect on him; he was so close to her and to be with her when it happened and then to find her body covered with blood…." Michael's voice barely spoke the final word of his sentence, picturing in his mind the scene and the experience his father had lived.

The old woman told Michael and Jenny that the following few years were difficult for all in the family. Yannelli tried to forget by going off to school in Constantinople. But his letters home revealed a deep and profound sadness about the loss of his sister. The other children were also affected and would not speak of their sister for the following two or three years. It was as if they could erase the event from their minds, perhaps hoping the reality was that it had never really happened. Katerina's mother became withdrawn and never again removed the black mourning dress and headscarf that she wore immediately following her daughter's death. Costa assumed the full guilt for what had happened, tormenting himself about what he had done, what he had insisted on, and what he had driven his daughter to do. He never again raised the issue of dowries for his remaining daughters, particularly with Stamatina, who was the next oldest girl and who would be at the age at which some arrangement would be made for a suitable husband. In Costa's mind, he would do whatever it was necessary to do to present some kind of dowry to the next prospective groom and his family. "But he never was really the same again," Mrs. Soukis said. "Within five years Costa was dead, suffering from heart failure, but a death as much caused by a broken heart. Vangeli eventually did marry again, but this woman was a widow from a neighboring village."

Katerina's death was, of course, a major event that caused discussion throughout the village. To some it was truly a tragic event that brought sympathy to the entire family. Others saw it as the work of the devil who had possessed Katerina and made her violate God's law and disgrace her family. For some of the villagers, mostly young but some who were older as well, Katerina's suicide was the inevitable result that was bound to happen sometime to someone's daughter. It was the tragic result of a system and practice deeply embedded in Greek rural culture but also deeply flawed, inhuman, and disturbing. What kind of system was this, they asked, that put a price known as a dowry on a woman? Were they no better than cows? Sheep? Olives? However, they eventually accepted the fact that it was their way of life and would most likely never change.

"There is an old village saying," Mrs. Soukis said, "that sums up how things were viewed at that time. It is 'that's how we found it, that's how we learned it, and that's how we leave it.' But time has changed things. The dowry is now a thing of the past." The old woman went on to explain another aspect of the rural Greek view of life that had affected the way people reacted to Katerina's death. She unconsciously, slowly rubbed the large crucifix, which hung around her neck, moving the cross methodically between the two wrinkled fingers of her left hand. "At that time," she explained, "and to an extent even today, we Greeks live with some mixture of Orthodox Christian beliefs and ideas, rituals, and symbols that have their origins in our pagan era. There remains a very powerful belief in *teexi* or 'fate.' The belief then and still today is that each of us has a fate that is written and cannot be changed. It is a belief that the main outlines and events of each of our lives have already been set and must inevitably come to pass. So, for reasons we as humans cannot understand, it was Katerina's fate that her life was to be played out and ended as it unfortunately did."

"I'm not sure I can buy into that," Michael said. "It sure doesn't square with the fact that the Church believes suicide is a sin. I find it hard to believe that God sets our fate to do something that He, through the Church, strongly condemns."

"But remember what I said," Mrs. Soukis responded. "I didn't say the two ideas of Christianity and pagan carryovers were logical or compatible, only that we have never fully abandoned some ancient pre-Christian ideas that were part of our history for thousands of years. Remember the characters and their fate in the great Greek tragedies? Do you remember the story of Oedipus? That's the kind of fatalism I'm talking about."

"That does make sense, Michael," added Jenny, "and I believe Mrs. Soukis is right: even today you can find that strong belief in *teexi* among all of us Greeks."

Michael began to sense that Mrs. Soukis was beginning to become tired. She had spent more than an hour relating Katerina's story and Yannelli's connection to it. She lifted herself from the chair to stretch, saying that if she sat too long the circulation to her legs would slow down and she would find it difficult to walk again. But she also seemed to enjoy the company of Michael and Jenny and the attention they were giving her. Where she had at first been reluctant to speak openly and freely, she now felt comfortable enough with her young guests to be completely forthright and candid.

"What else can I help you with, Michael," she asked as she slowly sank once again into her chair.

"Well, Mrs. Soukis, you have been very kind and generous with your time, and I very much appreciate what you have been able to tell me about my father and his family. But if you don't mind, and we could have a bit more of your time, I wonder if you could help with another thing I don't fully understand. And that is what happened to the next oldest daughter, Stamatina? My father's journal has an entry from 1913. But again I'm not sure what he meant."

Mrs. Soukis once again adjusted herself in the chair for a more comfortable position, placing both hands on the tip of the cane she carried but did not seem to need, and prepared to respond to Michael's question. Jenny now seemed even more focused on what was to be related, because Stamatina was Yannelli's sister and her maternal grandmother. "Stamatina." said the old woman in a barely audible voice. "Stamatina." she repeated. "Your father Yannelli was fifteen years old by then. And that's another complicated matter...."

Stamatina, 1913

FROM THE JOURNAL, 1913

SINCE MIHALI WAS IN AMERICA, I WAS NOW THE OLDEST SON IN OUR HOME. WHEN MY MOTHER SPOKE TO ME, I KNEW I HAD A DUTY TO DO SOMETHING. THE HONOR OF THE FAMILY WAS AT STAKE. MY FATHER WAS GONE. I WAS OBLIGATED TO DO SOMETHING, AND I DID.

The day was hot, and the humidity was high as Stamatina, her mother, and other women of the village of Agios Andreas slowly walked out of the village toward the community cemetery, which was on the road that led to the seashore. Within the next half hour, the rest of the family, including Yannelli and his other brothers and sisters, followed the same path toward the designated spot. That designated spot was the grave of Katerina, who had been dead for almost five years. The family had made the decision to bury Katerina there rather than in Prastos to attempt to avoid the gossip and speculation that had followed her death. The mission of all who now walked to the gravesite was to carry out a ritual and custom the origins of which were a curious mixture of Orthodox Christianity and legacies from an ancient pagan Greek past.

Stamatina was a small, frail girl, now seventeen years old. Her young face was framed by long dark brown hair, and her hazel, almond-shaped eyes gave her if not a beautiful certainly an exotic appearance. She was now the oldest of the daughters in the family, and since the death of her father and her sister, she had been the one to help her mother care for the younger children, assist in the necessary chores, and help raise her younger siblings. Stamatina was a quiet, somewhat withdrawn young woman, not prone to engage in the usual chatter and gossip like the other village girls her age, and she was interested in writing poetry, which she wrote in a small book that she kept with her in a large bag always hanging from her shoulder. She had been only twelve when Katerina died, but she missed her very much, thought of her often, and placed flowers on her grave almost weekly during the summer months. The ritual in which she now was to participate was not one she wanted to think about, because it was extremely sad and had a macabre element to it.

Upon reaching Katerina's gravesite, Despina, the mother of the deceased, began the traditional series of steps that would, as all understood, fulfill the family obligation to the one who had died and bring some finality and completion to the deceased's transition from life to death. At first the assembled women, those of the immediate family and then those from the village, began a slow methodical singing, known as the *myriologion* or funeral dirge. Some of the words were universal and could be applied to almost anyone, while others were specific questions to the dead Katerina: "Why did you leave us? We loved you and only wanted happiness for you. Why did you not talk to us again?" The singing, a remnant from pre-Christian times, was accompanied by women expressing their grief, publicly and loudly, releasing all the emotions they may have suppressed since the day of the person's death. This singing allowed the bereaved to maintain some kind of relationship with the deceased, a kind of conversation with the person. This conversation was carried out because of the belief that the dead continue to have a certain kind of consciousness and are fully aware of what the living who are left behind are doing for them.

As the singing ceased, Despina, Stamatina, and Yannelli then took turns digging the grave and removing shovels of dirt to the side. As the hole they were digging grew deeper, Despina began an uncontrollable sobbing and was immediately comforted by Stamatina, who in a matter of seconds, followed her mother's tears with her own. Yannelli, trying to display what he believed was his more masculine role, fought to hold back tears, but as his shovel finally struck the rotting wooden box, which served as the casket for his sister, he too lost control and a stream of tears flowed down his young face. When the dirt was finally cleared away, the wooden box was opened, revealing Katerina's remains: rotting clothes, bones, and a skull. Despina, Stamatina, and Yannelli did the sign of the cross as the mother reached down to pick up the visible remains of her daughter. The other villagers present and Despina's other children threw flowers into the open grave, and the family washed the remains in wine and water. The village priest, Father Petros Mylonas, dressed in his full clerical attire, approached the open grave to recite a prayer. Holding the incense dispenser was Yannelli's younger brother, Manoli, serving as the ceremony's altar boy. Manoli was perhaps the most devout of all the children, never missing the Sunday Liturgy and always available to assist the priest at funerals, baptisms, or weddings. The priest finished his prayers and slowly moved the censer so that the incense reached all who surrounded the grave. As he moved to bless the crowd, the large crucifix around his neck swung to the side, revealing another ornamental piece around his neck, a silver pendant with the Greek letters ΙΛ, *iota* and *lambda*, engraved on its front. Yannelli stared momentarily at the pendant but quickly dismissed it as he attempted to deal with the emotion of the moment as the priest continued his service chanting:

Everlasting be your memory, our sister,
Who are worthy of blessedness and eternal memory.
Through the prayers of our Holy Father, Lord, Jesus Christ our
  God,
Have mercy and save us.
Amen.

The priest then poured red wine over the bones with a hand movement that formed the shape of the cross three times. He then concluded by saying:

You shall sprinkle me with Hyssop, and I shall be clean.
You shall wash me and I will be whiter than snow.
The earth is the Lord's and the fullness
  thereof;
the World, and all that dwells therein.
You are dust, and
To dust you will return.

Upon the completion of the priest's words, Despina took the bones and skull of her deceased daughter, placed them in a box, and put them in a vault located on the cemetery grounds. The family then walked to their home, while the villagers who remained at the site were provided with red wine, a slice of bread, a spoonful of honey, pastries, and a handful of the special mixture presented at funerals and exhumations called *koliva*, which was parboiled wheat mixed with raisins, parsley, and walnuts and covered with a layer of sugar. The *koliva* was a symbolic offering representing resurrection and the belief that the deceased will someday, through God's grace, abandon death for a new life.

As the ceremony ended, the villagers departed for their homes, each softly repeating the words, "May God forgive her." The ceremony had gone as planned. The villagers had witnessed the solidarity of the grieving family, and it had accomplished its major purpose—the final acceptance by the family of the irreversibility of death and the fact that the dead no longer exist as individuals.

One of the villagers who had witnessed the exhumation ceremony was twenty-year-old Yorgos Athanasopoulos. He had dutifully followed the ritual but had focused his attention not so much on the ceremonial steps or the prayers of the priest but rather on the grieving daughter, Stamatina. He had seen her before as she had made her trips to the graveside of her sister to place flowers near the headstone, and he had gone into Stamatina's small family store to purchase cheese and bread where he had spoken to her briefly. Yorgos was a student of archaeology, and when he was not assisting his family with the raising of sheep, he could be found scouring the nearby countryside in the hope of finding some yet unearthed relic from ancient times, which might gain him some recognition and perhaps, more importantly, make a great deal of money for him. As Yorgos's visits to the store became more frequent, it became clear to Stamatina that his interests went beyond bread, cheese, and even her poetry; rather he seemed enamored with the young Stamatina herself. The casual conversations and store encounters continued for months, and at the end of more than four months of such visits and conversation Stamatina had developed a comfort level with Yorgos and returned his attention with flirtation of her own.

"Some lucky girl will steal you someday, Yorgos," she told him as he prepared to leave the store where he had purchased bread for his family's evening dinner.

"Maybe it will be you, Stamatina," replied Yorgos, suggesting through his voice and expression that he would be pleased if, indeed, it were to be her.

Stamatina smiled and said nothing. To Yorgos, her silence was not a denial but rather a signal that she would welcome being the one to capture his heart. For Stamatina it was merely part of a young girl's flirtation game with someone who seemed nice and whose attention she welcomed but in whom she had no real romantic interest. But Stamatina was carrying out her flirtation game much too long and much too well. And after five months, for Yorgos, it ceased to be a game.

On a warm October evening Stamatina hurried to finish her work in the olive groves before darkness set in. Her mother and younger sisters had just left to walk to their home to prepare dinner, and Stamatina worked alone to close out the day's effort. As she stooped to lift a basket of olives she had harvested, she looked up and was surprised to see Yorgos close beside her. "Yorgos," she said in a startled voice, "what are you doing here?"

"I am here so that we can be honest with one another," he replied. "I am tired of these village rules. From the day of your sister Katerina's exhumation ceremony, I saw something in your eyes that told me that you wanted me. There was a hunger there, a suppressed passion, which you could not conceal." He moved closer to her as Stamatina stepped backward as if she were in retreat from some unknown force. Yorgos suddenly lunged forward, grabbed Stamatina close to him, and moved his lips toward hers. Stamatina pushed him away with a surprising force, considering she was such a small young woman.

"Yorgos, stop! Stop! What are you doing? This is wrong. Yorgos you will disgrace our families, stop! Stop!" But he would not stop.

Throwing her to the ground, in a burst of violence and rage he struck her in the face with his open hand.

"I know you want me! I know! Don't play games with me. I want you now, now do you understand, and you want me, too!" He thrust his body over her, hitting her again as he tore away at her clothes and fumbled as he simultaneously moved to undress himself. Taking her headband, he stuffed it into her mouth so that her screams for help in this isolated area were muted and unable to be heard by anyone. Stamatina continued to struggle and pound Yorgos with her fists, but the weight of his body made it impossible for her to offer resistance. Within minutes he had entered her, and it was done. He rose, assembled his clothes, turned, and walked away, leaving his bleeding victim to grab for her clothes as she helplessly trembled and pushed her face into the dirt, unable to rise up or move at all.

Worried that she had not returned home, her mother had come back to the olive fields to find her. She came upon her daughter still lying on the ground, her knees curled beneath her and her hands covering her head. Despina cried out, "Stamatina! My child, Stamatina, what has happened?" But her mother instinctively knew exactly what had happened. She knelt down, cradled her daughter in her arms, gently lifted her to her feet, and together they slowly made their way to their family house.

In the following days Despina cared for her daughter, and Stamatina slowly and reluctantly related what had happened and who the person was who had beaten and raped her. Her daughter had been deeply traumatized and needed rest and time to recover physically, although whether she could ever recover emotionally was seriously in doubt. What Despina did know was that rather than confronting Yorgos and his family, the entire episode must be kept secret, for to reveal it would stigmatize Stamatina for life and bring great dishonor to the family. Since similar disgrace would come to Yorgos and his family, it was not likely that he would want the episode to be revealed. But, of course, some in the family, namely the oldest son living there, Yannelli, would have to be told, because living in the same house with his sister and mother, it would be inevitable that he would discover the truth. Despina sat with her fifteen-year-old son and related the facts to him. Yannelli listened intently as he unconsciously pressed his teeth together, his jaws tightening, as his nails from his one hand dug deeply into the other hand. "What must we do, Mother? What can I do?" he asked.

"Do nothing, Yannelli. God will guide us. Pray for your sister, say nothing. You must give me your word, say nothing." Yannelli continued to look into his mother's eyes. He nodded his head two or three times. He would obey his mother and say nothing and do nothing. Within the next six weeks, however, doing nothing was no longer an option—by every sign, Stamatina, at seventeen years old, was pregnant, and now Yannelli had little choice; he needed to speak to Yorgos.

He spotted Yorgos leaving the coffeehouse walking toward his home. Catching up to him, he briskly walked along Yorgos's side and opened the conversation. "Yorgos, I need to speak with you. It is important."

"What do you want, Yannelli? I'm busy now. I have no time."

Yannelli stepped in front of him to stop his forward movement. "You must make time, Yorgos. I know what a pig such as you did to my sister, and she is pregnant. You must marry her! Is that clear, you must marry her!"

Yorgos stopped. "Pregnant? That cannot be true, and I don't know what you're talking about. I had nothing to do with your sister. Maybe she is sleeping with someone else, maybe with many someone elses. Go back to school, Yannelli, and don't bother me with your accusations. I did nothing with your sister, nor would I ever want to. She is used property now, Yannelli, and I'm not interested in used property." Yorgos quickened his pace and walked away from Yannelli, leaving him standing silently in the street. Yannelli turned to return to his home. He was not afraid of Yorgos. Although he was five years younger, Yannelli was taller and heavier than the older and smaller Yorgos. No, he was not afraid, but he was not one to act impulsively. He needed time to think, and he needed direction from the only one he could trust to give it, his older brother Mihali who, unfortunately, was thousands of miles away, living with his new wife in Chicago. He did not know his older brother well. Mihali had left for America at the age of fifteen when Yanneli was only four years old. He had come back to Greece only once for his father's funeral, but since then he and Yannelli had exchanged letters five or six times each year. Now more than ever Yannelli felt the need to correspond with his brother again.

> *Dear Mihali,*
>
> *I hope you are well. I am writing to you with some bad news, and I need your help. Our sister Stamatina has been physically attacked, beaten, and violated by a man named Yorgos Athanasopoulos. He is twenty years old, so I'm sure you have no knowledge of him, but perhaps know of his family. Stamatina is now pregnant, she is in a state of shock and depression. She cries constantly and seldom speaks. She is ashamed to leave the house. I've spoken a number of times to this pig Athanasopoulos, but he denies he has ever been with Stamatina, ignores and dismisses me, and implies that we should talk to many men, for perhaps that is the character of our sister. So far we believe we have been able to conceal the pregnancy, but within a month or two it will be impossible unless Stamatina is sent away. If we do not, she and our family will be shamed. I seek your advice and I will wait for your guidance.*
>
> *Your brother,*
> *Yannelli*

Because of the slowness of the mail, which traveled by ship to America and by train from New York to Chicago, Yannelli waited impatiently for his brother's response. In what seemed like a year but in fact was four weeks, the letter from Chicago arrived:

Dear Yannelli,

Upon receiving your letter, I felt a surge of rage and disgust that I cannot convey in words. My frustration is that I am thousands of miles away, sitting here helpless as our sister suffers and this coward of a man walks the streets of our village. Yannelli, although you are still a boy, you know what you must do. Think carefully, but do not hesitate or delay. Remember always, "e time tou adelphou."

Your brother,
Mihali

Yannelli read the final words again out loud, "*e time tou adelphou.*" He knew well what that phrase meant and what it required. It meant, "the honor of the brother," and it dictated that no brother could stand idle while his sister's honor had been violated. He would first try, in some way, to salvage the situation so that not only Stamatina's honor would be protected but also that of the family name. If that effort failed and Yorgos continued to be defiant, the consequence was clear—Yorgos would have to die. Yannelli read his older brother's letter again. Think carefully, Mihali had said, before you do anything, and Yannelli began planning how he might penetrate Yorgos's hostility toward him, lower his defenses, and create a situation in which the two could be alone, in some remote spot where no one could see or hear anything. He finally decided that the one thing that might possibly break Yorgos's suspicion and defenses was the one thing that was his passion—his love of archaeology and his dream that someday he would become rich and famous by discovering some long lost treasure that would change the view of the past and make his name known throughout Greece and perhaps the world. Within the next week Yannelli looked for signs of Yorgos in the village. He did not want to deliberately seek him out but hoped he could have a chance meeting in the street where it would seem to Yorgos that it was simply a routine encounter like those that happen every day among all residents of the village.

Early one morning he finally spotted Yorgos sitting alone at the coffeehouse, savoring his morning drink and the bread and cheese that were his breakfast.

"Yorgos," smiled Yannelli as he approached small table, "good morning, how are you? I have not seen you lately, and I'm glad I found you. I've something important to tell you."

Yorgos looked up, placed a small cup of coffee on the table, and did not return Yannelli's smile or happy greeting. "What do you want, boy? You seem to have changed your tune. Did you finally discover your good sister was lying? Or maybe you found the man or men she had been with? Get out of here. We have nothing to talk about."

Yannelli smiled again. "Yorgos, I'm not here to talk about Stamatina. You are right, and I want to apologize for the things I said and how I acted when we last met. Let's get over all that. What I really want to talk to you about is something that only you can appreciate."

Yorgos seemed to change his attitude immediately. His body seemed to unwind as he sat back comfortably in his chair. His defensive posture disappeared, and a sense of relief seemed to envelope his body language and the tone of his words. "I'm glad to hear that, Yannelli. I'm glad you and your family know I have not lied. I've never lied. Now sit down, what is this thing that is so important that only I can appreciate?"

Yannelli had mentally rehearsed what he was about to tell Yorgos over and over in his mind. He had checked and rechecked history books on ancient Greece, so that he would seem knowledgeable and creditable when he spoke to Yorgos who was more informed on these subjects and was pursuing a university degree in archaeology.

"Yorgos, I was riding my horse along the seashore two weeks ago and had gone about one or two miles outside our village when I stopped to water the horse, rest a bit, and have something to eat. From the place where I stopped I began to wander farther in away from the shore when I saw a cave. Something about the entrance to the cave seemed unusual to me so I pushed away the brush and the rocks that had covered the entrance, and I walked in. It was still daylight out so the cave was not totally dark, and I found things that shocked me, but which I don't fully understand."

Yorgos' eyes now betrayed excitement that Yannelli immediately noticed. "What? What did you see, Yannelli?" he asked excitedly, interrupting Yannelli's story.

"I saw some bones, not many, but I saw what seemed to be spoons, vases, dishes, and a stack of what seemed to be some brownish gold jewelry. I remember from my studies that we were told that close to our village had been the ancient village of Anthene that Thucydides and Pausanias had mentioned in their writings."

"That's true," said Yorgos, "but scholars have been looking for decades to substantiate those ancient writers claims and have failed for the most part."

"That's what our teacher told us, and that's why I need your help. No one here knows these things better than you, Yorgos. If it is something new and important that I have found, maybe both of us can benefit, maybe museums will pay us money to lead them there. Who knows?"

Yorgos' defenses toward Yannelli had now totally disappeared, his eyes were open with excitement, and a broad smile finally could be seen on his face. "Yannelli," he said in a rushed and excited voice, "you must show me where you found those things. We will go together. Tell no one, because if this is anything that might be connected to the Anthene village, it will make us both rich and famous."

The two continued to talk and made preparations to meet at daybreak to travel to the site. For different reasons, neither told anyone of their previous conversation or what they had planned for the day. Riding their horses, the two, the twenty-year-old man and the fifteen-year-old boy, reached the site where Yannelli had said he had made his discovery. Dismounting their horses, they secured them with rope to a nearby tree and walked toward the opening of the cave. Unable to contain his excitement in anticipation of what he would find, Yorgos stepped into the cave, and Yannelli followed closely behind. Yorgos looked around, said nothing, and then frantically walked farther into the cave. "Yannelli, where are these things you have found? I see nothing here. Are you sure this is the same place you were before? I see nothing here!"

Yannelli did not respond. At fifteen he had grown and was now taller than his father had been and taller than his other brothers, and he was strong compared to the slight frame of Yorgos. He quickly grabbed Yorgos from behind, turned him around, and threw him to the ground. "No, there is nothing here, you lying pig! Nothing! Nothing but you and me." Yannelli began to strike Yorgos on the chest, and on his face, over and over and over again. Yorgos was helpless, pinned beneath the body and the raging fists that Yannelli continued to hit against his head. Yorgos was bleeding now, his left eye virtually closed.

"You raped my sister, you dishonored her and all my brothers and sisters, and you continue to lie, you lying bastard, you basket of shit!" Yannelli struck him again and again, each blow reflecting the young boy's rage and disgust.

"I did nothing—nothing!" pleaded Yorgos when he was able to articulate any sounds during the brutal beating he was receiving.

"Don't continue to insult me, you son of a bitch. Don't insult me, you lying bastard. Open your mouth. I said, open your mouth!" Yorgos struggled as Yannelli took his two hands and forced open Yorgos's bleeding mouth. Reaching into the bag that had been strapped to his side, Yannelli pulled out the pistol his father had always kept in the house and that Yannelli had learned how to use when he was nine years old. He jammed the muzzle into Yorgos's mouth as his victim screamed and a look of terror came over his face. "Now admit what is true!" Yannelli screamed, his hand carefully guarding the gun barrel now filling Yorgos's mouth. "This is your last chance to tell the truth, or you will never have a chance to lie again. You raped Stamatina, didn't you! Didn't you! I have been too patient with your lies, Yorgos. I will count to five, and then you will see *e time tou adelphou*. You understand that Yorgos, don't you?" Yannelli slowly began to count—one—two—three—"

" No, Yannelli, please stop!" Yorgos begged. "I will tell you everything."

Yannelli withdrew the pistol from Yorgos's mouth but kept it pointed directly at his face.

"I was the one," Yorgos said as he gasped for breath. "I was wrong. I made a mistake. What can I do? I'll give you money. I will leave the village. What can I do?"

Yannelli placed his face within inches of Yorgos's bruised and bleeding head. "Stamatina is pregnant. This is your child. You will marry Stamatina within the month, and you will care for her and the child."

"Yannelli, please, please," begged Yorgos again, "I will do anything else. I cannot marry her. I have my studies, my career, my future, it will be gone. I cannot, cannot marry Stamatina!"

The look that was now on Yannelli's face was one Yorgos, and probably no one else, had ever seen. It was a cold look of rage, as if any semblance of compassion or rationality had parted from his body. Taking the pistol, he again thrust it into Yorgos's mouth, cracking teeth that had obstructed its entrance. "I said, you will marry Stamatina, you dirty, fucking, lying, bag of shit! I have already counted to three. There are two numbers left to go before I hit five, and when I come to that last number you will depart from this earth, left to rot in this cave." Yannelli began to resume his count—"four…"

"Stop!" screamed Yorgos, "Stop! I will do whatever you say. I will marry your sister. I will. I will. I promise you, I promise you."

Yorgos had stared death in the face. He was shaking, crying, and Yannelli detected the odor of a petrified man who had lost control of his bowels. Yannelli rose from the position where he had pinned Yorgos to the ground, as his victim remained down, unable to move. Yannelli unbuckled Yorgos' pants, revealing the stench and filth of how he had in panic lost control and soiled himself. Ripping off a portion of Yorgos's shirt, Yannelli carefully lifted the feces in the feces-filled pants and pushed them into Yorgos's face.

"This is what you are, Yorgos, a lying piece of shit. Enjoy it and think hard about what you have done. Tomorrow you will come to my home, and you will ask me as the eldest male of the family for permission to marry my sister. You will be granted that honor, and we will announce that the marriage will take place next month. You will say that you seek no dowry because you love my sister and that having her as your wife is a gift more valuable than any dowry could be. And Yorgos, should you not do this or try to depart the village, I will find you, and I will kill you. If by some remote chance you have disappeared like the coward I know you are, your family will die for you. And one more thing. My brother Mihali sends you a message. He said that you should be on your knees and pray to God every day that he was not here to settle this score, for if he had been here, you would not be leaving this cave alive."

Yannelli placed the pistol back in his bag and turned away from Yorgos, whose body was still bleeding and trembling on the ground. "I will await your visit tomorrow," said Yannelli calmly as he mounted his horse and rode back into the village.

The following day Yorgos, still bruised and bandaged, arrived at Yannelli's home and made the request Yannelli had demanded. His battered appearance was explained to the village with a story that he had been accosted on an archaeological expedition by two thieves who had been so disappointed that he had no valuables that they could take that they left him beaten and bloody miles away from the village. The marriage was planned for the next month. Despina and Stamatina were not happy, but both knew this was a necessary step to protect the family honor, Stamatina's future, and the welfare of the unborn child. Stamatina spent hours alone crying, but on the day of the wedding managed to display an image of calmness and resignation. Yorgos, knowing that his options were now eliminated, stoically survived the day, drank too much, and managed to present a drunken façade of joy as he led dances at the small reception following the wedding ceremony. The hope of everyone was that perhaps once married, the two young people could develop respect and live a normal life, raising children and being a productive part of the village life.

The day following the wedding, Yannelli sat down at the old kitchen table to write to his brother in America. He was not in the mood to write a lengthy letter; as was his style, Yannelli had always been a person of few words, "laconic" as it was characterized:

Dear Mihali,

The issue concerning Stamatina is now resolved. The wedding is over. I did what I had to do. The honor of the family is preserved.

Your brother,
Yannelli

Michael and Jenny, 1980

I guess you can't say we come from a boring family," Michael said as Mrs. Soukis finished her telling of Stamatina's story and Yannelli's role in it. "That's really something, it's quite a story." Jenny seemed particularly quiet and gave no response to what Michael had said. "Are you okay, Jenny?" Michael asked.

"I'm fine," answered Jenny, "just thinking. You know," she continued, "I never knew what Mrs. Soukis just told us. Remember, Michael, remember who Stamatina was. She was my grandmother, and that first child who was born was my father." Michael paused. For some reason he had not made the mental connection as Mrs. Soukis was relating the details of the episode. It had escaped him that the child conceived by Stamatina was his older first cousin, Tassos.

"I'm sorry, Jenny, I wasn't thinking. I was so caught up in the story I just didn't make the connection. Of course, the baby was Tassos."

Jenny rose from her chair simply to become mobile and pace the floor. In a moment she turned to Michael and Mrs. Soukis and spoke of her father, of how he seldom mentioned his childhood or growing up in the village. She said her father had said that he had hardly known his father because he had died in a tragic accident and that he had loved his mother but worried as a child because her life in the village had been so difficult. As soon as he was of age, Tassos had left the village, had joined the Army, and had done well. He had been selected to attend the military academy to be trained as an officer and had established an exemplary record there. During World War II, he had distinguished himself leading Greek guerrilla forces in the mountains as they fought the Italians and Germans, and by war's end, he had earned the rank of colonel. He remained in the army as a career soldier, and eventually had been promoted to the rank of general, the rank he held when he finally retired. His had been a career of courage and distinction, a career that one would have thought he would have been proud to allow the village from which he had come to honor. But, said Jenny, that was not the case. In all the years since he had left, he only returned to Agios Andreas for specific occasions for which he felt a duty to be present, such as the wedding of his younger brother and the funeral of his mother. "I never fully understood that," said Jenny, "and he never would speak about it."

"I know the reason," said the old woman. "There was a reason for this. Life was not easy for your grandmother, Jenny, or for your father as he grew up. In a small village, few things remain secret, and it was quickly known what circumstances had taken place between your grandmother and your grandfather, Yorgos. And the role Yannelli played in this drama also became common knowledge. Your grandmother was not treated well by the women of Agios Andreas. The best that can be said was that they tolerated her but behind her back spoke disparagingly of her. She was a good, kind, decent woman, but to the jealous, mean, women who had few pleasures other than to gossip about others, she was often the target of their hateful words. Your father, Tassos, in some ways, fared even worse. Behind his back he was known as the 'bastard boy,' and soon that label was no longer a secret kept from Tassos himself. He increasingly felt shunned, ashamed, and, for a while, ashamed of his own mother. The village had no attraction for him. The army did, and he went there as quickly as he could."

"I can understand that," said Jenny. "Given the position of the women of the time, I could see where my grandmother would be the one to bear the burden of the shame, even though she had done nothing to deserve it. I'm sure my grandfather suffered little."

"Very little," said Mrs. Soukis, "but he was not a happy man. He always harbored resentment that he was forced to marry a woman he did not want and raise a child who was a daily reminder of the life he had wanted but could not have. He was forced to leave the university, abandon his hopes for a career as an archaeologist, and spend his time raising olives and sheep like every other man in the village. There were rumors that he dealt violently with your grandmother and his child Tassos, but I really can't say if those rumors were true or not. I personally just don't know. It may have been just some other examples of village gossip, which too often destroyed people's reputations."

Mrs. Soukis's story had also raised questions in Michael's mind about his father. In all the years of his childhood and adult life, he had never once seen evidence of his father losing his temper or raging against anything. Never once had he heard him use obscenities, either in English or in Greek, and Michael, for all of his lack of knowledge of the Greek language, had managed to learn a few of the choice Greek obscenities. The father he knew was a quiet, serious man, not the person Mrs. Soukis had described as a half-crazed individual beating people and sticking guns in their mouths and threatening to kill a person or his family.

"Mrs. Soukis," he finally said, "I must tell you, the story you have told of my father's role in Stamatina's life sounds like another person, whom I never knew. It just doesn't sound like something my father would do, it just doesn't."

"Mihali," she replied, "generally it was not characteristic of your father, but I know it is difficult for you, coming from a city like Chicago more than sixty years later, to really understand the codes, values, and rituals of a small rural village such as this at that time. Remember, most people, while literate, were not educated. Most seldom left their village, even to travel short distances to a neighboring village. We lived an isolated life, where everything was everybody's business. And you must particularly try to understand the power of the idea of 'honor,' and how it affected every family. To lose one's honor or to be dishonored was, in fact, to lose everything and to be virtually ostracized from everyone. It was something that had to be protected and defended at all costs. In truth, the fact that Yannelli spared Yorgos his life and forced him to marry Stamatina was an act of compassion. In most cases, he would have been killed."

"And what about the two other sisters," asked Jenny, "are there more surprising and shocking stories about them?"

"No," said Mrs. Soukis, "for those women, at least, I think the fate of the older two was probably enough for any family. The two younger girls had difficulty finding husbands because of the lack of a dowry the family could offer any prospective groom. That is one of the main reasons Yannelli eventually went to America, to earn money that could be used as a dowry for his sisters. The older brother, Mihali, for some reason I don't understand, never did offer to help his sisters very much. I'm not sure why. Eventually, the two younger girls did marry and have families, which are now scattered throughout Greece, and I believe a few have gone to South America as well."

"And what about my father's brothers, Christos and Manoli? What was their story?" asked Michael.

"And before we leave you, Mrs. Soukis, people keep referring to the tragic death of my grandfather, Yorgos," interrupted Jenny. "Do you know anything about that?"

Mrs. Soukis was visibly tired; she had spent more time than she had intended with Michael and Jenny. Dusk had set in, and it was her habit to be in the comfort of her home to watch a particular television program every evening before dark. She reached for her cane, rose from the chair, and moved toward Jenny and Michael to bid them goodbye, hugging each of them and kissing them lightly on the cheek.

"I hope I have been helpful," she said. "I'm not sure there is much more I can tell you. But, Mihali, I think you should speak with Phillipos Alfearis who lives in the house with the brown shutters just before you leave the village. He was your father's friend, only a year or two older than Yannelli, and they served in the army together. I know he can tell you more than I can about Yorgos, Christos, and Manoli."

Michael and Jenny thanked Mrs. Soukis for the time she had devoted to them and for the information she had provided. They sensed, however, that while she claimed some lack of knowledge of the lives of the men they had asked about, she probably knew more than she was prepared to tell. As they got ready to go to the local restaurant for dinner, they wondered why.

The next morning, Michael and Jenny walked to the house where Mr. Alfearis lived. It was early—the day had not reached the blistering hot temperature that was to come by afternoon—and they found him sitting at the side of the small house, his chair and table shaded under a canopy covered with vines. The old man looked up and greeted them with the phrase, "Tse piu?"

Michael and Jenny turned to one another with looks of surprise. Jenny said in Greek, "Pardon me? What is it you said?"

Reverting to the language Jenny understood, the old man responded, "I said, how are you? It's Tsakonika, a dialect many of us old men and women still speak here, particularly when we don't want our grandchildren to understand. It's an ancient tongue, carried down, we believe, from our Dorian ancestors." He smiled and said, "Please be seated. I don't know who you are, but I welcome the company. Please sit down."

Michael and Jenny shook the old man's hand and told him who their relatives were who had been born and lived in the village many years before. Phillipos smiled broadly and seemed genuinely pleased that his visitors had arrived. "I knew your grandmother and grandfather well, as young people," he said to Jenny. "And I knew your father Tassos only slightly, because I was in the army at the time he was growing up here. When I returned and married, he was in school and then left for the army himself. But Mihali, your father and I were like brothers. I knew him so well I could sometimes know what he was thinking. We lived in the village and played together as children, and after he and I had grown to manhood, we both went to the army on the same day and served together. I had heard he recently died. I'm very sorry, May God rest his soul." Mr. Alfearis finished his condolence statement by doing the sign of the cross three times. "Now," he began again, "what can I tell you?"

Michael explained to him that they were on a journey of discovery regarding his father, Yannelli, and that he wanted to know as much as he could about him and his family, because he had asked so little and his father had spoken so little of his past. "Mrs. Angeliki Soukis suggested that you could be of help to me. So that's why we have come to meet you."

The old man smiled again and systematically swirled a string of beads he held in his hand. Michael recognized them as "worry beads," which could be found in every souvenir store in Greece. "Before we start," asked Michael "is there any significance to the use of those beads?"

"I don't know," answered Mr. Alfearis. "All I know is that I have seen them all my life, and there was a time when I was young when almost everyone had them. Today, it's only old men like me, with nothing to do to pass the time, who use them."

"I do know something about them," said Jenny. "We were given some background in my tourist guide training because so many foreign tourists are curious about them." Jenny explained that there are variations of such beads among Muslims and Buddists, as well as Greeks, and that in Greece they are commonly believed to have their origin in the monastery of Mount Athos in northern Greece during medieval times. "There," Jenny said, "strands of beads made of woven knots were tied on a string and used to count and recount prayers. The Greek word for them is *komboli*, derived from the word *kombos* which means 'knot' and the verb *leo* which means 'to say.' Thus the combination of saying a prayer with each knot."

"But these beads are really not religious now, are they?" asked Michael.

"No, not at all," responded Jenny, "but you can see, I'm sure, the similarity to the rosary beads used by Catholics. Today, *komboli* are used only for fun and relaxation. Playing with them in a methodical swirling motion, while you feel each marble bead slip over your fingers, allows you to pass time, relax, and take your mind off daily cares and troubles. But Mr. Alfearis, you are correct, I see few younger people using them today. Enough though, with all my official tourist guide lectures. Michael, let's ask Mr. Alfearis to help you seek more answers."

Michael began his questions about his father's brother Manoli. All he knew, he said, was that Manoli was a withdrawn individual, who went to church often and studied the Bible and the writings of the Church Fathers constantly. "Most people, my father once said, were sure he would either become a priest or spend his life in a monastery, but he never did and I am eager to learn more about him and his relationship with my father."

"And if you can help, Mr. Alfearis," asked Jenny, "I want to learn more about my grandfather's accident. No one seems to know much, or at least no one wants to talk about it."

The old man looked at both of his visitors intently. The smile that had seemed a permanent fixture on his face now disappeared. "I will tell you what I know," he finally said, "but I'm not sure you will want to hear it all...."

Manoli and Stamatina, 1915

FROM THE JOURNAL, 1915

I WORRY ABOUT THE TROUBLES IN MY FAMILY. MY BROTHER MANOLI IS TOO QUIET, TOO WITHDRAWN. I KNOW HE IS VERY RELIGIOUS, BUT SOMETHING IS WRONG. AND MY SISTER STAMATINA IS SO VERY UNHAPPY. MAYBE IT WAS A MISTAKE TO FORCE YORGOS TO MARRY HER. I JUST DON'T KNOW. SOMETIMES ALL OF THIS BOTHERS AND CONFUSES ME.

In 1915 Yannelli was now seventeen years old. He had grown into a handsome young man, tall for his age in comparison with others, slim, and with gray eyes, fair complexion, and somewhat thin sandy brown hair. He was, since Mihali was in America, the oldest male in the family, who now, after the death of his father, assumed the role of head of the family. The family continued to operate their small village grocery store and grow and harvest olives on their small parcel of land. All of Yannelli's younger siblings worked and helped in some way to sustain the family economically. Their economic situation, after the death of Yannelli's father, Costantinos, was such that none of the other children had the opportunity to be sent to Constantinople for their schooling and instead went to the village school. Yannelli's contribution to the family's finances came from a modest salary he now earned as a mail courier. Each day he delivered mail and packages from village to village and town to town in various parts of Arcadia. He had become an excellent horseman and would ride his horse, Bucephalus, named in honor of the mount of Alexander the Great, from place to place with a large leather bag strapped across his shoulders and two others that hung from both sides of the saddle. It was difficult work, riding on poor roads through hot summer days and cold winter ones, as he traveled his usual route from Agios Andreas to Nafplio to Tripoli and sometimes as far away as Sparta. As difficult as the work was, however, Yannelli loved it. It allowed him to be his own boss, enjoy the natural beauty of each route he was on, and see different communities that others from his own village never in their lifetimes saw. He met new people, learned new things, and acquired information and gossip about people and events in each village in which he worked. The travels associated with the work allowed him, at least for some hours of the day, to enjoy other people, listen to their problems, and temporarily put aside those problems that he now, as head of the family, would have to face.

Listening to the problems of others in other villages, however, was only a distraction, and at the end of each day Yannelli pondered what he could do, if anything, to address those he saw in his own family. He was particularly worried about his younger brother, Manoli. Manoli was now thirteen, still growing but inches shorter than Yannelli, with dark brown hair and hazel green eyes. He was always willing to help with the family chores and work and had never caused any problems for his mother, except for the one that was detected when he was only nine years old. One day, at that very young age, Manoli complained that he felt very sick, that he had a terrible headache, was short of breath, felt nauseous, was losing his sense of balance, and could speak words only with great difficulty. Seeing her young son in such a state, his mother at first panicked, not knowing what to do. Perhaps he ate something old and rotten or even poisonous, she thought, but then quickly dismissed the idea since he had been with her all day and they had both eaten exactly the same food and drink. Not knowing how to deal with the situation and help her son, she told one of the other children to go to the next house to a friend of the family, Fotini, to see if she might have some answers and know what needed to be done. The moment their neighbor entered the house and saw the condition of Manoli, she announced her diagnosis: Manoli had been subjected to the "Evil Eye."

The idea of the Evil Eye had a history in Greece going back to ancient times. Representations of the Evil Eye from pagan times more than two thousand years ago have been found by archaeologists in Greece. The concept, like so many other pagan ideas and symbols, was incorporated into Christianity when the Greeks were converted, and it remained an accepted idea in the Greek Orthodox Church, which referred to it as *Vaskania*. The Church believes it is a form of Satanism, which comes mainly from a sense of extreme jealousy or from coveting the beauty or material things of others. Through the generations many practices were developed to ward off or defeat this curse. Wearing a crucifix was said to defend a person against the Evil Eye; a clove of garlic was said to do the same. Some people wore amulets containing splinters of holy wood or earth from Jerusalem. Others wore a blue charm that had an eye painted in the middle. Sometimes blue beads in the form of a necklace or bracelet were worn as protection against the curse. The color of blue was significant, because individuals who had blue eyes were thought to initiate the Evil Eye with more frequency than individuals with different eye colors. So in many villages people were suspicious of compliments received from a blue-eyed person. In Manoli's village, as in many others, there were individuals who were said to be able to effect a cure by reciting certain prayers, although the Church opposed such practices, believing that only a priest could actually help the afflicted individual through prayers that he offered to God. Customs, developed over countless generations, also were used to determine who in the village might be giving the *kako mati* or Evil Eye to someone as well as who might be capable of eliminating the curse from the afflicted person. It was believed by some that persons whose eyebrows met together or those with green eyes had the ability to cast out the Evil Eye. In other instances, tests of some kind were given to individuals to see if they might be the ones giving the curse. One such test involved getting close to three possible suspects and asking each suspect to throw cloves into the fire. If the clove thrown by a particular person "popped" in the flames, he or she was the guilty party.

As the neighbor Fotini rendered her assessment of Manoli's condition, Yannelli, who was then thirteen, entered the house that was already filled with his brothers and sisters anxiously watching Manoli and listening to what Fotini said needed to be done to relieve the child of the curse. "Bring some garlic," said Fotini, motioning to Manoli's younger brother, Christos. The young boy dutifully walked over to the area where his mother prepared their meals, secured a clove of garlic, and handed it to the neighbor woman. Fotini placed the garlic on Manoli as he lay on the bed, staring at her with a strange and distant look.

"What's that supposed to do?" asked Yannelli, breaking the silence and somber mood that had filled the room. "Manoli needs a doctor. He doesn't need magic tricks and superstitions from long ago, and if Manoli has been cast demons by the Evil Eye, who gave it to him?"

"Yannelli," his mother said sternly, "this is no joke; this is serious. Something is wrong with your brother, and someone has brought this upon him. It could be anyone, someone you know or don't know. Often it is cast by a person with blue eyes."

"Blue eyes, blue eyes!" exclaimed Yannelli, his voice rising to a pitch and tone of disbelief. "If it's a blue-eyed person who is responsible for this, then a few members of our own family and at least a quarter of the village could be the guilty ones. It's all ridiculous, let's get him to a doctor!"

Although Yannelli was thirteen and may have taken on the role of male family head, to his mother he was still her child, subject to her teaching, guidance, and discipline. "Enough Yannelli!" Despina's strong voice clearly conveyed to her son that she had heard enough of his opinions and that Fotini must be allowed to do what she had do to cast the spell from Manoli. As all in the room sat silently and watched, Fotini began to quietly recite prayers over Manoli as he lay on the bed with the garlic clove on his chest. Holding a crucifix in her left hand, she began reciting the words,

Christ and the Virgin Mary
Passed through a crossroad

They spread their golden apron
And ate, crumbs fell upon the apron
They took those crumbs
And tossed them into the sea
The sea waters were stirred up
And man was cured

Then in a louder voice, audible to everyone in the room, Fotini continued, "Holy Virgin, Our Lady, if Manoli is suffering from the Evil Eye, release him from it." She repeated this three times, made the sign of the cross three times, and then spit into the air three times. She turned to Despina and kissed her on the cheek, saying, "Now we must wait, wait to see if our prayers are answered." Wiping droplets of sweat from her forehead, she nodded to the children and walked through the door to return to her home.

Within the next two days, it became clear that Fotini's prayers had not been answered. The symptoms displayed earlier by Manoli had not changed, and it was clear to Despina that the evil had not been cast away from her son. Yannelli continued to ask his mother to seek medical help, at least to let the doctor who traveled among the three or four villages look at him, but his mother kept insisting that Manoli's problem was not medical. "You don't understand, Yannelli," she said, "doctors and medicine are of no help here. Something beyond what doctors know is needed. We will wait one more day. If Manoli is not better, we will call the priest."

The fact that the priest had not been summoned immediately was indicative of the attitudes toward religion and priests in many rural Greek villages. On the one hand, the Greek Orthodox religion had provided guidance, strength, and hope for Greeks through centuries of hardship, slavery, war, and foreign occupation. Through four hundred years of subjugation by the Ottoman Turks, the Church was the key in maintaining the Christian faith against Islam, preserving national identity, and providing education and the transmission of language, history, and culture from one generation to the next. The pagan Greeks of antiquity took to Christianity with ease, since the conversion utilized and incorporated much of what was familiar to them into their new religion. This adaptation did not require a complete break with their pre-Christian beliefs. What had formerly been pagan gods were transformed into Saints. For example, Helios, the sun god, became the prophet Elias, Athena Parthenos became the Virgin Mary, and during the Middle Ages the Parthenon became the Church of St. Mary. In these and many more instances, the new Christian religion was melded with the old paganism. Yet while most villagers took the rituals and the doctrines of religion seriously, they were always ambivalent toward the priests. The fact that the local priests could marry and raise families that gave them the ability to identify with the issues and problems families in their congregations faced was a positive thing. In many villages the priest may have been one of the few literate persons living there. He most often was a person respected in the village. However, the priest, in the eyes of some villagers, could also be an individual to avoid, a bearer of ill omens. Often individuals believed that any encounter with a priest would bring bad luck. For example, a farmer, setting off on some journey or beginning some new venture would, if he met a priest on that particular day, turn around and return home or not embark on his new venture because seeing the priest could be a sign of failure or bad luck. Gestures such as hitting a companion on the shoulder when meeting a priest signified that the individual doing the hitting was passing on the potential bad luck to the other individual that was accompanying him. These, of course, were superstitions, passed down through generations, but they were strong indicators that the priest was not always viewed as a welcomed holy man in many village homes. It was for reasons such as this that the village priest was not always the first person an individual would summon in a time of family problems or crisis. But Manoli's mother had tried the cure of the village wise woman to no avail. After another day had passed with the boy showing no signs of improvement, the village priest was called to the bedside of the stricken child.

Father Petros Mylonas arrived at Despina's home early in the morning. He came in his traditional black garments and stovepipe-looking hat. He was a young man, in his mid-thirties, and wore his dark, somewhat wavy hair tied back tightly, combing it at the back of his head in a short ponytail. Upon entering the house he greeted the family, offered each his hand, which each child, except one, respectfully kissed. Yannelli took the priest's extended hand, gently held it, bowed slightly, and released the priest's hand as he stepped back. The priest starred at him momentarily but said nothing. Yannelli, even at thirteen, had become uneasy with the rituals of the Church. He knew that kissing the priest's hand was supposed to be a gesture of reverence and respect, but he could not get himself to do it. In his mind, the act put the worshiper in a subservient position, not as an equal among all of God's children. He chose to be respectful to this priest and all priests but not through ritualistic gestures that had no meaning for him.

"Father," said Despina, "please help my son Manoli. It appears that the *kako mati* has stricken him."

The priest moved closer to the bed where Manoli was resting, but the boy was still obviously not normal as a boy of his age should be. "I cannot help your child, Despina," he said, "only God can. And through the prayers of our Holy Greek Orthodox Church, we can, through our Lord Jesus Christ's intervention, restore him." With a large silver crucifix in his left hand, Father Petros began reciting the Church-sanctioned ancient prayers against the Evil Eye from the Greek Orthodox book, *The Euchlogion*:

> *O Lord, our God, King of the ages, Who holds all creation and*
> *Is all powerful, Who made all things and wrought all things*
> *By a single command, Who changed the seven-fold furnace*
> *And flame in Babylon into a cool rain and Who protected*
> *the three holy children unharmed, the physician and healer*
> *of our souls, a bulwark of all those who believe in You; we*
> *pray to You and we beseech You, remove and cast away*
> *every diabolical energy, every satanic assault and every*
> *attack, every harmful and wicked curiosity and the evil eye*
> *of the wicked and sinful persons from your servant Manoli;*
> *and whatsoever has happened, either by beauty, or by*
> *courage or prosperity of jealousy or envy or by the evil*
> *eye, do You, O loving Master, stretch forth your strong*
> *hand and send to him an angel of peace, a strong guardian*
> *of soul and body, who will cast out and drive away every*

*evil will and every poison and the evil eye of the envious
and evil people....*

Upon completing the prayer the priest asked all who were present
to join in silent prayer asking God to remove the curse from the boy
Manoli. When all had completed their prayers, the priest shook the
censer, and incense filled the room, particularly over the bed where
Manoli lay. Father Petros made the sign of the cross three times
over Manoli and turned to his mother who was standing close by.
"It is in God's hands now, Despina. We must wait, but we will soon
know."

Despina took the priest's hand, held it tightly in her own, bent
her head, and kissed the clergyman's hand. "Thank you, Father,
thank you." The priest gathered his belongings, patted some of the
younger children on the head, and left the house. The family could
do nothing now but wait.

Within two days Despina and her family were convinced they had
witnessed a miracle. On the first day after the priest's intervention,
Manoli had already shown signs of recovery. He seemed to be
breathing easier, and his eyes seemed to be returning to normal
rather than having that distant, staring gaze. But on the second
day after the prayer offering to God by the priest, Manoli seemed
totally cured, himself again, a normal nine-year-old boy, speaking
to siblings and eager to see his friends again and resume the normal
life of a healthy village boy. Everyone in the family, even Yannelli,
was astonished.

"You see the power of prayer, the power of God, Yannelli,"
his mother said. "You should not be so quick to criticize and to

question our religion. A good man, like Father Petros, working as God's vehicle, can do miracles." Despina did the sign of the cross. "You should go to church more often, my son, it might do you some good." For once Yannelli had no response. Something, he wasn't sure what, had happened. His little brother Manoli was well. The Evil Eye had been defeated. He smiled at his mother, walked over to her, placed her head between his two hands, and kissed her gently on the forehead.

"I thank God Manoli is well, Mother. I do thank God."

In the weeks that followed Despina went to church, prayed to thank God for her son's recovery, and made a pledge to the Virgin Mary. In thanks for God's intervention and cure of her son, she would instruct him to devote his spare time in service to the Church. He would not only serve as an altar boy but make himself available to help the church and priest in every way, learn deeply about religion, and, if it was God's will, perhaps become a priest himself.

For the next four years Manoli, through his mother's encouragement and insistence, devoted first some, then virtually all, of his time at the church helping Father Petros and learning about the Greek Orthodox faith from him. The experience had a profound impact on the boy. Manoli, who had been outgoing and gregarious, had now become, at thirteen years of age, quiet and introspective. He never missed Sunday services and spent his time reading not only the Bible but also the works of the Church Fathers and theologians as well. And he would accompany Father Petros into the mountains to visit monasteries and nunneries and to enjoy the wonder and beauty of nature that was God's creation. At first the family saw the changes in Manoli as a good and positive thing. He genuinely seemed to be deeply religious and gave every sign of wanting to enter the seminary and become a priest someday. But gradually his quietness, his withdrawal, his desire to be alone became pronounced. He was in the house for days, saying nothing unless someone initiated the conversation. He would not seek out other boys who had been his friends and refused to join them when they sought his friendship and companionship. At times, he would sleep for long hours, seemingly uninterested or unwilling to remove himself from his bed. It became increasingly clear to friends and family alike that something was not right about Manoli. Some speculated that perhaps he had been cursed again, thinking that perhaps another person, willingly or unwillingly, had again given him the Evil Eye.

His mother, once happy that he had so diligently followed her offer to God, was now troubled by what she saw in her son. Perhaps she had gone too far, she thought, put too much pressure on Manoli to devote so much of his time and life to the Church. Perhaps he was feeling pressure to become a priest when, in fact, he really had no desire to follow that calling. Her son's behavior troubled her greatly and she once again turned to her older son, Yannelli, for help.

"I'm worried about him," she said to Yannelli, "I don't know what's wrong. He has changed. I saw some of it two years ago, but it has been worse this past year. You need to talk to him. Find out what's bothering him. Tell him that he can stop the work at the church if he wants to. I'm not forcing him to be a priest. I just want him to be the happy boy he was a few years ago, just a happy boy." Despina's voice trailed off; a sense of pain and desperation was in her plea to her older son. Yannelli, too, was worried, very worried, and he decided the time had come to speak with his younger brother.

The next day, after Yannelli had made his mail run to Nafplio and back, he asked Manoli to accompany him for a swim in the sea. The seashore was only a short distance from the village, and a small area had been developed to be used by the local population as a beach. The day was warm and clear, and the water took on an exceptionally vivid, deep blue color that made the area resemble a picture that might be found in a tourist guidebook on Greece. Yannelli and Manoli first spoke generally of things happening in the village or at Manoli's village school, although Yannelli seemed to force the conversation by asking questions to which his brother gave short answers and then became silent as if he were waiting for Yannelli to once again lead the conversation. After a short swim, the brothers sat on nearby rocks to eat some bread, cheese, and olives, which they had brought along from their home. Once again Yannelli took the initiative to begin talking, only now to address the strange behavior of his younger brother.

"Manoli," Yannelli began, "I'm glad we have a chance to talk. I'm worried about you, and so are our mother and everyone in the family. You always seem so sad, you stay mostly to yourself, you seldom speak to any of us. You spend so much time at the church, we hardly see you, and I honestly don't know if you are doing your school studies or not. You need to talk to me, Manoli. I'm your brother, I love you, and I worry so much about you. You need to talk to me. Whatever it is that is bothering you, I can help you, whatever it is. You can tell me and trust me. Are you in some kind of trouble? Are you not feeling well? Or are you worried about something? Please Manoli, you need to talk, let me help you. Whatever it is, it will stay between you and me."

As Manoli listened to his older brother's plea for information, his face turned down, his eyes unable to meet Yannelli as he spoke. He clenched both hands in a tight fist, then opened his hands, rubbed them together, then closed them again in a tight fist configuration as if he were straining to be away from his brother's questions. He seemed eager to get up and walk or even run away. He then bowed his head, placed his hands along side of his head, and began to cry.

"Manoli," Yannelli said as he went to his brother, wrapped his arms around him and held his head close to him. "Manoli, it's all right, I'm your brother, I want to help you, whatever it is I will help you, protect you. Together we can solve anything that is bothering you." Manoli continued to cry, now more forcefully than before as if an emotional barrier had been broken and all his inner feelings were being released in a flood of tears that seemed to have no end. Finally as the tears subsided, he looked at Yannelli with an expression on his face that conveyed the message that he was ready to say something.

"Yannelli," he started, "I'm so confused, so scared, I don't know what's right, what's not. All I know is that I'm so depressed. I feel ashamed. I feel so unhappy, I'm just so confused." Manoli's voice was a voice of desperation, pleading for help, guidance, and answers. He began to cry again and again, as Yannelli continued to hold and attempt to comfort him.

"Talk to me, Manoli, talk to me. I promise you I will help. Please talk to me."

Manoli paused, rubbed the tears from his eyes and began what was the most difficult conversation he had ever had in his still very young life. "It's the church, Yannelli, it's the church, and what the priest has told me and is teaching me. I do spend a lot of time at the church and with Father Petros. I want to be a good person and follow the Church, but what I am learning scares me. It confuses me. I just don't know, I just don't know."

"What is confusing you, Manoli? What is the priest saying to you?"

Manoli proceeded to explain what had transpired in the four years since the priest, through his prayers, had seemingly cured him of the Evil Eye. Following his mother's wishes, he had become an altar boy and gradually began to spend more time at the church. For the first two years, until he was about eleven years old, things seemed normal, and he was relatively happy. But in the last two years, he said, things had changed. Yannelli's attention was now intently focused on Manoli's words, gratified that he had begun to speak but curious and apprehensive about what direction Manoli's story was about to take. Manoli continued speaking, saying that the priest began telling him of the customs and heroes of some individuals in ancient Greece and how it was always considered normal, proper, and even essential that older men mentor young boys and that the mentoring and guiding had a necessary physical side to it. That physical mentoring was homosexual love, the priest said, and it was part of God's plan for mankind, as was heterosexual love. Yannelli did not interrupt, but his face seemed to tighten, the veins in his neck became more evident as he unconsciously pressed his upper and lower teeth together. Manoli paused, collected his thoughts, and continued.

"Father Petros wears something around his neck, alongside the cross," Manoli said. "Maybe you have seen it. It is inscribed with the letters I and Λ."

"I have seen that," Yannelli finally said, "but I never understood what that was for or what it meant. I just assumed it was just some Church thing."

"No," Manoli responded, "it's not a Church thing, although in some ways it is." He went on to say that the letters in the pendant represented the Greek words Ιερὸς Λοχός which meant "The Sacred Band of Thebes." The Sacred Band was an elite group of one hundred and fifty pairs of ancient Greek soldiers. The pairs consisted of older men and their younger companions. They were not only pairs of battle comrades, they were also homosexual lovers. The reason for the establishment of The Sacred Band was that it was believed that the lovers would fight more fiercely and bravely at each other's side than would strangers who had no such homosexual bonds. The pendant with the letters of the Greek alphabet, Manoli said, meant that Father Petros was one of a modern group of warriors for God, who share the same philosophy as the ancient warriors and that one of their goals was to initiate and enlist younger men like Manoli himself into this new religious Sacred Band who would carry on the work of fighting against Satan. In fact, Manoli said, Father Petros taught him that only our Church knew of a great secret—that the philosophy of the ancient Greek Sacred Band became the strategy followed by the Twelve Apostles.

"What?" exclaimed Yannelli. "This is ridiculous! Your saying the priest told you the Twelve Apostles were pairs of homosexual religious warriors operating on the same beliefs as the so-called Sacred Band? And the priest told you this? Ridiculous!"

"I'm just telling you what he has been teaching me, Yannelli. You told me you wanted me to talk, to tell you what's bothering me, didn't you?"

"I'm sorry, Manoli, but it's so hard to believe he told you this and he believes it. So, Father Petros, married and respected in our village, a father of two children, is part of a secret group of homosexual priests who claim they are doing God's work. What else did he tell you?"

"He said…" Manoli started to speak and then stopped as tears once again filled his eyes. "He said that if I wanted to do God's work and be part of this Sacred Band, I would have to submit to his will and do some things that would bond us forever…." The tears now came gushing down from his eyes, and he was unable to continue.

"You can tell me everything Manoli. Remember, I am your brother, and I love you. Everything you tell me will stay with me alone. And I will help you. Take your time and tell me everything."

Manoli took a long deep breath, wiped more tears from his eyes, waited a moment longer to regain his composure, and related the rest of his story. The priest, he said, had told him that as God's representative on earth through the Church, he knew what Manoli should do. He should devote his life to the Church and become a priest but a special one, like himself, a member of the Sacred Band. Manoli went on to relate how the priest had convinced him that to become a true member of the Sacred Band he would have to be initiated through sexual encounters with him and that those had begun about eighteen months ago.

Yannelli seemed unable to speak, a curious combination of shock, anger, confusion, and then rage racing through his mind and body. With a deliberate effort to control his emotions and in an effort to not frighten Manoli from not saying more, he quietly asked, "And where did these encounters take place, Manoli?"

"In fields when we were alone. And in the church, behind the altar." Manoli again began to cry, "Yannelli, what have I done? I'm so ashamed. I trusted him. I believed him! I thought, he is a priest, he must be telling me the truth. I believed him! I'm sorry! I'm sorry! I'm so ashamed. Please, Yannelli, help me, help me!" Manoli's cry of desperation once again moved Yannelli to comfort his brother. He did not chastise him and tried to reassure him that he had not sinned and that what he had revealed would remain only between the two of them.

"Manoli, I don't want you to worry. You're young, you still are. You trusted someone who deserved no trust. He violated you, and God will deal with him. Promise me this—that you will not return to the church or see the priest again. You must promise me this, do you understand? If he asks why, you tell him that you are sick or must catch up on your schoolwork or must help at our store—just tell him something but do not, I repeat, do not go to the church or with him anywhere. Trust me to deal with this, trust me."

Manoli seemed relieved that he had unburdened himself of this secret that had torn at him for more than a year and relieved that his older brother had not chastised him or shown anger at what he had done. He admired his older brother, he trusted him, and if Yannelli said he would deal with the problem, Manoli was confident that he would. He promised Yannelli that he would do what he was told to do and would stay away from the priest and let his brother handle everything. When the two brothers finished what had been a cathartic but emotional encounter, they both walked back into the village, conveying to no one what had transpired between them.

Yannelli returned home, hoping to find time to mentally explore what he could or should do next. He needed a few days to think, he decided, but his mother approached him with news that was to deny him the luxury of a few days of thinking time. Now it was Stamatina, and she needed help.

Stamatina had come to her mother's house exhausted and disheveled. Her clothes had dirt smudges on them, her arm was bruised, and the left side of her face was red and swollen. She had confided to her mother what Despina had long suspected, that Yorgos had struck her and that the beatings were a frequent occurrence in her household. When Yorgos drank too much wine, the beatings were more frequent and severe, but they did not only occur because of alcohol. At other times when he was totally sober, she had told her mother, he repeatedly struck her for what were the most trivial and unimportant reasons—the food was not heated well enough, or their child was unruly, or his clothes had not been washed as yet. Stamatina had tried to shield all of this from her sons and her mother and siblings. She could not, she felt, disgrace herself or her family by complaining or attempting to leave Yorgos. And where would or could she go if she tried? How would she live? Who would support her sons? She had no answers. There seemed to be no answers, so she took the abuse, prayed every day that God would help her or save her, and did what she could to protect her young sons. It was a life of misery, she thought to herself, but maybe this was the price she was destined to pay for the shame she held in her own mind of being a victim of rape. The thoughts made no sense, they followed no logic. She had done nothing wrong. Yorgos was the one who should be the one with shame and guilt, but it seemed she was being forced to suffer the consequences of the code, which was designed so that her family would not be shamed. But now, she could no longer pretend, no longer remain silent. He had physically hurt her too often. She had been bruised, bloodied, beaten, and left to heal herself while her husband offered no apologies, showed no remorse, and openly sought the arms and beds of other women. So now, finally she had come, along with her children, bruises, and tears, home to her mother—and she needed help. As Despina finished telling Yannelli Stamatina's problems, her son felt helpless. Manoli and now Stamatina, what could he do? He was being asked to assume a role more properly carried out by a father—his father—but he was gone. Yannelli at seventeen years of age was having thrust upon him two serious and potentially explosive problems. Circumstances had placed him in a man's role, but even at seventeen, he was really still a boy. He knew he had to respond to his mother's pleas that something had to be done to help Stamatina, and he also knew that he could not let his mother know that he was attempting to decide what, if anything, he needed to do to help Manoli.

"I know, Mother," he finally said. "I know something has to be done. I just need some time to think things through. Tell Stamatina and her boys to come to our house for a month or two. She can tell the neighbors that you were not feeling well and that we needed her here to help with the household chores and to help at our store.

We'll tell everyone it's just for a few months and then she will be returning to her own home. I will take care of telling Yorgos the story of why we need her here."

After speaking with Yorgos, Yannelli helped his sister bring her sons and some clothes and belongings to the family home. Yorgos seemed to accept the story and did not seem particularly upset that he would be alone for a few weeks. Once again, he thought, he could pretend to be a bachelor, no cares, no wife, no responsibilities, and no one watching. But for Yannelli, Stamatina's move was only a temporary reprieve from dealing with the core issue. He was still confused about what he could do. And he was deeply troubled by the issues surrounding Manoli. The priest had not been pleased when Manoli and Yannelli together had gone to him and said that the boy was needed at home and that he had much school work and work for the family business to do. Within a month or two the priest was told, he would have more time and could again devote the bulk of his efforts to the church. Father Petros, not wishing to place too much undue attention on the matter, said he understood and looked forward to having Manoli working back at the church as soon as possible. Manoli's situation filled Yannelli with anger, but he felt helpless. What could he do? Confront the priest and let the entire village know what had happened? Yes, the priest and his family would be disgraced, but what about his brother? What would happen to him? What label and stigma would he carry with him for his whole life? What woman would ever want him? Would Manoli, publicly disgraced, follow with a second family suicide? The questions were too difficult. There were, it seemed, no answers, and Yannelli's frustration mounted as he tried, unsuccessfully so far, to deal with these two seemingly unsolvable problems. He needed some guidance, he thought, and once again he sat down to write to his older brother Mihali, who was now twenty-eight years old and still living in Chicago in far off America. Yannelli wrote to Mihali explaining every detail of what Manoli had told him and what had happened to him. He wrote of his anger, sorrow, and rage about what the priest had done—how he had manipulated their young brother and affected his brain with doctrines and stories that the boy's mind could not comprehend and that Manoli had become a depressed child, filled with shame, almost unable to function. Yannelli continued in his letter with Stamatina's problems, how she had been consistently subjected to verbal and physical abuse and how Yorgos had beaten her, called her names, and disrespected not only her but her children and the entire Bakalis family. He wrote of his anger regarding this situation as well but explained his frustration about the consequences of taking strong action in each case.

Within weeks Yannelli received a response to his letter. Mihali wrote that words in a letter could not convey the outrage he felt upon reading Yannelli's letter. He told Yannelli to do nothing, that he had decided to return to Greece for Easter and see his mother, Manoli, and Stamatina. He had booked his place on a ship that would leave within a week, and he would speak with Yannelli when he arrived at the village. He closed his letter writing, "Yannelli, please do not worry, comfort Stamatina, Manoli, and our mother. I will take care of this. I promise you, I will take care of this."

Mihali from America, 1915

FROM THE JOURNAL, 1915

MIHALI WAS HERE FOR EASTER. WE ALMOST DIDN'T RECOGNIZE EACH OTHER. I HAVE GROWN, AND HE IS TWENTY-EIGHT NOW, AND HE WEARS GLASSES AND HIS HAIR IS BEGINNING TO THIN. HE WAS ONLY HERE FOR TWO WEEKS. STAMATINA'S AND MANOLI'S PROBLEMS HAVE BEEN SOLVED. I DON'T ASK TOO MANY QUESTIONS, BUT THEY HAVE BEEN SOLVED. MIHALI LEFT QUICKLY. I DIDN'T HAVE A CHANCE TO SAY GOODBYE.

Within two weeks after he had responded to Yannelli's letter, the oldest of the family, Mihali, arrived in Greece from America. It was only the second time he had returned to the country of his birth and the village of Agios Andreas. The first time had been when he returned for the funeral of his father, Costandinos. He Had left Greece for America when he was only fifteen, having convinced his mother and father that they should allow him to leave so that he might find employment and send money back to Greece to help the family, which was struggling to live slightly above the poverty level. In the first years he was in Chicago he had sent money to his parents, but what had been a regular monthly amount had now become sporadic, with some months in which the family received no financial help at all.

Coming to Chicago in 1902, he had worked in any job that would take a young immigrant boy who spoke no English. He helped the Greek fruit and vegetable peddlers who sold their produce on small carts on Chicago's State Street. Later he worked as a dishwasher and waiter in the growing number of Greek-owned restaurants that had quickly sprung up throughout the city as more and more Greek immigrants flowed into Chicago. Most of the immigrants came from the Peloponnese area of Greece, in villages close to his own, so there was a natural connection among many of the newcomers, which helped Mihali and others as they sought employment, housing, and people to whom they could relate.

When he had first left Greece, Mihali was fifteen and Yannelli was only four years old, so they had had no close relationship because of the difference in their ages. Coming home for his father's funeral earlier, the two brothers had gotten to know one another personally, although they had corresponded by letter for a number of years. Having gone to America at such a young age, Mihali had grown into a different kind of person from those he had left behind in Agios Andreas. He had escaped the narrow world of the Greek village and had come to manhood on the urban immigrant streets of Chicago. He had gone to Jane Addams's Hull House to learn English and in those classes received an international education as he sat in classes with immigrant Italians, Russians, Poles, Serbs, Jews, and numerous other nationalities as well. And he had quickly learned that being a Greek immigrant was no guarantee that other Americans welcomed you. He learned to defend himself with his fists and the strength of his body as he faced discrimination and was subjected to derogatory remarks and name-calling.

"Greaseball" and "dirty Greek" were words he had heard numerous times and had ignited in him a passion and a rage that found outlets in Mihali's involvement in numerous physical altercations. He was tough, very tough, and his demeanor was that of a person with ice in his veins. He offered no apologies or felt no regrets when he attacked anyone who dared insult him or his nationality. Deep emotion was not part of his makeup. Even when his father died and the rest of the family was stricken with grief, none had witnessed a trace of sadness or tearful eye in Mihali. He bought and rode some of the first motorcycles that appeared in Chicago and traveled at, what were for the times, record speeds on the city streets. When cars became available at a reasonable price through the vision and foresight of Henry Ford, Mihali was among the earliest to own the black Model T. And in driving his new automobile he once again displayed a reckless and confrontational part of his personality. He would deliberately hit another car with his own vehicle if that other driver had cut him off or driven too close to him.

The other side of this outwardly risky, confrontational, and sometimes violent behavior was the Mihali who was a calculating planner, a consummate actor, and a successful charmer of women. His high-speed escapades on his motorcycle had resulted in a crash three years earlier, and he had been seriously injured. Taken to the hospital for treatment and recovery, he had been cared for by a nurse who devotedly worked to bring him to full recovery. The woman was a decade older than Mihali, had never been married, and could be described not only as "plain" but essentially as physically unattractive. During his lengthy stay in the hospital Mihali discovered that the woman had considerable wealth, partly from her savings and partly from an inheritance from her grandfather. Mihali paid her special attention, flattered her, and made her feel as if she were the most important person he had ever met. The woman, desperate for companionship and affection, fell victim to Mihali's charms, and within weeks of his release from the hospital, they were married. Marriage, however, would not be a restriction on Mihali's eyes for women, or his charms, and a succession of other women became part of his life as he continued in his marriage.

After docking at the Port of Pireaus on his latest return to Greece, Mihali made his way to his home village. It was two weeks before Easter and already the residents of Agios Andreas had begun the religious and traditional activities that preceded this, the most important event in the Greek Orthodox Church. His first day at the family home was spent speaking with his mother, Yannelli, and the other siblings who still resided in the house. The conversations were mostly one-sided; everyone wanted to know about America, what it was like to live there, what Chicago was like, what did the Greeks in Chicago do, were the churches there like those in Greece, what was his wife like, and did he ever want to return to Greece? Mihali patiently answered all the questions and sat down for a family dinner with everyone. Immediately after dinner, Mihali asked Yannelli to meet with him alone. Although they had seen one another just a few years earlier, both had changed in their appearance. Yannelli had grown taller, surpassing the height of his older brother. He seemed to Mihali to be more mature, a function of his having had to operate as head of the household. To Yannelli, Mihali had also changed. He was twenty-eight years old and a married man. He now wore glasses, and his dark brown hair showed signs of premature thinning. Yannelli informed his brother of the details concerning Manoli and the priest, as well as Stamatina's problems with Yorgos. Both their brother and sister, Yannelli said, were mentally, physically, and psychologically in terrible shape. "I know something has to be done," he said, "but I'm not sure what to do. There seem to be no good or easy answers."

"You're right," responded Mihali, "there are no good answers and certainly no easy ones, but let me take a few days to think about this. I don't want you to do anything. Promise me that you will not. Let me try to find some solution to all this."

"Okay, Mihali. I'll do that. I think we should all try to forget all of this for a while and deal with it after Easter."

Mihali spent the week prior to Holy Week in the village, reacquainting himself with people he had known as a child and meeting new individuals for the first time who had not known him before he had departed for America. He visited his sister Stamatina and his small nephews as well as her husband Yorgos, whom he had not known before. Mihali made a special effort to speak, laugh, and joke with Yorgos and have him get to know him as the good-natured, fun-loving, brother-in-law from America. He also took time to visit the church, light a candle, pray before the icons, and acquaint himself with Father Petros and the priest's family.

"It's good to see you back in Greece, Mihali," the priest said. You look well, and I pray that America is being good to you. I hope we will see you at services during Holy Week. "

"Good to see you, too, Father," Mihali said. "It's good to see my family again. I love America, but I miss my mother, brothers, and sisters. Father, you have a wonderful family as well. And I will be in church during Holy Week, and I look forward to it."

In America Mihali almost never went to church, nor did he partake in the sacraments of the Church. He certainly believed in God, but in America he had been exposed to a different way of life. No particular religion played such an overwhelmingly important role in the lives of people as did the Church in Greece. He had even had a brief exposure to the writings of Karl Marx who had characterized organized Christianity as being the "opium" of the people, in the sense that it acted as a drug, making people immune to and accepting of the evil, violence, disease, poverty, and injustices of this life by offering the hope of salvation that would then give them eternal life in a heaven with no such problems or afflictions. In addition, the multiplicity of religions in America and the clear doctrine of separation of church and state made for a more secular outlook and environment. But here, in his home village, Mihali was prepared to play the role of a devout Greek Orthodox follower of Jesus Christ.

Holy Week in the village was a time of church attendance, prayer, ritual, and tradition. It was also a time of mourning for the crucified Christ, followed ultimately on Easter Sunday with joy and celebration of Christ's resurrection. Each day of the week church services were held commemorating key moments in Christ's road to death and resurrection. Mihali did not attend each day's liturgy but did attend on Holy Wednesday when the priest administered the sacrament of Holy Unction at which time each member of the congregation is anointed with oil on the forehead, chin, and cheeks, the motion symbolically making the sign of the cross and symbolizing bodily and spiritual health for each participant. As Mihali approached the priest for the anointing, Father Petros nodded and displayed a slight, controlled smile, signaling his approval of Mihali's attendance at the service.

Outside the church the week was filled with tradition and custom. On Holy Thursday few people worked after noon, for as the villagers stated, "It was on this afternoon that Christ was seized." Good Friday signaled a day when none of the villagers worked. During the day flowers were gathered to place around the bier upon which the representation of a crucified Christ would be placed and which would be carried through the streets of Agios Andreas as a soulful, mourning procession before it was returned to the interior of the church. Mihali and the entire family attended the Good Friday service, and even he was moved by the drama and symbolism of the entire sequence of events. On Holy Saturday Mihali once again attended church. This was the Resurrection Liturgy, which was celebrated at midnight with lighted candles illuminating the darkness of the church and the priest's loud message of *Christos Aneste*, Christ is Risen! Leaving the church Mihali saw Yorgos and approached him.

"*Christos Aneste*, Yorgos."

"*Alethos Aneste* (Risen Indeed)," responded Yorgos.

"Yorgos," said Mihali, "There's something I want to speak to you about. Let's have coffee, next Tuesday or Wednesday."

"That sounds good, Mihali. Let's make it Wednesday. I'll meet you about 10 o'clock."

Mihali nodded approval and waved to his sister Stamatina and her sons as he left for home for the traditional meal that was served in Greek homes after the Holy Saturday Resurrection service. Easter Sunday Mihali spent with his mother, brothers, and sisters. All were eager and excited that he had come from America, if only for a short time. Some of the children had not yet been born when as a young boy he had set out for a new life in the United States. They spoke and laughed at the dinner table, eating lamb, cheese, salad, olives, and the special *Tsoureki* Easter bread. At the meal all engaged in the traditional ritual of cracking eggs that had been dyed a dark red, the color representing the blood of Christ. Two persons cracked their eggs against one another's, until one person was left with an uncracked egg. The person holding the last uncracked egg was considered the individual who would have good luck. As each member of the family took a turn cracking the egg of another, only one person remained with a whole egg that had not been damaged. It was Manoli.

"Manoli!" exclaimed Yannelli, "you did it. Luck will be coming your way soon."

Manoli smiled, nodded his head up and down, and said simply, "I hope so."

It was a good day for the family. For at least one day, nothing interfered with all of their being together, meeting, laughing, teasing one another, and simply enjoying each other's company. Mihali finished the evening thinking that this was something he had missed by leaving home at such a young age so long ago. He knew he was here for other reasons, but on this night he was happy to be home. On the Tuesday following Easter Sunday, Mihali walked to the church where he found Father Petros sweeping and cleaning the church of the candles and other items left by the large crowd that had filled the church on Holy Saturday and Easter Sunday.

"Good morning, Father." Mihali said greeting the priest, who then stopped cleaning the floors.

"Mihali! Good morning. I was pleased to see you in church last week. *Christos Aneste*!"

"*Alethos Aneste*," responded Mihali. "Father, I can't stay long, but I need to ask a favor of you. I'll be leaving to return to Chicago on Saturday, and I would like for you to hear my confession before I leave. I know this should have been done before last week, but I was reluctant to relate to anyone what was on my mind. I am away from the village during the day, so I am asking if we could meet Friday evening about eight o'clock at the church. Is that possible?"

The priest was surprised and yet intrigued by Mihali's request. Confession was not something many in the village were comfortable doing, and only a few people actually did it. But he was also curious about what was on Mihali's mind. What could he have done? What sin or sins might he have committed?

"Mihali," the priest said, "I sense that perhaps you have come home not only to your village but perhaps to your religion and God's grace as well. Of course, I will meet with you. I will be waiting at the church on Friday evening at eight. God bless you, my son."

"Thank you, Father, I will be there."

The next day, on Wednesday, Mihali met Yorgos at the coffeehouse in the center of the village. It was a bright, sunny spring day; children were out running around and playing. Almost every table was taken with older men, some playing cards, others dominoes, while still others were talking in an animated fashion, saying as much with their hands as with their mouths. The two men sat at a table. Mihali ordered coffee and some Greek cookies known as *koulodia* for both of them.

"What's on your mind, Mihali? You said you wanted to speak about something."

"It's something I think you'll like, Yorgos, but it's something you must promise to keep between us only. Can you promise me that?"

The secrecy of what Mihali was hinting at both intrigued and excited Yorgos. While he didn't know Mihali very well, he had heard much about him, how he was an adventurer, a risk taker, and someone who could get things done. "I don't know what you want to share with me, Mihali, but I can give you my word, whatever we say here will go no further. I pledge that to you as my wife's brother."

"Yorgo," began Mihali, "I have heard much about you. I know in one way, you're a person much like me in one way at least. You like women, all women very much. Am I not right?"

Yorgos hesitated, not knowing how to respond. He was talking to his brother-in-law, the brother of his wife. He contemplated how to respond. To say no would be the safe but false answer. To say yes could incur the wrath of Mihali, defending the honor of his sister. Mihali, sensing Yorgos's discomfort with the question spoke again before Yorgos could answer. "Yorgo, you and I are both married men, but things are different among men. Yes, I am married, but in Chicago, I see many other women. It harms no one, and it pleases me."

"But," interrupted Yorgos, "Stamatina is your sister!"

'I know, I know, but I sense you are an unhappy man. Listen to me. I know of two young beautiful women, Bulgarian girls, who are working for families in Prastos. I know they are very lonely and are seeking companionship of handsome, virile men, like you and me. On Friday morning I'm going to meet one of them for sure, and I need a partner for the second girl. Will you come?"

Yorgo momentarily contemplated what Mihali was saying. Suddenly he was no longer his brother-in-law, the brother of his wife, but rather another man speaking as a friend about what he talked about with his other men friends. And the prospect of a liaison with some young girl, who probably couldn't speak Greek and whom he would never see again, excited his imagination. All his apprehension and hesitation were suddenly gone, eased by the thrill and excitement of what he could imagine. "I'll go, Mihali, I want to go," said Yorgos, "but as you said, it remains between us only."

Mihali smiled, then laughed. "Good decision, Yorgo. You won't regret it. I have seen these girls, they are beautiful and uninhibited. Your wish is their command." Yorgos found it difficult to contain his excitement. "I'll meet you early, about seven o'clock in the morning, on the road to Prastos," said Mihali. "And remember, tell no one where you are going."

"Seven o'clock. I'll be there, Mihali. You can be sure, I'll be there."

On Friday morning as Mihali waited for Yorgos to arrive, he sat under the fig tree, slowly savoring the taste of the figs he had just picked. Yorgos arrived, but the look on his face conveyed a message of concern and apprehension. "Come, Yorgos, sit with me before we start up the mountain to Prastos. The figs are good and sweet."

"Mihali," Yorgos said, his voice filled with a sense of worry, "I don't think it's a good idea for you or me to sit there, and I'm not sure today is a good day to leave Agios Andreas."

Mihali seemed perplexed by Yorgos's words and the mood he was in. "What's wrong, Yorgos? What's bothering you?"

"This morning," said Yorgos, "I awoke and saw two crows, obviously fighting over something, flying directly over my house. It's a bad omen, Mihali, it means that someone in that house will die soon. And then I come here this morning, and I find you sitting under the fig tree, another bad omen. Mihali, it was under the fig tree that Christ was sitting when he was taken by the soldiers, which eventually led to his crucifixion."

"Yorgos!" exclaimed Mihali, "are you really serious? Do you believe that ridiculous stuff? I'm surprised, I thought somebody with your knowledge of books and archaeology would know better. Forget that nonsense. You should be thinking of what awaits us in Prastos. I'm telling you, you have never met girls like the ones waiting for us. The only omens you should consider are good ones, two twenty-three-year old beautiful Bulgarian girls waiting to please us."

Mihali's picture of what rewards awaited them in Prastos once again cleared Yorgos's mind of the omens he believed he had encountered, and as Mihali continued to describe what was to come, Yorgos smiled, looked at Mihali, and said, "Let's go."

Prastos, located high in the mountains was difficult to access. What was considered a road was in reality a dirt path, wide enough for only a small cart pulled by a mule to pass. The road was dangerously close, at some points, to the edge of the mountain. Looking down from the edge was to look into a cavernous hole, miles down in depth, making objects at the bottom appear as miniature toys that might be found in a house made for dolls. And the village of Prastos sat at the very top of these high mountains. Mihali and Yor-

gos slowly and carefully made their way up the mountain; they estimated it would take an hour, or perhaps two, before they reached
their destination. Mihali had argued against going by horseback,
because some of the twists and turns of the dirt road up the mountain would be too difficult for the horses to make, and they might
bolt or panic at the extreme heights and throw both men over. Better to be safe and go more slowly, Mihali had cautioned. After more
than an hour of walking, the two men had climbed approximately
two thirds of the mountain's height, and Mihali suggested they stop
to rest.

As the two men sat on some nearby flat rocks and shared some
water, suddenly everything changed. Mihali's smiling face had
lost its smile, his eyes betrayed a man changed from who he had
been just moments before. Without warning, he sprang on Yorgos,
throwing him to the ground, and began pounding on his face with
closed fists, over and over and over again. Yorgos, totally shocked
and surprised at this attack, tried to protect his face but could not.

"You cowardly bastard," yelled Mihali, as he continued to pound
on Yorgos's now bloodied face. "Maybe now you'll know what it
feels like to be beaten, the same way you have beaten my sister. Can
you only hit women, you piece of shit? Is that it, can you only hit
women?" As Yorgos gasped for breath, Mihali continued his brutal
assault on him, hitting his face, chest, arms, and head with an un-
controlled fury of rage.

"Please, Mihali, please," pleaded Yorgos when he could manage
to speak at all. "Please forgive me. I was wrong. It will never happen again, I promise you. Please stop!" Blood now covered his face,
dripping down onto his shirt, his eyes half closed from the brutality

of Mihali's attack. Finally Mihali stopped, pulled out a small pistol from his pocket, and ordered Yorgos to stand. Yorgos struggled to get to his feet but finally managed to stand while holding on to a nearby tree for support. Mihali raised the gun and placed it firmly against Yorgos's head.

"Empty your pockets, take off the chains around your neck, and take off your rings," Mihali ordered.

"Please, Mihali, please. Why are you doing this? I will give you anything. I will never hurt Stamatina again! I promise you that on my word!"

"Your word," said Mihali, a coldness in his voice that Yorgos had never heard before, "is as valuable as your piss, do you understand? You are as valuable to me or to my sister as the rocks we see here all around us. But I'm going to give you a choice, Yorgo—one you should seriously consider."

"What is it, Mihali, what is it? Please don't hurt me anymore." Yorgos' face and eyes now conveyed messages of fear and panic that he had never before experienced, even greater than the time Yannelli had placed a gun in his mouth and told him that he must marry Stamatina. For some reason, he had felt that Yannelli would spare him, but he had no such feeling about Mihali. Continuing to hold the loaded pistol to the side of Yorgos' head, Mihali put forward the choice he was presenting to Yorgos.

"I will either put a bullet in your head and leave you here for the vultures to feast on…" Mihali paused as tears began streaming down Yorgos's face, "or give you a chance to live or die on your own. You see how close we are to the edge of the mountain? The second of your choices is to jump off this mountain, Yorgos. If you die, you will have deserved it; if by some miracle you live, I will forgive what you have done to my sister, all will be forgiven, you can go on with whatever life holds for you. What is your choice, Yorgos?"

Yorgos's body was now shaking, the tears continuing to flow from his eyes. He tried once again to plead with Mihali, "Please, please, Mihali, please don't do this. Your sister will be a widow, who will care for my sons? Please, Mihali, I will never hurt Stamatina again, never, never, never!"

Mihali said nothing. Pressing the gun more firmly against Yorgos's head, he said in a whisper, "What is your choice, Yorgos?"

Yorgos knew that either choice was a probable death sentence, but if, by some unlikely miracle, something could break his fall from the mountain, or if he could somehow latch on to some strong branch protruding from the mountainside, perhaps he could survive. He knew all of these things were unlikely, but somehow a leap off the mountain at least gave him some chance; a gunshot to the head did not. "Don't shoot, Mihali, I will take my chance."

Mihali, still holding the gun at Yorgos's head, led Yorgos to the edge of the mountain. Saying nothing further, Yorgos did the sign of the cross three times and lunged over the side. Mihali's eyes followed Yorgos's body as it fell farther and farther until he could barely see it any longer. Then it stopped its descent, splattered against an extension of the mountain that was protruding from its side. Mihali picked up Yorgos's belongings and began his descent down the mountain. It was still daylight, and he had another appointment later this Friday evening.

Just before eight o'clock in the evening Mihali approached the village church of Agios Andreas. The church was located directly at the head of the village square where usually, at this hour, the tables would be filled with villagers drinking coffee or sipping ouzo, but on this night the weather had kept everyone in their homes. A severe spring thunderstorm was passing through the area, which gave no sign of slowing down. Thunder and lightning continued as Mihali approached the door of the church, his clothes already soaked by the downpour of rain. The church and the village were named after Andrew, who had been the first called by Christ to be an Apostle. He was the brother of Peter, and both had been fishermen. After Christ's crucifixion, Andrew preached Jesus' Gospel in Asia Minor and Greece. His life ended when he was crucified in Patros, Greece.

Mihali entered the church, which was dark except for the multiple lit candles that provided not only some light but a small measure of warmth for his rain-soaked body. He reached for the tray in which small orange-colored candles were placed, took one, lit it from the flame of one already burning, and placed it in the receptacle in which parishioners placed their candles. He walked over to the icon located to the left of the candles, made the sign of the cross, and bent down to kiss the holy picture. Churches always had a special smell, Mihali thought, the smell of incense. It was an odor he had almost forgotten, since in Chicago he almost never went to church or partook in any church rituals or sacraments. He did not yet see any evidence of the priest, so he entered the church area where on Sundays the worshipers gathered. Pictures of the Saints looked down on him from every wall.

"Mihali," the word came from the entrance to the church. It was Father Petros. "Mihali, I am sorry I am late. The water from the rain was coming into my home, and I had to do some patchwork so that the whole house would not be flooded. It looks as though you did not escape the rain either. Fortunately I had a rain covering and an umbrella. Come with me, I have some towels and you can dry yourself off, at least as much as you can."

"Hello, Father," said Mihali. "It's really very bad out there. It is a night to be home, and I very much appreciate your meeting me on a night like this. If I were not leaving to return to Chicago tomorrow, I would have waited until a better time. And I will take that towel, thank you." Mihali attempted to dry himself as best he could, wiping his hands, face, and head. His clothes remained wet but were slowly drying in the warm interior of the church. "Except for last week, Father, it has been such a long time since I was in this church. It feels good."

"I was glad to see you and your family during our Easter services. I know you were an altar boy here, when you were about eight or nine. We have some new icons in the sanctuary, and it has been remodeled. Would you like to see it?" The sanctuary of the church was a holy place in which only certain persons could enter. Those who were non-Orthodox, as well as women, were forbidden from entering. And only the priest was allowed to stand in the area where the priest conducts church services.

"I would like that," said Mihali, "it has been years since I was in there." The priest led Mihali to the door to the left of the *iconostasis*, which divided the church between where the priest conducted services and where parishioners sat or stood during the Holy Liturgy.

"Come, Mihali, follow me, through this door with the image of St. Michael, the Archangel, your Patron Saint. It will bring you good luck through God's blessing." Mihali followed the priest through the door into the sanctuary. He could not remember all the details of how it had looked when he was a child, but it did look different; it was cleaner, and it had icons with more vibrant colors and a greater number of gold and silver candelabras.

"This is very nice, Father, it does look different from what I remember. It's all very beautiful. I get a good peaceful feeling standing here."

"Yes, it is beautiful. And I, too, have that same feeling when I'm conducting the Sunday Liturgy. But, Mihali, what is on your mind? How can I be of service?"

Mihali hesitated, as if he was reluctant to say why he had requested this meeting. Finally, he did speak. "Father, I am here for confession, something, I must admit, I have never done before, but I feel that now I must talk to a priest."

"Of course, Mihali, I am glad you feel that way. Confession is one of our Holy Sacraments. It is something all should do, but unfortunately, most do not."

In the Greek Orthodox faith confession takes a different form from the image commonly held of that same Sacrament in the Roman Catholic Church. In the Orthodox Church there is no wall or screen barrier between the priest and the person offering confession. They sit openly, discussing the issue face-to-face in a conversational mode. The Greek word for "sin," *amartia*, is not an exact translation of the English word. In Greek, the word means missing the mark in the same way an archer might miss his target. Confession provides a way for the penitent to hit the proper target once again and unburden himself of the *amartia* that has brought the person to the priest for confession. It also allows the individual to partake of the Eucharist or Holy Communion with a clean heart.

"Mihali, let's stay here, in the sanctuary, in an atmosphere that, I think, allows us to speak openly about what is on your mind and in your heart. Here, let's sit on these benches and talk." The two men sat on the wooden benches, which were placed against the back wall of the sanctuary. Candles flickered around them, and the smell of incense was particularly strong, since it was in this area where it was regularly used by the priest during every church service. Mihali now began the scenario he had rehearsed in his mind over and over since he had first received Yannelli's letter telling him about what the priest had done to Manoli.

"Father," Mihali began, his head bowed down, seemingly unable to look the priest in the eye, "in the past few years I've had some thoughts and desires I never had before and still don't understand. You know, I am married, but something is wrong. I have thoughts and fantasies about not being with my wife, or even other women, but with men. I think I physically desire men, and I don't know what to do, Father. I don't know what to do. Please help me. Have I sinned? What will happen to me?" Mihali was now giving his best performance and was pleased with the irony of the entire scene. He, who loved women, and continued to have many of them, was telling this filthy pedophile priest that he was homosexual, and he was thoroughly enjoying the charade. "Is homosexuality a sin in our Church, Father? Is there any hope for salvation, if that is what I am?"

The priest listened intently, surprised and temporarily unable to think about what his response would be. Finally, he responded to Mihali's questions. "Mihali," he began, "the teachings of our Church go back centuries ago. Issues pertaining to sexual matters are wholly determined by the Church's view of marriage and the family. It is the family, as history has shown, that has been the unifying element in our society. The Church teaches that the only morally correct place for sexual relations is marriage and that marriage can only be between a man and a woman. Homosexuality is thus an attack on the institution of marriage and the family. The Church condemns homosexuality, and it is considered a sinful failure. An individual who is homosexual, the Church doctrine states, degrades his own sex and is out of line with God's intent in creation. It is a moral perversion."

Mihali listened intently, careful to pay attention to every word of the priest's statement of official Church doctrine. "But Father," he said, "if what you say is so, why did God create individuals who have these desires and thoughts about the same sex?"

"None of us can fathom all of God's actions or intent, Mihali. We cannot fully understand why diseases afflict people, why infants and children die, why earthquakes kill innocent people. We know that evil exists in the world, we know that Satan continues to influence us and cause wrongdoing, but the honest answer is that we simply don't know. We cannot, as humans, understand all the ways of our Creator."

"I believe that, Father, but who are these flawed humans, whether Church Fathers or anyone else to sit in some ecclesiastical meetings and pretend to issue Church doctrine in God's name?"

"These are men ordained by God to interpret His will, Mihali. We cannot question what they determine is Church doctrine." The priest seemed to be increasingly uncomfortable with Mihali's questions, and Mihali sensed the discomfort.

"But what do you believe, Father? Not what Church doctrine is, but what do you personally believe?"

The priest now moved nervously on the bench, his fingers quickly stroking the pendant hanging from his neck, the pendant with the inscription of the Greek letters, 'ΙΛ'. Mihali fixed his eyes on the priest, watching as he moved the pendant through his fingers. "I'm a priest, Mihali," he finally said, "I follow the doctrine of the Church. I believe the doctrine of our Church. But you must understand something else. While our Church condemns the thoughts you are having, it also believes you can change those thoughts through prayer and help you find your way back to what is morally right. The sins that have entered your mind and cloud your thinking can be forgiven. Let me pray for you, Mihali. Let these prayers cleanse your mind, your heart, and your soul."

Mihali now knew that the moment he had planned for, the reason he had come to the church at this time, had come. "Thank you, Father. Please pray for me. I don't want to sin, I don't want to sin." Mihali bowed his head and wiped his eye as if to clear away a tear, although there were no tears.

"Mihali," said the priest, "please kneel before me so that I may recite the prayer of absolution." Mihali knelt before the priest, and bowed his head as the priest placed a stole on his head and then placed his own hand upon the stole saying,

Whatever you have said to my humble person, and whatever You have failed to through ignorance or forgetfulness, Whatever it may be, may God forgive you in this world and in the next. Have no further anxiety; go in peace.

As the priest removed the stole from Mihali's head, Mihali slowly rose from the position of kneeling, reached into his coat pocket, and withdrew his pistol. "And you go in peace as well, you lying, perverted hypocrite."

Horror consumed the priest's face. He stood motionless, unable to understand what he was witnessing. "Mihali! Mihali! What are you doing? We are in the sanctuary, Mihali! This is a holy place! What are you doing?"

"The question, you perverted pig, is what did you do to a child, my brother Manoli? But you know what you did. Perhaps you can't satisfy your good wife, Father? And not even grown men? Only a child, only a boy? The boy who is my brother! The boy whose life you have ruined forever!" Mihali was now shouting, enraged by the thought of what this man had done to his young brother.

"Mihali, I don't know what you are talking…" The priest did not finish his sentence as Mihali pulled the trigger on the pistol, as the discharged bullet entered the priest's forehead splitting his skull, as blood burst out, and he fell to the ground.

"That was for the Father," Mihali said. A second shot entered the priest's heart. "That was for the Son, holy man." As the already dead body lay motionless on the floor, Mihali fired a third shot, this time the bullet entering the groin area of the priest. "And this is for the Holy Spirit, so that you will never again violate my brother or any other child." Mihali looked around and gathered some gold candelabras as well as the gold cover that held the Holy Bible. He moved to the nearest icon, made the sign of the cross, and softly uttered the words, *Kyrie Eleson*, Lord have Mercy. He walked out of the church in what was a continuing downpour of rain. Drenched again by the water, he began his journey to the Port of Pireaus, prepared to board the ship, which would take him back to America the next morning. As he walked in the rain, he felt a sense of relief. Now Stamatina and Manoli were safe. They would not be abused again. They did not have to live a life of shame and fear.

Michael and Jenny, 1980

The old man continued to systematically swing the beads as he concluded his story of Manoli, Stamatina, and Mihali. It was almost an unconscious movement of hand and bead coordination that could, in some ways, be annoying when one was trying to have a serious conversation. But Phillipos Alfearis had not allowed the beads to distract him from his thoughts or interrupt the flow of memories and words that came from his mouth. "It's quite a story, isn't it," he said. "Quite a story."

Michael and Jenny had listened intently as Phillipos had related his tale of abuse, violence, and revenge. "It is quite a story," Michael said. "In fact, it's almost hard to believe. First of all, how do we know it's true, since you said that no one knew of the meeting my Uncle Mike had that one day with Yorgos and then the priest?"

Mr. Alfearis temporarily stopped twirling the beads and then thought for a moment before he answered Michael's question. "For a very long time," he said, "absolutely no one knew what had happened. It was only years later when your father had gone to America that he asked his brother if he had, in any way, been connected or involved in the two deaths. Your uncle, after time had passed and he was safely in America, did finally tell your father the truth. And Mihali never returned to Greece again, mostly because he had severed the connection with his homeland but also, I would guess, because of his concern that somehow if he returned something might develop that would tie him to the two deaths."

"And how did you come to know the facts of the story, Mr. Alfearis?" Jenny asked.

"Sometime after Yannelli found out the truth from his brother, I made my first and only trip to the United States. My brother was living in Rock Island, Illinois. I stayed in Illinois for about nine weeks and made a trip to Chicago to see your father. Remember we had been friends since we were boys, fought side-by-side against the Turks. We were closer than brothers, and Yannelli told me what he had learned."

Michael rose from his chair and began a small circular walking movement around the area in which they were sitting. This really is incredible, he thought. He knew his uncle was different from his father, but had never imagined he was that different! "You know," he finally said, "I'm named after my uncle. I saw him, not often, but enough to get to know him, I thought. But I guess I really didn't know him."

Jenny felt conflicting emotions as she listened to the drama the old man had related about her grandfather and grandmother. She had been born after Yorgos's accident but had known her grandmother and had visited with her in the village numerous times. She loved her grandmother whom she knew as a kind, hard-working woman. "At the time," she asked, "how was my grandfather's death explained?"

"It was well known that there had been bandits operating on the mountain road from Agios Andreas up to Prastos," said Mr. Alfearis. "Yorgos's body was not found for days, and when it was, it was barely recognizable as him. When it was discovered that the few valuables and the money he had were missing, it was assumed that bandits had robbed him and killed him. I assume that's what Mihali had in mind when he took those things and I imagine disposed of them somewhere."

"And what about my grandmother? What was her reaction?" asked Jenny.

"Jenny, your grandmother Stamatina must have found herself in a difficult situation. She was a good, kind woman who would not have wished such a terrible death on anyone. I don't think she ever found out the real story of what had happened. She was suddenly a widow with two children and no real way to support herself and her sons. In the village Stamatina did the customary things widows do about husbands who have died. She wore black at all times, mourned at the funeral, and dutifully participated in the exhumation ritual of Yorgos's remains after two or three years. But I also believe she must have also felt a sense of relief and freedom, freedom from the violence that her husband had been constantly inflicting on her. She remained in her house, and her adult brothers did help her and she was able to get by until, as you know, about six years later she married again. The man she married was a widower himself who had no children. He was a good man and treated Stamatina well. They were, for the most part poor like all of us, but I think they were happy."

"But the priest's murder must have been a tremendous shock to everyone in the village. What did people say and think?" asked Michael.

"It was a tremendous shock," replied Mr. Alfearis. "I'm not sure that even to this day, when people relate the story, they understand any motive. The one motive that at least had some credibility was that it was a robbery that had somehow gotten out of control. Once again Mihali's taking of gold objects, which, I was told by Yannelli, he later discarded, planted the idea that thieves were at work. The priest's wife and children did not remain in the village, but I have never heard where they went or what had happened to them. Fortunately for Manoli, no one ever discovered what the priest had done to him as a child. Manoli, as you know, did eventually marry and have a family, but he was never really completely right."

"Right?" questioned Michael.

"I guess that's the correct word," said Mr. Alfearis. "He continued to be withdrawn and moody. It seemed as though he found it difficult to be amused by things or find jokes or situations funny. Before he married, he did spend a short time in the seminary to become a priest, but here too he could not follow through. Perhaps the whole idea of the priesthood brought to mind too many bad and hurtful memories. I just don't know."

Michael tried to picture himself in all of the situations Mr. Alfearis was describing. "How did my father deal with all of this?" he asked.

Mr. Alfearis thought for a moment and then offered his explanation to Michael. "I think Yannelli must have known all along that two such violent deaths happening on the same day with people from the same village were more than coincidence or the work of greedy bandits. Your father was too smart to buy the commonly accepted explanations. Add to this the fact that your uncle left in the middle of the night, speaking to no one in the family and never returned to Greece. Yannelli must have lived with these facts and doubts for a long time but still needed absolute confirmation directly from his brother, which he finally received years later. He questioned his brother's method of solving the problems of Manoli and Stamatina, but he was loyal and respectful of his older brother so would not question or criticize what he had done. And besides, although it was not in Yannelli's makeup to say so, he probably felt that Yorgos and the priest got what they deserved. And it did relieve him of worries that he had carried constantly and allowed him now to plan and live is own life."

"Mr. Alfearis," said Michael, now hoping to change the subject, "I'm also curious about something else. In the next few years after the episode we are talking about, my father became eighteen, nineteen, and twenty years old. It's hard to think of your own father this way, but he must have been interested in girls, or a particular girl sometime in those years. Was he? And what can you tell me about it?" Michael waited for an answer. It was something he had always wondered about but would have never directly asked his father.

Mr. Alfearis smiled. "Well, of course, he was interested in girls, and so was I. In fact, I still am at eighty-five, although now all of it is just interest. I may be old, but I'm not dead," he said as his smile now broadened into a full-blown laugh. Michael and Jenny laughed along with him as they waited for him to provide more details. "Michael, your father was a young man who was very much interested in a girl from our village named Alexandra Rigatos. He was about nineteen, she was about seventeen or eighteen. She was a beautiful girl, very fair with almost blond hair and green eyes. I knew her, too, and she was a very nice girl. But remember, being interested in a girl around 1917 was not the same as today. The traditions and customs of the village basically set the rules of what you could or could not do, although there were some important differences in our village because of the Spartan influences from ancient times."

Michael was intrigued by what Mr. Alfearis was saying, as his mind attempted to construct a mental picture of his father as a young man liking, or possibly loving, this young girl. "Obviously my father and Alexandra did not marry since he met and married my mother after he came to the United States, but what happened to this girl? Did she ever marry? Is she still alive? Is she still here in the village?"

"All I know," answered Mr. Alfearis, "is that after your father left for America I think they wrote letters to one another for a few years, but then Alexandra married someone from the island of Hydra. I really don't know if they ever had any contact after that. As far as I know,

Alexandra is still alive, she's about eighty now and still lives on Hydra where she moved with her husband when they married." The fact that she was still alive intrigued Michael. He wondered what it would be like to meet the woman and whether she would be prepared to talk about her connection with his father that had happened so many years before.

"Do you know if Alexandra has a family?" Michael asked.

"I believe she has a son and a daughter," said Mr. Alfearis, "and I think the son lives on Hydra as well, but I'm not sure. Until today with your visit I really haven't had any reason to keep up with Alexandra or her family."

Michael and Jenny had enjoyed not only Mr. Alfearis's account of the family history but his company as well. He was a very pleasant man, seemingly content with his life now that he was in his mid-eighties. He seemed to genuinely enjoy telling his stories and simply having the company of both Michael and Jenny. After giving Mr. Alfearis their thanks and appreciation for the time he had spent and the information he had provided, Michael convinced Jenny that they needed to make the trip to Hydra. He felt he needed to see and meet this woman who was perhaps his father's first real love. And he wondered what might have happened had his father not gone to America? Would they have married? Was this woman in love with his father? And if he did actually meet the woman, would she be willing to talk freely and candidly about their relationship, whatever it was? He decided that even if Alexandra was unwilling to speak of those long ago events, he still needed to meet her, to see the only woman he had ever heard about, besides his own mother, who had had an emotional connection to his father.

Leaving from Nafplio, Michael and Jenny took the motorized hydrofoil boat to the island of Hydra. The trip took about an hour, which was shorter than the three-hour trip by ferry boat. Arriving at the port they were struck by the picture beauty of the location. Shops surrounded the bay area, and houses were situated in higher elevations in the mountains. It was an exceptionally warm, clear day, and the sun's rays made the dark blue water of the sea seem even more blue than usual. The island had a special feel of quietness and tranquility since no motorized vehicles were allowed. In past history the island had served as an escape destination as people from mainland Greece had come and sought refuge there from the Turks during their domination of the country. The island had also been the base for many entrepreneurial Greeks engaged in commerce throughout the Aegean. By 1980 it was a popular tourist destination for day trips from Athens and was home to many people engaged in various forms of the arts. Tourists were also attracted to the fine jewelry shops, the beaches, the monasteries that they could visit, and the active nightlife in numerous music and dance clubs.

After lunch at one of the seaside cafes, Michael and Jenny began the search to locate Alexandra Rigatos. To their surprise, it was easier than they had anticipated. Excluding tourists, the actual resident population of the island was just over two thousand people, and most residents either knew one another or knew someone who knew someone else. Within a short half-hour of questioning various shopkeepers, they received the information they were seeking. Alexandra Rigatos was a widow who lived about a quarter of a mile up the mountain immediately behind the bay of the island. More questions resulted in an address of the woman as well as a telephone number. Jenny placed a call that Alexandra answered. Jenny explained that she and Michael had relatives from Mrs. Rigatos's girlhood village of Agios Andreas and that they were doing research on the village and simply wanted to ask her some questions about her memories of her childhood there.

Jenny deliberately said nothing about Yannelli, not knowing how the woman would react to questions about him from people who were total strangers.

Alexandra had been surprised by the call but was friendly and gracious in her reply. She invited Jenny and Michael to her home and said she would look forward to their visit and company. Since there was no access to the house except by foot, Michael and Jenny slowly walked up what appeared to be marble steps that led from the seashore to the homes built in the mountainside. Finally reaching the house, they stopped to catch their breath, wondering how an eighty-something-year-old woman could make such a trip day after day. Approaching the front door of the house, Jenny knocked. Michael seemed nervous. In a moment he would be looking at a woman that his father may have loved. It was a strange sensation, and he waited as someone opened the door.

"Welcome," the woman said, "please come in." Michael stared at the woman, immediately noticing her clear green eyes and then abruptly caught himself.

"Mrs. Rigatos, my name is Michael Bakalis, and this is my cousin Jenny Berdalis. Thank you for allowing us to visit with you."

The woman had fair skin, remarkably free from the wrinkles associated with someone in her eighties. Her hair was white, and she was a small woman, perhaps just over five feet tall. She was still an attractive woman, and Michael tried to imagine what she might have looked like as a young girl of seventeen or eighteen. Alexandra seemed to be returning a penetrating look to Michael as well. Looking at him she said, "I heard your name, Michael, Mihali I assume in Greek, but what did you say your last name was?"

"My name is Bakalis, Mrs. Rigatos," Michael answered, pronouncing his surname with the best Greek accent he could imitate. "It's Ba-Kalees." Alexandra seemed frozen; she did not move for what were only a few moments but seemed like more.

"Which Bakalis are you?" She finally said. "Who are you related to?"

"My father was Yiannis Bakalis. I believe he was known as Yannelli as a boy. I am Yannelli's son."

Alexandra remained silent, just looking at Michael, looking and looking at him. Tears now came to her eyes. She slowly walked toward him and then embraced him. Michael, not knowing exactly how to react or what to do, placed his arms around the old woman. "Are you all right, Mrs. Rigatos?" Michael asked, not knowing what else to say. Through Jenny's function as an interpreter, she said she was fine, just pleasantly surprised to meet the son of a friend from so long ago.

Michael explained why they had come to visit her and that he had heard that his father and Alexandra had been friends when they were young. He was cautious with his words as he spoke, not quite knowing how to describe or characterize the relationship. He was careful not to suggest that they might have been lovers or even in love with one another, fearing that such a suggestion would offend the woman and make her reluctant to speak to them about what the connection might have been. But Michael and Jenny were surprised by Alexandra's response. Rather than being reluctant to speak about the past, she seemed eager to do so, as if to these strangers she could now speak of things that she had held within for decades.

"I am an old woman now," she started, "and I am a widow. My good husband died ten years ago. We had a good life together, and I know he would not object to my speaking to you about things that happened before he and I met and before your father and mother met. Yes, Yannelli and I were friends, but we were much more than that. Let me explain…"

Alexandra, 1917

FROM THE JOURNAL, 1917

THINGS HAVE BEEN BETTER THE LAST TWO YEARS. MANOLI IS MUCH BETTER AND MAY STILL WANT TO BE A PRIEST, AND STAMATINA ALSO SEEMS BETTER THAN I HAVE EVER SEEN HER. MY YOUNGEST BROTHER CHRISTOS IS WORKING AS A MAIL COURIER AS I AM. HE SEEMS TO BE INTERESTED IN A GIRL HE HAS SEEN IN ARGOS, AND I HAVE AGAIN MET ALEXANDRA WHO I REMEMBER AS A CHILD, BUT NOW I SEE AS A BEAUTIFUL YOUNG WOMAN. I LIKE HER VERY MUCH AND THINK OF HER CONSTANTLY.

For once Yannelli was experiencing what he considered to be normal times. In the two years since his brother Mihali had returned to America, the days had been characterized as routine and peaceful. Manoli still seemed to be very religious, but the stress and guilt he had experienced seemed to be gradually disappearing. Stamatina, although now a widow with two children to support, was struggling financially but was clearly less stressed and generally considered herself happy with the quiet and peace that had finally come to her life. The major worry confronting every village and city in Greece was the increased prospect that the country would be drawn into the conflict now raging on the continent. What would later be labeled World War I was killing young men on both sides of the war in record numbers, and the government of Greece was attempting to walk a delicate line of neutrality but only with great difficulty. To most informed observers it seemed as if it would only be a matter of time before Greece would be pulled to ally itself with one side or the other.

Yannelli was very much aware of what was transpiring across the continent and knew he would soon be called to the military service commitment required of all Greek males. But as yet his age and the fact that he was the head of a household that required his economic contribution to survive meant that he would probably have perhaps another year before he entered the army as long as Greece remained neutral in the European conflict. It was a commitment he actually welcomed and looked forward to, but he also knew that he had the major responsibility to oversee his younger brothers, sisters, and mother and to organize the ways each contributed to the well-being of the entire family. But in spite of the clouds of conflict that were hovering over Europe, life in the village, as yet untouched by war, went on as it had for countless generations.

Within every Greek village the daily unchanging routines of life were broken by Holy Days, ceremonies, baptisms, weddings, names days, and village festivals. In villages such as Agios Andreas, which had been named after the Apostle Andrew, once a year a festival was held honoring the particular Saint associated with the village. Although the official day commemorating St. Andrew was actually in November, the village elders for many years had decided to hold the festival in May when the weather was more conducive to outdoor activities and the intense heat of the summer had not yet arrived. This event, while essentially a community activity, also brought back to the village individuals who had been born there or lived there in past years, but who, for a variety of reasons, had left the village to reside elsewhere. It was a time to see and socialize with current and old friends. It was also a time when the young men and women of the village had the opportunity, in full view of their parents as overseers, to meet and speak with one another. The festival was filled with music, dancing, and a continuous presentation of food, wine, and Greek sweet pastries.

Agios Andreas, in particular, presented an environment seldom found in most rural Greek villages. What made Agios Andreas different was the unique view and place of women in the social structure of the community. In contrast to many Greek villages, women played a more open and visible role, much of it a direct heritage of the Spartan influence that had been so prominent in ancient times and continued on from generation to generation. The role of women in ancient Sparta was truly unique for the time. Women there were not sequestered but were visible, prominent, independent-minded, and powerful. Girls were given an education and were literate. They participated and competed in athletic contests, often against boys. Women in Sparta could own property, and they were freed from everyday household chores, mostly because other Greeks the Spartans had enslaved did all of those tasks. In fact, in his work *Politics* Aristotle presented the view that in Sparta the women ruled the men, and he called such a power a "gynecocracy." Such a powerful tradition, now greatly changed and reduced over the centuries, still could be seen in some aspects of Agios Andreas society. To be sure, women were not viewed as equals of men but were in no way forced to not openly mix with men in church or at festive occasions. The dowry system was still in place, but Yannelli's older sister, Katerina, was not the first or last to reject it or in some way rebel against it. In some villages even conversation was prohibited between underage people of the opposite sex, but no such extreme prohibition existed in Agios Andreas as long as it was in full view of village adults. Boys and girls and unmarried men and women could speak to one another although almost always in the presence of observing older married adults. There was, of course, no such concept as dating. although most young men and women found creative ways to escape the watchful eyes of parents and village gossips and find some time alone.

The weather was perfect for the festival of Agios Andreas in May of 1917. Yannelli, now nineteen years old, had grown to what was to be his full height. He was slim and considered handsome by the older village women who had the freedom to tell him so. After church on Sunday the musicians had assembled, the food and wine were brought out, and the festive activities were about to begin. It was there that Yannelli first noticed Alexandra. It was not the first time he had ever seen her, but on this day she looked different. She was seventeen years old, but he remembered her as a small child, a pretty girl but, as he recalled, no different from all the other little girls in the village. But now she was clearly not a child but had grown into a beautiful young woman, and it seemed as though his eyes kept returning to where she was standing with her mother, watching as the people of the village joined in each of the many varieties of Greek folk dances.

Yannelli walked over to where the three musicians were located, one playing the clarinet, one the bouzouki, and a third maintaining a rhythmic beat with his old set of drums. Yannelli was preparing to lead the next dance and requested his favorite song, one entitled "Itia" that was done through a special kind of folk dance called the *Tsamiko*. Greek dances had always expressed the emotions not only of the individual person but also often of the community and even the nation. This particular dance, the *Tsamiko,* followed a slow tempo and gave the lead dancer the dominant role. It was a dance done in past Greek history almost exclusively by men, and the particular song Yannelli requested was historically connected to the 1821 Revolutionary Era in Greek history. In Agios Andreas the women regularly joined in dances with handkerchiefs separating the hands of men and women in the circle dances. As Yannelli prepared to lead the next dance, Alexandra and her mother joined the circle as Yannelli assumed the first position in the line. As the music began Yannelli executed the dance perfectly according to his own improvisation. Alexandra's eyes were fixed on Yannelli as he, with strength, style, and grace, did the intricate steps of the dance. Other men, in similar circumstances, took every opportunity to literally engage in acrobatics, jumping into the air, slapping their hands against the soles of their shoes, and doing backward bending contortions of their bodies, hoping to impress the onlookers and especially the women with their athletic prowess and dexterity. Yannelli was the complete opposite. His dance was graceful, and there were no jumping, no slapping, no attempted high leaps in the air, just calculated moves that made him appear the smooth master of the music being played. Alexandra was fascinated by Yannelli's every move and by the fact that he seemed to be trying to impress no one but rather was in his own world, captivated by the music and its historic meaning. As the music ended, those surrounding the dance spontaneously broke into applause in recognition of what they had judged to be a masterful rendition of the historic dance. Alexandra, her mother at her side, made her way over to Yannelli.

"Yannelli," she said. "I don't know if you remember me. I am Alexandra Rigatos. I just wanted to say your dancing was wonderful. I have never seen anyone do it better."

Yannelli greeted Alexandera's mother, then simply said. "I do remember you, Alexandra, although I have not seen you for a number of years. You are grown now, and I can hardly recognize you. But thank you for your nice words about the dance. It was good to see both of you. I hope you enjoy the festival."

In the weeks that followed Yannelli kept thinking about his meeting with Alexandra, and Alexandra confided in her younger sister that she, too, was having similar thoughts about Yannelli. A few times they met by chance at the village post office, and then each began thinking how they might see one another again. As a few more months passed. Yannelli felt a growing need to see and speak to Alexandra but was frustrated by the customs and traditions that forbade him from doing so. Eventually he concocted a way to contact her. He decided to use his younger sister Erini and give her the task of secretly conveying the messages to Alexandra's younger sister who was in the same class as Erini. His first note was bold and risky. He wrote that he would like to meet with Alexandra just to speak with her as a friend. Yannelli's note was risky, because there was a chance that Alexandra would not be interested in meeting him or that her mother might access the note and complain to Yannelli or to his mother that he had violated village norms and would be subject to gossip and ridicule. But such worries were needless because Alexandra not only was quietly given the note by her sister but quickly and enthusiastically responded in a positive manner. Of course, she wrote, she would love to meet with Yannelli as friends and have a chance to speak and get to know each other better. When Yannelli received Alexandra's reply, he was excited, experiencing emotions he had never had before. The notes between Yannelli and Alexandra continued for the following weeks, carried by each of their young sisters who were enjoying their role as couriers of what they knew was forbidden correspondence. Finally Yannelli and Alexandra did agree that on a certain day they would meet for a brief time in the village cemetery that they determined would have no visitors during the early morning hour they had agreed upon.

"This is a strange place to meet, Yannelli," said Alexandra, taking the lead to open the conversation. "Here we are among people whose lives are over, and ours are really just beginning."

Yannelli sat on the grass, motioning Alexandra to do the same. He was somewhat surprised by her opening comment, not expecting something that was almost philosophical in nature. "I hadn't really thought about it that way," Yannelli answered, "but I guess you are right. So tell me. Alexandra, since you are just beginning, what would you like to do with your life? Do you want to stay in the village? Get married someday? Have children? Or get lost in Athens or maybe Thessaloniki?" Yannelli was straining to make conversation not knowing exactly where to begin. He continued to look at her. How beautiful she is, he thought. Alexandra had let her light-colored hair down, and it rested on her traditional village blouse made up of multiple colors. She smiled at Yannelli.

Of course, she said, someday she would want to marry and have children, but she had doubts about remaining in the village. "It's nice here," she said, "but I think I want something more, maybe to go to the university, maybe to be a teacher. I'm not sure, but I know I can't tell my mother or father because they would not approve."

"I don't know if any girls from Agios Andreas have ever gone to the university," said Yannelli, "but if that's what you want, you should do it."

Alexandra was surprised and pleased by Yannelli's answer. Most men in the village would have ridiculed the idea and immediately argued for the traditional role they believed all women should play—that of wife and mother. "And what about you, Yannelli? Do you have plans or dreams or hopes?"

"I know what I would like to do, but I also know what I have to do. If everything were perfect, I would want to go to the army for my whole life, maybe rise to be a colonel or even a general, but what I know I have to do is care for my mother and my brothers and provide a dowry for my two younger sisters."

"The dowry! The dowry!" Alexandra broke in. "I hate that stupid thing. I'm not going to pay or bribe any man to marry me. If I don't want him, and he doesn't want me without a dowry, then I'll never marry. It's that simple. I'll never marry. But why would you want to be a soldier? Especially for your whole life?"

Yannelli did not comment on Alexandra's opinion of the dowry. He agreed with what she had said, but the topic was too painful in his memory to discuss the merits or demerits of the practice. But the military, he said, offered things he wanted and valued. Defending the country itself was important, but the military was an institution built on order, discipline, loyalty, trust, and purpose. "Those things are important to me," Yannelli said. "They are the things I believe should direct all of our lives. But I don't know if I will be able to do it. I'll probably be here in Agios Andreas when I'm sixty or seventy, running our small store and playing with the *komboloi* at the coffeehouse."

"Won't you marry?" asked Alexandra.

"Probably," answered Yannelli, "probably someone unlike you, who doesn't object to the idea of the dowry and will make me a rich man. Then I'll have nothing to worry about." Yannelli smiled, knowing he would elicit some response from Alexandra with his remark.

"Yannelli!" she protested. "you will not do that! I don't believe you, and if you really believe that, I'm going home right now and this meeting to see if we could be friends is over!"

"All right," said Yannelli. "I'll tell you what. If I end up marrying you. I'll forget the dowry. Is that okay?"

Alexandra smiled and rolled her eyes in a gesture conveying her message of what other ridiculous things are you going to say? But she enjoyed the friendly banter with Yannelli. She felt comfortable with him, and she, like the old women in the village, found him to be an attractive young man. They both decided that they should not remain much longer in the cemetery since someone from the village would eventually come to visit or care for the grave of a loved one.

"Can we meet again?" Yannelli asked.

"Yes, I would like to," answered Alexandra.

Over the next weeks the notes, carried by the two younger sisters, continued between Yannelli and Alexandra. Somehow they found a way to meet and just talk, often for only fifteen or twenty minutes at a time. They gradually began to feel as if they knew each other, and they were pleased with what they were learning. Alexandra saw that Yannelli was unique among men in the village. He respected women, did not assume they were inferior or overemotional as so many of the other men did. He clearly did not see women as objects to have children and serve their husbands as their sole purpose in life. She could talk to him about ideas and thoughts she dared not bring up in her home, in her school, or even among her female friends. "I think women are every bit as smart as men," she told Yannelli, "and I don't think God made us so that we could just be mothers in the house, cleaning while men went out every night to coffeehouses or to have sex with other women or with prostitutes." Rather than arguing her points, Yannelli genuinely agreed with them. The more the two young people were together, the more they found common ideas, values, and future aspirations. This is what good friendship was all about was the thought that both began to realize. But from the increasingly solid friendship something else was developing, something neither were at first prepared to acknowledge. Yannelli finally confided to his mother that he had been seeing and talking to Alexandra.

"Well, I'm not surprised," she said. "You're nineteen now, and I guess I would worry if you weren't interested in someone. But you must be careful. In this village if the word gets out that you two are secretly meeting, her reputation will be ruined, and every mother will shy away from having you as a prospective son-in-law whenever that time comes. And you are still young, Yannelli, too young. You have responsibilities here and military years you must serve. Don't do anything foolish. After the army if you both still feel strongly, that may be the time to think of marriage."

Yannelli listened to his mother. It was interesting, he thought to himself, why she and others in the village used phrases like "if you both still feel strongly"; it was as if they did not acknowledge or could not articulate the word "love." Why could she not have said if you both still love one another? Even Yannelli himself was reluctant to admit to himself that his feelings for Alexandra went beyond being friends probably, in fact, best friends and that on that foundation of friendship he had grown to be in love with her. But why couldn't he tell her that? Had he been so conditioned by his own parent's relationship and that of virtually every person in the village that he could not articulate what he felt?

"Don't worry. I won't do anything either you or I will regret," said Yannelli in hope of easing his mother's concerns.

Alexandra, too, felt the need to convey her thoughts to someone as well. She knew she liked and respected Yannelli very much. But did she love him? How could she know, she thought; she had never been in love before. Her mother had always been there to talk to her when she had any problems so she turned to her once again. Alexandra tried to explain what she was feeling—a mixture of ease, contentment, joy, comfort, laughter, and a longing to be with Yannelli all the time. Her mother's immediate reaction to Alexandra's words was shock and disappointment that Alexandra had been secretly meeting with Yannelli.

"Alexandra, I will not tell your father, but if he knew or if he finds out, you know it will not only be you who will be in trouble but Yannelli as well. You must not see him; you will bring disgrace to

159

the family." Alexandra respectfully listened but, as always, showed no reluctance to voice her opinion.

"Mother, I hate this village. I hate these stupid rules. Does it matter that I think I love Yannelli and I believe he loves me too?"

Her mother had known that the day would come when she would have this conversation with her daughter. She had always been a headstrong girl with an independent streak that concerned the family. At seventeen she was approaching the age within the next two years when most girls' families in the village arranged for a husband to marry their daughters. So the time was fast approaching when they would have to do the same for Alexandra, and they worried about what her reaction would be.

"Alexandra," her mother began. "I do not approve of your meetings with Yannelli. You know that. From everything I know and have heard about him, he is a fine boy, but you are still young and there are other good boys in the village as well. Don't rush into things."

"But Mother, I love Yannelli. I love him, not some other boys in the village!" Alexandra began pacing around the room, unconsciously clenching her fists in frustration for what she perceived was her mother's lack of understanding.

"Love, love, love," her mother repeated. "I think you have been reading too many of those foreign novels. Love is greatly overrated, Alexandra. What you think is love today becomes routine boredom tomorrow. You must know and respect your place as a woman and marry a good man who will respect you and provide for you. That's what love is about. Nothing more."

"Don't you love Papa, Mother? Don't you love him?"

Alexandra's mother gave no immediate answer and looking at her daughter said, "He is a good man. He has provided for all of us."

Alexandra looked back at her mother. "I really feel sorry for you, Mother. I really, really do. I will not live your life. I will marry a man I love. I will. I will!"

"But listen to me, Alexandra, please listen to me." Her mother now began to change her argument from cautioning her daughter about being too young and not knowing what love was to concerns about Yannelli's family. "His family has had so many problems, Alexandra. Why would you want to be part of that? Remember what happened to his sisters Katerina and Stamatina, and Manoli does not seem well either. None of us knows what happened to Stamatina's husband, but there is much gossip."

Alexandra was now angry and frustrated with her mother. "Gossip, gossip, that's all you or anyone else cares about. I'm tired of gossip. I'm tired of being viewed as a child or as if I'm no better or no more intelligent than our dog. I'm tired of it! I'm tired!" Alexandra quickly walked out of the house, not bothering to hear or acknowledge her mother's pleas for her not to leave. For days Alexandra and her mother spoke little, and her father was kept ignorant of the exchange they had had. Her mother, however, had spoken in general terms to her father about Alexandra's future.

"She's only seventeen," her mother said, "but we will want to marry her in a year or two. We should begin looking for a suitable husband." She suggested to her husband that perhaps he should start talking to the father of another young man in the village, Leonidas Matsos, who would someday inherit his father's vineyards and olive groves and be able to provide a good life for their daughter. He would ask for a dowry, Alexandra's mother said, but it would most likely be a modest one. Her husband, seeming to be in no such rush to begin such a dialogue, nodded his head and said he agreed with his wife and that he would consider doing it soon. Alexandra's mother did not wait for her husband to open the discussion with the Matsos family. She informed Alexandra that her father was considering the Matsos boy as a possible husband for her. If the terms were agreeable, they could be engaged and wait a year or perhaps a little more and then be married. Alexandra was stunned and said nothing but then suddenly came forth with a burst of raw emotion.

"No! No!" she screamed. "No! I will not do it! Do you hear me? I will not do it! You told me to remember Yannelli's sister—well, I will, and I will follow her to the grave! Do you hear me? Do you?" Her mother reached out to physically calm her daughter and contain the outrage.

"Don't talk like that, Alexandra, please don't say that! Leonidas is a good boy from a good family. He will make you happy."

"But I love Yannelli, Mother. I love Yannelli! You really don't understand, do you? You really don't understand what it means to be in love with someone!" She began crying, unable to speak and exhausted from screaming. She turned her back on her mother, walked to the door, and disappeared into the night.

Within the next two days Yannelli and Alexandra had, through their two sisters, again made contact and arranged to meet. Alexandra began telling Yannelli of her ordeal with her mother and what her mother had told her were the plans of the family for her with the Matsos family.

"Yannelli," she pleaded. "I can't let them do this. I need to tell you something. Whenever I marry I want only one person to be my husband—you. Yannelli, you! I love you, Yannelli. I love you!" Alexandra finished her sentence crying, relieved that she had finally articulated what she felt and wanted Yannelli to know. Yannelli took Alexandra in his arms, wiped the tears from her eyes, looked at her in a way she had never seen before, and gently pressed his lips against hers.

"Alexandra," he said. "I love you, too. With all my heart. I want you to know, I love you, too." Yannelli and Alexandra remained in each other's arms and kissed again and again. "I want you, too, Alexandra. I want you to be my wife. No one else."

"But what can we do, Yannelli? What can we do?"

Yannelli thought for a moment. It was clear he had no good answer, but they both needed some answers that could give them hope. "Maybe," he said, "the best thing for you to do is to say you have thought about things and have changed your mind. You can say that you realized that you don't really love me and that we will not be together. Tell them that you intend to marry no one until you are at least twenty or twenty-one and then, when you have matured and understand things better, you will comply with their wishes to marry someone of their choice. But now they should forget Leonidas Matsos. By that time, Alexandra. I will have completed my time in the army. I will return here, and we can marry. And then we can leave here, maybe go to Athens, Salonika, or even America. I will wait for you, Alexandra, because I love you. Will you wait for me?"

"I will, Yannelli. I will. I love you so much, more than you will ever know. I will wait for you."

Yannelli received his notice to report for the army a month after he had presented his plan to Alexandra. He was told that he was to report to the training camp at a date two months from the receipt of the notice. But with Alexandra and leaving for the military on his mind, he first had to deal with yet another serious family problem before he left. This time it involved his younger brother. Christos.

Michael and Jenny, 1980

ichael was surprised at how open and candid Alexandra had been. It was almost as if she had wanted to relate the story to someone, a story she had apparently kept to herself for all these years. Alexandra had prepared some tea and brought cups to the table along with some pastries that were covered with honey and sprinkled with cinnamon. She poured the tea for her guests and resumed the conversation.

"What else can I tell you?" she asked. Michael, caught somewhat off guard by her question, took a moment to drink from his cup of tea.

"Well, something must have happened," he said. "Obviously, you did not marry my father. Was Leonidas the man who did become your husband?"

"No," she responded. "Leonidas went to the army and unfortunately was killed in fighting between Greek and Bulgarian forces in Macedonia. Your father left for the army, then returned to Greece, and then left for America. We exchanged letters for a year or two, and then I met my husband, Taki, who was from here, Hydra, but was visiting some relatives in Agios Andreas. My father and his family eventually made the arrangements, and we were married in 1925. I then moved to Hydra where my children were born and I have lived here ever since."

"So then, your marriage was arranged?" asked Jenny. "From what you have told us, it seems as if you were strongly against that practice. What made you change your mind?"

Alexandra lifted her cup, sipped tea, and reached for one of the honey pastries she had baked. "These are very good, you both should try one." Michael and Jenny sensed that she was not comfortable with the question and was debating in her mind as to whether she should respond to it. She then lifted the plate with the pastries and presented them to Michael and Jenny. Assuming that the question that had been posed to her would receive no response, both took the pastry.

"These are very good, Mrs. Rigatos," said Jenny.

Alexandra did not want to embarrass her young guests, so she never corrected them about her name. *Rigatos* was her maiden name which she hadn't used in years, but she said nothing.

"Yes, they are excellent," echoed Michael, hoping that the conversation would now take a different direction. But both Michael and Jenny were surprised when Alexandra, after this long pause, responded.

"Sometimes in life," she started, "things only happen once. Those things are so good, so special, that they can never be repeated. That's how I felt about Yannelli, your father, Michael. Taki was a good man, a good husband, and a very good father. I had a good life with him. I do not regret marrying him, but some things really do only happen once. I guess that was not meant to be." Alexandra's voice trailed off to almost a whisper. She slowly lifted herself from the chair and walked over to a small chest. She placed it on the table, opened it, and began to show its contents to her guests. She handed some old faded photographs to Michael. Michael looked at the photographs, saying nothing. He continued looking at them, placing them down, then picking them up again for a second and third time. They were images he had never seen before. Images of his father as a young man of nineteen or twenty and pictures of a beautiful young woman smiling as she held Yannelli's hand. The young woman was Alexandra. There were pictures of them sitting by the seashore at Agios Andreas and even one of his father leading a *Tsamiko* dance at some village festival. Michael wondered why she had kept these photos all these years. Did her husband or children know about them, he wondered? Michael handed the photographs back to Alexandra, understanding now how powerful the bond between her and his father must have been.

"Thank you for showing us these pictures, Mrs. Rigatos. These are the only pictures I have ever seen of my father at this young age. I'm sure they must mean a great deal to you."

"Yes, they do," she answered as she moved to return the photos to the small chest.

The pictures raised some troubling questions in Michael's mind. What he had heard and seen was a story of two young people very much in love who, for reasons he still did not fully understand, went separate ways in their lives. It was obvious that Alexandra still had vivid memories and strong feelings about his father, but had his father felt the same way years later? His father, he thought, had not as yet met his mother, and every indication Michael had as a child growing up was that his father and mother had a loving relationship in a good solid marriage. But, he wondered, had his father ever thought of Alexandra after he had married? Did he feel, as she did, that the bond they shared only happened once in a person's life? These were questions that he knew he could never answer, but he continued to wonder what those answers might be. Still, even if he could never answer every question, he had found out a great deal about his father, things he had never known before. As he and Jenny prepared to leave, he thanked Alexandra for the time she had spent with them and asked if she would mind if Jenny took a photograph of them together. Alexandra seemed eager to do so, perhaps seeing Michael as the living connection to the man she had loved long ago.

"Of course," Alexandra said, "but only if you promise to send me a copy of the picture."

Jenny answered that she would. Michael, however, had one final question to ask Alexandra before they departed.

"Mrs. Rigatos, in my father's journal he made reference to a family problem pertaining to his younger brother, Christos. He says he needed to deal with it quickly because he had been called to serve in the army. This was in 1917. Do you know anything about this? I am just wondering if my father talked to you about it or confided in you in any way."

"Yes, Michael, your father did tell me about this issue with Christos. It was a complicated and sad story and another of the many family issues your father had to resolve. Let me tell you what your father told to me..."

Christos, 1917

FROM THE JOURNAL, 1917

MY BROTHER CHRISTOS HAS CONFIDED IN ME THAT HE IS IN
LOVE WITH A GIRL IN ARGOS. HE SAYS SHE LOVES HIM AS WELL.
BUT SOMETHING STRANGE HAS COME UP THAT IS A PROBLEM I
NEED TO DEAL WITH, AND I DON'T HAVE MUCH TIME BECAUSE
I'M LEAVING FOR THE ARMY VERY SOON. CHRISTOS'S ISSUE IS
LIKE SOMETHING OUT OF AN ANCIENT GREEK TRAGEDY, SOME-
THING THAT SOPHOCLES OR EURIPIDES MIGHT WRITE ABOUT.

Yannelli's younger brother, Christos, had just turned eighteen in February, 1917. For the past year he had, like Yannelli, taken a job as a mail courier, delivering letters and
packages among various towns and villages in Arcadia. He, like his
older brother, had become a skilled horseback rider, able to lead his
mount over difficult roads and streams using the shortest routes between destinations. Yannelli and Christos traveled different routes,
but on weekends, back in Agios Andreas, they would discuss their
week's work and compare notes on what they had seen and heard.
Both liked their job very much since it allowed them to leave the
village, meet people, and hear of the things that might have never
reached their home village.

Christos's route took him to a number of smaller villages, but his main destination where most of his mail was to be delivered was the larger city of Argos. Argos was one of the oldest cities in Greece and one of the few that had a continuous history from ancient times under the same name. It had been the chief Greek city in the Heroic Age, but was taken over by the Dorians when they invaded Greece. It was then later overshadowed in importance by Sparta. The Argos Christos encountered in his work had few historic sites of interest left and had become a center for orange growing and small manufacturing. The streets were narrow and winding, and Christos did not find it an attractive city. Something, however, was attracting him to the city, so he looked forward to each week when he would deliver his mail to the local postal center. What he looked forward to was seeing Ioanna, the young girl who worked sorting incoming mail at the center. She was about a year younger than Christos, a pretty girl with dark eyes and long black hair that she usually tied to the back of her head but at times would leave flowing over her shoulders. Week after week, as Christos made his required stop at the postal center, the two young people would talk and laugh about various aspects of the work. Christos and Ioanna seemed to have that rare element of total compatibility that made them completely comfortable in the company of each other. Christos began scheduling his work so that he arrived in Argos about the time Ioanna was taking a break from her work to eat in the early afternoon. He would then join her, sometimes sitting outdoors at the table that was located to the side of the entrance to the postal center. The meetings, discussions, and lunches went on for months, and it became clear to both Christos and Ioanna that something was developing between them that went beyond simple friendly conversation. Christos was feeling things he had never felt before, things totally new to a young person his age. He finally found the courage to confess these feelings to Ioanna, and, to his great pleasure, she responded that she too was having similar emotions.

"I miss you, when I leave here," Christos revealed to Ioanna, "and I think about you every day, all the time."

"And I miss you too, Christos. I get excited by the thought that on a particular day you will be coming to Argos and coming here."

Christos and Ioanna both, of course, realized that they were young, really too young for anything more permanent to develop from their relationship. Even though Argos was a larger community, there were still rules, traditions, and customs that had to be followed and activities between men and women that were not accepted. They would wait, they decided, until they were at least twenty or twenty-one and then talk to their parents about their plans to marry. Neither had spoken much about each other's families; they only had discussed in the most general terms how many siblings they each had and how it was to grow up in a small village and in a larger town such as Argos. Christos, however, felt he needed to share his plans and feelings with someone and felt Yannelli would understand, since he knew of his brother's feelings about Alexandra. On a cold spring evening Christos sat with his older brother on two old chairs that were always located directly in front of their home. The rest of the family was busy with one thing or another; some were in the house, others were playing with friends in a nearby open area. Christos took the lead in opening the conversation with Yannelli.

"Yannelli, I know that I'm young, but what I need to talk to you about is real, and what I am about to say I feel very deeply. I have met this girl in Argos. She works at the postal center. We get along really well. She just makes me feel good every time I see her, and when I don't see her, I miss her very much and she is on my mind constantly. Yannelli, please don't laugh when I tell you this, but I believe I love her and she tells me she loves me too."

Yannelli did not laugh. He was only slightly older than Christos, and he was experiencing the same feelings and emotions about Alexandra. He knew these feelings were real and powerful and Christos's age made them no less real.

"I would not laugh, Christos. I understand what you are feeling. I'm sure this girl is a fine person, but you are young and when I leave for the army later this year, you will be the oldest male still at home. You will have the responsibility of looking after our mother, our brother Manoli, and our sisters. I'm not saying you should forget about Ioanna, but there will be a better time when things can work out the way you want them to."

Christos felt better that he had confided in his brother and knew that Yannelli's advice was correct. He would soon have greater responsibilities, and he could, at least, keep seeing Ioanna when he could. Yannelli, too, was pleased with their discussion. Christos was an intelligent, rational person, not given to impulsive thought or action. He would follow his brother's advice, wait, fulfill his obligations, and when the time was better talk to Ioanna's family.

In the weeks that followed, both Christos and Yannelli followed their normal routines and worked on their mail delivery routes. It was on his route, with a stop in Nafplio, that Yannelli first encountered a rumor that troubled him greatly. Sitting by the seaside café while eating his dinner of lamb, salad, potatoes, bread, and wine, he met two older men who were sitting nearby and eventually struck up a conversation. Yannelli was the first to introduce himself. "I'm Yannelli Bakalis," he said, "and who are you two gentlemen?"

The two men introduced themselves. Costas Marangos was about fifty years old, had a full thick black mustache, and wore loose-fitting clothes that it seemed he might have worn at a time when he had been forty pounds heavier. The second man, a tall thin man, was Demetrios Athanasopoulos, who said he was in Nafplio for business but said he resided in Argos. By the time Yannelli had begun any conversation with them, the two older men had obviously consumed large quantities of food and wine, and unfortunately, it was mostly wine.

"Bakalis? Bakalis?" repeated the man with the mustache, "I know I have heard that name. What is your father's name, Yannelli?"

"My father died a few years ago, but his name was Costandinos, but everyone knew him as Costa," answered Yannelli.

"Oh," said the man from Argos, "I'm sorry to hear that. May God rest his soul, but I have met your father. I'm in the business of raising and selling vegetables, and your father would come to Argos to buy my produce that he would then sell in his village and other nearby villages. He could be one smooth talker, you know, he could always get me and others he bought from to give him the lowest price. Sometimes it seems like we just barely made any profit at all."

Yannelli listened carefully to what the man from Argos was saying. "I guess I never had the occasion to see that side of my father,"

Yannelli said, "he always seemed so matter-of-fact to me. I don't think I even saw him laugh very much."

"Oh, he laughed plenty," said Mr. Marangos. "I met him once or twice here in Nafplio when he came here to do business. He had many stories to tell, and I think he liked the ladies, too, at least that's what I heard." The wine had now taken control of both men's tongues and there was little caution or discretion in what was coming out of their mouths. Dimitri now added to what was becoming an increasingly uncomfortable situation for Yannelli.

"There were rumors about Costa in Argos as well," said Dimitri, "that he came there so often not because of grocery business but because of woman business. I heard he was seeing two or three women there. I don't know if it's true, but that's what the rumors were about. Your father, Yannelli, was quite a man. Maybe the rest of us are just jealous."

Yannelli was shocked by what the men had said. He knew his father had been gone from Agios Andeas for days at a time but always assumed it had been part of his business routine. Never had he heard a mention from anyone about rumors of his father being with other women. He refused to believe it, attributing what the men had said to the malicious gossip of people who had nothing better to do than watch other people's lives and fabricate stories that deliberately hurt people. Tired and troubled by what he had heard, Yannelli told the men he had to leave to move on to complete his mail route. He paid his bill for the dinner and went on to his next destination, now concerned about what he had heard. Could it be true, he asked himself? Had his father been living some lie? Did he have some secret life that, until now, years later, none in the family or in the entire village knew about? The questions would not leave him, and he knew he had to get to the core of the matter. He had to find out the truth, whatever the consequences of that truth might be. As he rode his horse, Bucephalus, he debated how and where he should start.

Yannelli began by trying to remember where his father had gone to buy and sell food products in the villages nearby Agios Andreas. Going from one village to another, first to Astros, Leonidion, Cosmas, Paleohori, and others, he would stop in the town square, seek out older residents, and begin to ask questions. His questions were always general, asking if the person knew of Costas Bakalis, the grocery man. Most had no knowledge of him, but a few who had business with him did remember him. Everyone who had met Costa reported dealing with a very businesslike individual, one who, to be sure, drove a hard bargain but was always a pleasure to deal with. None who had met him offered any negative comments, and none even hinted that Costa had any connection, liaison, or relationship with any woman in their villages. None said that there were even rumors of such things.

Yannelli was pleased with what he had heard in the places he had visited. What he had heard was a verification of everything he knew and believed about his father. He would not, he told himself, let the gossip of two drunks destroy the image he had of his father. With no particular sense of urgency Yannelli visited other villages he knew his father had also frequented in his business dealings and received the same positive reports—there was no negative information whatsoever. Anyone who had dealt with Costas spoke well of him, and again none reported rumors of any kind. But Yannelli knew, if only to satisfy himself, that he had to complete his task by going to the largest town on what had been Costa's route, Argos. Once again he repeated the pattern he had established in every other place. He talked to people who had been business acquaintances of his father, probing them with questions and once again receiving the same answers as he had received everywhere else, until one day when he was preparing to return to his home he spoke with a man named Fotis Lekakos who had sold chickens and eggs to his father. What he heard startled him.

"I did hear," Fotis said to Yannelli as they sat next to his chicken house, "that Costa did have some relationship. I think it went on for a year or two with a woman in Argos, a woman named Melina. I don't know her last name. A few times Costa told me he was having dinner at Melina's house, but I never asked any questions. I figured it was none of my business, so I left it alone. Yes, I'm sure the name he told me was Melina."

What Fotis had said was not something Yannelli had expected or hoped to hear. He tried to ask more questions, but Fotis could offer no further information or, as Yannelli thought, maybe simply didn't want to say more. But the only clue he had was one first name, Melina, and there were probably dozens, if not hundreds, of Melinas in Argos. Realizing that he could not obviously go house to house, he knew he had to begin somewhere so he chose a logical beginning point, the office of the town president and the tax and census records that were stored there. And, the thought now crossed his mind, if this connection with this woman Melina were true, was it simply a love affair or something more permanent like his father having a second family and even children?

Yannelli went to the town hall and said he was doing some research and asked to have access to the latest census records, those for
the year, 1910. Leafing through page after page of the documents,
he lost track of time, and the woman working in the office told him
they were about to close. He had been there for four hours and had
not noticed the passage of time. He told the clerk he would return
in the morning, which he did, exactly at the time this same woman
unlocked the front door signaling that the office was open for daily
business. By noon, he had found twenty households with the name
of one adult head named Melina. Further sorting eliminated ten
of them—some who were very elderly, some had left the city, and
a number were deceased. Sorting through the remaining entries,
he decided to first target the three households with an adult head
with the first name of Melina who had children. Yannelli's mind
was now filled with thoughts he tried not to consider but could
not dismiss. Did either of these women have a daughter named
Ioanna? The first entry of the woman with the name of Melina had
children but none named Ioanna. Looking further he found that
a second household did have a child named Ioanna, but that she
had been eighteen at the time of the census. That would make her
twenty-five now, thought Yannelli, so she couldn't possibly be the
person Christos was talking about. He breathed a deep sigh of relief as he inspected the third entry. The remaining entry described
a household headed by a Melina Boulos, a widow with three children, a daughter Ioanna, aged ten, and two sons, Strati, aged eight,
and Nicholas, aged seven. Yannelli did not move and continued to
stare at the document. He quickly mentally made the calculation
that immediately gave him a sense of fear and anxiety. If, in 1910,

the Ioanna listed in this document was ten years old, she would be seventeen now, the age of the girl Christos had mentioned. Yannelli's fears became even more pronounced. Could this possibly be the same girl? He quickly copied the information down, put the paper with the woman's address in his pocket, thanked the clerk for her help, and headed for the address of this woman, Melina Boulos. His heart was beating faster; what had started out as a walk now turned into a sprint. He did not know what he would learn, but he knew he had to find out something.

Yannelli finally approached the house with the address he had copied from the census records. It was a two-story structure with an open third floor, as if the construction had not been completed. He carefully rang the exterior bell, which gave no sound. Trying again, the result was the same. Seeing that the bell was not working, he knocked softly on the door, but there was no response. Trying again, he now knocked more forcefully and repeated the knock three more times. He waited, and just as he was about to knock again, the door opened and a woman stood there. "Yes, can I help you," she asked. The woman seemed to Yannelli to be about forty-five or fifty years old, not heavy, but rather plump, with a full face and ample arms and breasts. She was wearing what appeared to be some kind of Greek traditional dress, particular to a special village or section of Greece, although Yannelli could not identify its origin.

"My name is Yiannis Bakalis," Yannelli said, using his more formal first name. "I wonder if I might have a few minutes of your time to ask you some questions?"

The woman's eyes conveyed a strange reaction to her visitor. As she heard Yannelli introduce himself and say his last name, she asked, "Are you from here in Argos?"

"No," Yannelli answered, "my home is in Agios Andreas, a village close to Astros."

The woman's tone now became apprehensive and almost defensive. "What do you want with me? What questions can I answer for you? I'm not sure we have anything to talk about." She reached for the door, looking as if she were preparing to close it and end the conversation.

"Please, please!" pleaded Yannelli. "This is very important. It may involve your daughter Ioanna. You must talk to me!"

"Ioanna!" exclaimed Melina, "What did Ioanna do? Is she all right? Is she hurt?"

"She is not hurt, Mrs. Boulos, but she could be unless we talk. Please let me in."

The possibility that something was wrong with her daughter changed Melina's attitude and tone. Opening the door more widely, she invited Yannelli into her home, asking him to join her at the table where they could speak. Yannelli began the conversation speaking about his brother Christos and how during his mail courier routes he had met a girl named Ioanna at the postal center. "Is your daughter Ioanna the one who works at the center?" asked Yannelli.

'Yes, she has worked there for about two years," said the woman.

"Well, Christos and Ioanna seem to have become more than just friends. My brother told me that he was in love with Ioanna and that she felt the same way about him."

Melina now became more visibly nervous, rubbing her hands together, and then pulling at the crucifix that was on the chain around her neck. "But they are so young," she finally said. "They are hardly more than children."

"I don't disagree, Mrs. Boulos. I really don't disagree at all. But from what I understand they plan to wait until they are twenty or twenty-one and then come to you to ask for permission to marry."

Melina seemed stunned. Her daughter had casually told her that she had met a very nice young man who delivered the mail and that she enjoyed speaking with him but had said nothing more. There had been no talk of romance, of love, or of some eventual marriage. She was genuinely shocked by what Yannelli was telling her. Regaining her composure, Melina now posed a question to Yannelli. "Mr. Bakalis," she asked, "what was your father's first name?"

Yannelli was hesitant to answer, fearing the ultimate revelation that his answer might bring. "Costandinos," he replied, "but most people called him Costa."

"Yannelli, if I may call you that, I must tell you something I have told no one for almost twenty years. Please listen carefully to me, and you will understand why I am speaking the way I am."

Melina slowly and methodically began to tell Yannelli a story he had hoped he would never have to hear. Years before, said Melina, she had met Yannelli's father Costa when he was making his food and produce travels from town to town. Her father raised goats in a village ten miles outside of Argos and was also a maker of feta cheese that Costa purchased at regular intervals. She was only in her twenties, he somewhat older, but she found him handsome, gregarious, and a pleasure to talk to. He had told her he was a widower, which she later discovered had been a lie. He had told her that he loved her and would someday marry her, which she also said she soon discovered was a lie as well. Believing that he loved her and would take her as his wife, they became intimate, the lovemaking going on for four or five months. She had become pregnant, and when it became clear that Costa would not only not marry her but, in fact, had a wife and family, she was at a loss for what to do. She had contemplated an abortion but decided she could not do it. Her family disowned her, particularly when she would not identify the father, so she left the village and located in the much larger town of Argos, hoping to find anonymity. She concocted a story, she said, that her husband had been killed in a farming accident and began a new life in Argos. She met a man who accepted her story and married him and had two sons. Just last year, she continued, he had died of tuberculosis, but until this moment her secret had been secure. No one, her daughter, her husband, her sons, or anyone else, had ever discovered what had happened with Yannelli's father. But this situation, she said, had now changed everything.

"They cannot be together, they cannot marry! Yannelli, Ioanna is your brother's and your half-sister! She is his half-sister!" Exhausted from unburdening herself, she placed her head between her hands as she cried out, "God, God, why have you done this to me? Why?" Tears were now rolling down her face, a seemingly unstoppable torrent of water, a cleansing of a secret she had hidden for decades.

Yannelli did nothing. He did not reach out to comfort the woman. He had a complex mixture of strange feelings and thoughts. It seemed as if some ancient Greek tragedy by Sophocles or Euripides was being acted out before his eyes. He felt sympathy and some contempt for the woman who had slept with his father. But then he quickly realized that his father had violated the vows of faithfulness he had made with his mother and that he had lied to this woman. Now his anger, for the first time in his life, centered on his father. Why had he done this? His mother was a good and faithful wife. Perhaps, he thought, this was the inevitable result of marriages arranged as business transactions, which brought virtual strangers together and asked them to share a marriage bed, show intimacy and love even when there was no love and one or more of these forced unions desired no intimacy. But, he then thought, perhaps this was just some kind of rationalization. His father had been deceitful and unfaithful; he had fathered a child and then come home to his wife and other children. Yannelli felt disgusted; he could never again retain the fond memory of his father as he had done since his death. This situation reinforced his belief that he would live his life with Alexandra, a woman he truly loved. Finally, when all these thoughts had raced through his mind, he spoke to Melina.

"Mrs. Boulos, I'm in no position to pass judgment on you. You were young, we all do things we regret. You did not know my father was married. But let me ask you something, did my father know about Ioanna?"

"He did, and in the beginning he would visit us in Argos while on his business route. He tried to help us out financially for a few years, but when I married, he stopped helping and stopped coming as well. It was only later that I had heard that he had died."

"Mrs. Boulos," said Yannelli, "both you and I must do something, something that may be the hardest thing each of us has ever done. Of course you are right, Ioanna and Christos cannot marry, and you must tell Ioanna the entire truth, and I must do the same with Christos."

182

"I know you are right," she said, "and we must do it very soon."

Yannelli left Melina's house, and both she and Yannelli spent the remaining hours of the day contemplating how they would relate the revelations to Ioanna and Christos. Melina felt she could not wait, wanting desperately to further unburden herself of a part of her life she had successfully hidden for so long but, more importantly, to save her daughter from an inevitably tragic situation. That evening, when her two sons had gone to bed, she asked Ioanna to sit with her, saying that she had something important to tell her. Relating the details to Ioanna, her daughter sat listening in horror, as if some bad book was being read to her. She cried, listened, and cried and cried again. Finally she screamed out, "Mother, why are you telling me this! You have ruined my life! You have ruined my life!" Ioanna quickly jumped up from the chair, thrust open the door, and began running, running, running, to no destination. She only knew she had to run, to somehow escape this nightmare that she had just experienced. There was nothing else at this moment she could think to do. Just run.

Yannelli waited one day. He needed to carefully think of how he would deal with the issue and what he would say to Christos. He was not one to avoid problems and decided that probably the best thing to do would be to simply tell the story as Melina had told it to him—straight and to the point. This way, he thought, he would get it over with and then deal with whatever reaction Christos would have. The next morning Yannelli asked Christos to join him in a private spot where they could speak, a spot down the dirt road from their home. Sitting on two large rocks, Yannelli related to Christos his meeting with Mrs. Boulos and the information about their father's affair with her and the daughter to which she had given birth. "That daughter," said Yannelli, "is Ioanna. She is your half-sister and mine as well."

Christos blurted out, "That can't be true, Yannelli! That can't be true! There must be some mistake!"

"I wish it were not true, Christos. I really wish there was some mistake, but it is true, there is no mistake."

Christos rose from the rock he had been sitting on and paced back and forth, over and over again. "Our father," he said, "our father did that! My father ruined my life! I hate him! I hate his memory! He disgraced our family, and he ruined my life, ruined my life!" Christos continued to repeat the same phrase over and over, "He ruined my life! What can I do? I love Ioanna, I love her!"

"Christos," said Yannelli, trying to calm his now distraught and hysterical brother, "you must learn to love her in another way. You can never be together as you both want. You can never marry Ioanna. She is our sister Christos, she is our sister."

Christos had nothing more to say. "Yannelli, please leave me alone. I need to think. I need to sort out all of this craziness." Yannelli nodded, got up from the rock that served as his chair, and began walking back to the house.

In the weeks that followed both Ioanna and Christos attempted to mentally process this unexpected blow that had stuck them. They made no attempt to see or contact one another, but both eventually reached the same conclusion—that they could never marry or be together and that the only way to deal with this was to sever all contact and correspondence. Within the next six months, Ionna made a decision that would alter her life forever. She informed her mother that she was joining the monastery to pursue the life of an Orthodox nun. If God had forbade her to be with Christos, she told Melina, then no other mortal man would replace him. She would become wedded to the Church and to the mission of Jesus Christ, our Lord and Savior.

Christos told Yannelli that he wanted to get away from everything and join the military, but Yannelli had other thoughts. "Christos, you know I have been called to serve in the army. I'm leaving in a matter of weeks, and you can't leave, too. Someone must stay here to provide for our family and protect them. By the time I return, it will be your turn for the army. Stay here in Agios Andreas, have faith, things will get better for you." Christos followed his brother's advice and became the family head as Yannelli now left the village to begin his mandatory military service.

Christos stayed with his family but lived with an emptiness that he could not fill. He would never be the same again.

Michael and Jenny, 1980

Alexandra finished relating what Yannelli had told her about Christos and Ioanna. Michael was deep in thought. Her story triggered something in his memory that had happened a few years before in Chicago and that he could never totally dismiss from his mind.

"That is a very sad story," said Jenny before Michael had the opportunity to react to what Alexandra had related. "What happened to Ioanna?" asked Jenny, "Did she become a nun and remain in the monastery? Do we know if she is still alive?"

"She did become a nun and as far as I know remained there her entire life. As far as I know she is still there, but I'm not really sure. If she is, she is now in her eighties."

"And Christos?" broke in Michael, "what about him? From what I know he seems to have fared better."

"Well," responded Alexandra, "he eventually did go into the army after your father returned, and a few years later he did marry a woman from the village. They had children and as far as I know lived a fairly normal, uneventful life. The family is still there, so if you haven't seen them yet, I'm sure you will. But from what I was told, Christos never spoke of Ioanna again to anyone."

Michael said that he and Jenny intended to stop by Agios Andreas one more time before he returned to Chicago because they wanted to speak again to Mr. Alfearis about Yannelli's army experiences and that they would try to visit Christos and his family when they arrived at the village.

"And Melina? What happened to her?" asked Jenny.

"She was very saddened by what had happened. She tried to persuade Ioanna not to become a nun but could not change her daughter's decision. She visited Ioanna at the monastery often, mostly during important religious holidays. Her sons grew and married, and one went to America, actually, I believe, to Chicago. I had heard that Melina died about four or five years ago."

Finally Michael spoke out about what had been on his mind earlier. He told of visiting a friend's business establishment in Chicago and noticing a picture the individual said was that of his grandfather. At the time, Michael said, he kept looking at the picture over and over. He said that he had seen only one photograph of his own grandfather, Costandinos, and that it looked exactly like the one in his friend's office. "I wondered," Michael continued, "how could these photos be almost identical? It seemed very strange to me, and since that moment the feeling has never left me. Now, with the story we just heard, I really do wonder, could the two photographs have been of the same man? Now I wonder if my grandfather might have been involved with some other woman and that my friend is possibly the child of that relationship? It's all just too confusing, but I guess I'll never know every aspect of my grandfather's life."

"I'm afraid I can't help you with that," said Alexandra, "and I don't think your father could have either. In 1917 he had had enough drama and crisis at home. He was about to start another stage of his life. Greece's role in the European conflict had changed, and Yannelli was called to the army sooner than he had expected. By the middle of the year he was headed for the military and to the front at Thessaloniki. But I do think you do have to go back to Phillipos Alfearis to get the full story because they served together in Thessaloniki and later in Smyrna."

Michael and Jenny headed back to the next scheduled hydrofoil that, within an hour, would take them back to Nafplio. It was another beautiful, warm day when they reached Nafplio and again took Jenny's old French model car for the drive to Agios Andreas. The next morning they again met Mr. Alfearis sitting in the exact same spot he had occupied days before and, it seemed, wearing the exact same clothes. Once again he greeted them twirling his *komboloi* or worry beads in a constant rhythmic motion that allowed two beads to strike one another at regular intervals. It was as if one were listening to a clock hand making a sound as it clicked off second after second.

"So, you're back," he said with a smile, his mustache still somewhat moist from the cup of coffee he had just lowered from his lips. "Did you meet Alexandra? Is she still beautiful? Is she still a widow? Maybe she will consider marrying me," Mr. Alfearis smiled, acknowledging to Michael and Jenny that he was, of course, attempting some early morning humor.

Michael told him that they had net Alexandra and that she still was an attractive woman, but he didn't think she was interested in having another husband.

"Well," Mr. Alfearis said, "I don't blame her. I don't want another wife either." He smiled again. "Now what can I tell you, Mihali? What more do you want to know about your father?"

"Mr. Alfearis, you were my father's closest friend from childhood until he left for America. You served together for years in the army. I want to learn something about that time."

"That was so long ago," Mr. Alfearis started with a deep sigh, "we had some good times together, but mostly it was hard. We saw things we never forgot. We shot at people and killed some. We did some good things for our country, but our country did some bad things, too. I never really liked the army, but your father loved it. I probably stayed as long as I did only because of him. Let me think of how to begin..."

Salonika, 1917–1919

FROM THE JOURNAL, 1917

MY UNIT IS BEING SENT TO THESSALONIKI. I HAVE NEVER BEEN THERE, BUT MY GUESS IS THAT WE ARE BEING SENT TO STOP THE BULGARIAN ADVANCE INTO MACEDONIA.

By 1917 war and politics had transformed the geography and place of Greece on the international stage. For most of the nearly one hundred years after Greece secured its independence from the Ottoman Empire, the nation had become obsessed with what came to be known as the "Great Idea"(Megali Idea). The essence of the Great Idea was that Greece had a destiny to put under one nation all ethnic Greeks who lived in the Balkans and in Asia Minor. A leader of the Greek Revolution of 1821, John Kolettes, summarized the essence of this grandiose dream stating, "A Greek is not only a man who lives within his kingdom, but also one who lives in Janina, in Salonika, in Seres, in Adrianople and Constantinople, in Smyrna, in Trebizona, in Crete, in Samos, and in any land associated with Greek history or the Greek race…. There are two main centers of Hellenism: Athens, the capital of the Greek kingdom…and 'the City'(Constantinople), the dream and hope of all Greeks." As the Ottoman Empire, "The Sick Man of Europe," began unraveling and approached its final death, various European powers began positioning themselves to pick at the carcass of what was slipping from Turkish hands. Italy and Bulgaria had their eyes on establishing a foothold in Macedonia. Britain, France, and Germany also believed they had interests in these areas as well as in parts of Asia Minor.

In 1910 the Greeks had elected Eleutherios Venizelos as prime minister. A charismatic leader of great eloquence, he initiated much needed domestic and military reforms and implemented a foreign policy that nearly doubled the size of the country. If any one leader seemed capable of making The Great Idea a reality, it was, in most Greek minds, Venizelos. In 1912 he had gone to London and secured the friendship and support of the Chancellor of the Exchequer, Lloyd George, who continued to support Greek foreign policy and aspirations for the next decade. In October 1912 the Greek army entered Salonika unopposed and established control over the city that had, at that time, only a minority population of Greeks. With Venizelos's leadership and the role of the Greek army, the size of the Greek kingdom was greatly enlarged after the first and second Balkan wars. The nation now encompassed southern Epirus, Macedonia, western Thrace, the islands of Crete and Samos, Salonika, and the commercial centers of Janina and Kavala. In addition, the population of Greece had dramatically increased from 2.7 to 4.75 million people. Such success gave all Greeks the confidence that the Great Idea, while not yet fully realized, was, in fact, a real possibility.

Although he had been young at the beginning of the Balkan wars, Yannelli was fully aware of what was happening. Newspapers from Athens did make their way to Agios Andeas and Prastos, although sometimes one or two weeks after their publication, and the men in the coffeehouses were always involved in political discussions. After the successes of the Balkan wars, Yannelli secured a large photograph of Venizelos that he proudly hung in the space over his bed. There had not been a Greek leader like Venizelos for generations, and the young Yannelli absorbed whatever reading material he could find about this dynamic personality who was changing the image of Greece internally and in the eyes of the entire world.

"I admire this man so much," he told his friend Phillipos Alfearis, "and I hope he stays as our leader for life. I would not be against that."

"For life?" responded Phillipos, "We Greeks won't keep anybody for life, not even our kings. I think it's because we think we know more than any of them and that we could do the job better. Don't forget we invented the word that gave a name to this condition, we named it 'ego.'"

Yannelli didn't disagree with Phillipos. He had come to believe that within the Greek character was one element that could lead them to greatness and also subject them to crushing defeat, and that one thing was "individualism." Individualism, he thought, fostered great innovative ideas, democracy, and incredible achievements in art, drama, literature, architecture, philosophy, and science but also was an obstacle to unity, cooperation, and collective action. Phillipos was probably right, he concluded; everyone wants to be Venizelos and nobody wants to be one of his followers.

As the World War I erupted in 1914, Greece was officially neutral, but within the ruling factions there was strong disagreement as to whether neutrality was the wisest course the country should follow. Venizelos strongly believed that Greece should enter the war on the side of the Triple Entente of Britain, France, and Russia. His logic was that this would eventually be the winning side and that they would be most supportive of his agenda for completing the goals of the Great Idea. The king, with family ties to Germany, strongly opposed the Venizelos position and believed the country needed to maintain its neutral stance. The result was a national schism, during which Venizelos was forced to resign, and he began to function extra-legally, as a virtual alternative government. The Entente, eager to get Greece to enter the war on its side, made extravagant promises of land that would come to Greece after victory had been won and openly began efforts to depose the king. In January, 1917 their efforts succeeded, and King Constantine left Greece as his son, Alexander, succeeded him. By June 1917 Venizelos had returned to power as prime minister.

As he approached the age of mandatory military service, Yannelli watched these events with greater interest than ever before. He remained a staunch supporter of Venizelos. To him, the fact that his country, the people who had invented democracy, was led by a monarch had always seemed absurd. Obviously, there still was a king after Constantine left, but he hoped that perhaps by war's end that, too, would change in a new Greece. As he left his home for the military in June, 1917, he was optimistic about the future of the country and excited about what he might do as part of the army of his nation.

Arriving in Athens, he prepared himself for the weeks of training that would precede his deployment to some location. The various aspects of the training period were rigorous, but they were routines Yannelli almost enjoyed. He thrived in a structured environment where everyone was expected to know their place in the military hierarchy. He had little to learn in the small time allotted to training in horsemanship, which now had a diminishing combat role in what had now become an increasingly mechanized mode of warfare. But it was believed that soldiers on horseback might still play some useful role at a particular time, so all recruits were required to spend some time in this aspect of their training. Yannelli was also an excellent marksman but became even more proficient using the rifles issued by the army as well as learning how to utilize for maximum efficiency the rapid firing machine gun weaponry. Here, for the first time, he met men from all parts of Greece with backgrounds, customs, modes of dress, and dialects far removed from the limited world he had known in his home villages and in the surrounding area that had constituted his mail carrier route. "Sometimes I can't even understand some of these men," he complained to his friend Phillipos. "I'm not even sure they're speaking Greek."

"I wouldn't be so quick to criticize," said Phillipos. "They probably think the same thing about us when we start doing our Tsakonika dialect."

Yannelli smiled. Phillipos was probably right, he thought. He sometimes forgot that many people from his area spoke a version of Greek that only others from that region could comprehend. "And you know," continued Yannelli, "for the first time I'm really getting a sense of who we Greeks really are. I see blue-eyed blond men, some with fiery red hair, some with fair skin, and some so dark I think they are probably part African or Arab, sort of like you, Phillipos," Yannelli laughed as he gave Phillipos a friendly light punch to the side of his arm.

"I'm not African or Arab!" protested Phillipos, "I'm every bit as Greek as you are, and you know it." Phillipos did not always appreciate Yannelli's humor. He had always been sensitive to his coloring and physical features from the time he was a child at school and some teased him about really being a Turk, a product of the four-hundred-year domination and occupation of Turks on the Greek mainland.

Yannelli's instincts had been correct about where he, Phillipos, and the others were going to be sent. The Greek victories and gains in the two Balkan wars had given Greece more territory but no guarantees that others would accept this as a permanent condition. Other nations, for historic, economic, and strategic reasons, continued to covet the fertile plains of Macedonia. At the end of the training period Yannelli and his comrades boarded trucks that were taking them to Thessaloniki, known primarily at that time simply as Salonika. It was July 1917.

Although Greece now controlled Salonika, it was hardly a Greek city. Bordering not only the rest of Greece but also Albania, Serbia, Bulgaria, and Russia, it had been controlled for centuries by Muslim Turks and had a long history as a safe haven for Jews who had been expelled centuries before from Spain and Portugal. Salonika in 1917 was an international city, a mixture of races, religions, and cultures. The most recent census of 1913 reported a city with a population of 157,889 people, of whom fewer than 40,000 were Greeks while 45,867 were classified as Ottomans, which really meant Muslims, and 61,439 were listed as Jews. The Jewish population was most prominent, and the city had more Jews than all of Serbia, Bulgaria, and Constantinople combined. The census also revealed how intermingled the various ethnic and religious groups were in the city. The city had no ethnic ghettos, and there were only a very few neighborhoods that belonged exclusively to one group or another.

Arriving in the city Yannelli was fascinated by what he saw. It was, of course, a city, not a village such as those that had been his life experience thus far. It seemed alive with energy and people, more people than he had ever seen in one place and more people than he had encountered in all his mail courier routes. But it was the diversity of the city that intrigued him. The streets were filled with entrepreneurs of every background, selling their wares from stores or street carts or simply by walking the streets. He had never before actually met Serbs, Albanians, Turks, and Jews. He found the entire environment fascinating and wondered how all these different people actually got along so well. If it could happen here, he thought, why could this not be duplicated elsewhere? Why had there been a need for two Balkan wars or the World War now raging, or even for him and his fellow soldiers to be sent here? Maybe, he hoped, things would calm down. Maybe they would not have to engage the "enemy," whoever they might be. But the calm Yannelli hoped for was not to be.

Internal conflict in Greece came to a head by the end of 1916 and into 1917. King Constantine's position of neutrality in the war was now no longer acceptable to the Triple Entente. A blockade of southern Greece and the Peloponnesus had been ordered to force the royalist government to capitulate. In January 1917 when Constantine agreed to abdicate, the blockade was lifted, and Constantine was succeeded by his son, Alexander. In June, when Venizelos returned to power as prime minister, Greece officially entered World War I on the side of the Triple Entente. Coming to Salonika in July, 1917, Yannelli and his fellow soldiers awaited their orders as to what front, if any, they would be sent to engage the enemy. But the first battle they would fight was not against the Turks, Bulgars, or Germans but rather against a devastating fire which consumed the city in the hot summer days of August 1917.

At 3:00 p.m. on August 18, a spark of fire from a kitchen in a house fell into a pile of straw situated nearby. A fire started, which for some unexplained reason was not immediately extinguished. A strong north wind carried the flames to the next house, then the next, until house after house and building after building were consumed by flames that appeared to be unstoppable. Fire trucks were dispatched to stop the spread of the flames, but they were old wooden fire vehicles that moved slowly and had little power to project large streams of water on such huge fires. There was also an acute shortage of water. Salonika had become a transit center for Triple Entente troops, and there were thousands of British, French, and now Greek soldiers based on the outskirts of the city with great need of water for their camps. As the fire continued hour after hour to devastate more and more blocks of the city, the Allied forces appeared to be the only ones who could act, in some way, to prevent total devastation, so British, French, and Greek soldiers were ordered to engage in firefighting, rescue operations, and care for those who had lost their homes and businesses. Soldiers from all three countries now fanned out throughout an increasingly chaotic city. Women, clutching their children were frantically running away from their burning residences. Muslims and Jews were desperately attempting to salvage valuables or records from their businesses. The streets were filled with screaming, crying men, women, and children running, seeking safe ground from a fire that continued to seem unstoppable as the strong north wind carried it farther and farther within the city.

Yannelli's unit was ordered to go to the part of the city where it was believed the fire originally started to determine how they might rescue people and property. Running from house to house, Yannelli directed panicked people to safe areas and helped elderly Jews remove what they could salvage from their places of business. The heat of the August day combined with the roaring flames was intense. Hour after hour Yannelli directed men, women, and children away from the flames toward the refugee areas that were being established close to the sea. He was exhausted, his body now was operating on pure determination and will power. He ran past houses looking and listening for any persons who might still be trapped within. At one home flames were engulfing the old wooden building, and intense heat was emanating in every direction. Running by, Yannelli stopped, believing he heard a human voice. Looking up he saw a woman screaming in a language he did not understand. She was at a window, not yet consumed by flames, but soon to be, and she was holding a small child. Yannelli froze. The woman continued screaming and the sight of the child affected him deeply, but the intense heat of the flames made him question whether or not he could enter the building. He had little time for contemplation or debate. He called for one of his fellow Greek soldiers who was nearby, although he did not know his name. "Soldier!" he yelled, "come with me. There is a woman and a child trapped in the building. I'm going in to get her. I will drop the child from the window, and you had better be there to catch it!"

The soldier, with a military rank no lower than Yannelli's responded hesitantly to the command given by Yannelli's strong, confident voice. "I don't think you can make it in there," he said. "The flames are too high and too hot, you won't make it. But if you do go in, I'll be down here waiting for the child." Yannelli nodded, ran into the entrance of the house, and climbed the stairs to the second floor. Flames that had destroyed the back part of the house were now dangerously close to where the woman and the child were huddled. The heat was intense, and smoke was everywhere as Yannelli burst into the room, coughing up smoke as he raced toward the woman. Grabbing the small child, he wrapped it in a blanket, hoping to offer some protection, and dropped the small boy into the hands of the soldier waiting below. The force of the fall pushed both the soldier and the child to the ground, but both were unharmed. Yannelli quickly took another blanket off a second bed in the room, lifted the woman in his arms, covered her as well as himself, ran down the stairs now caught up in flames, and headed for the first available door. The blanket was now burning, and Yannelli, with a quick motion, threw it to the ground. He then brought the woman to her son who embraced the little boy who was crying. Looking at Yannelli, she said something in a language he did not understand, but he knew she was saying, "Thank you, thank you."

It was now almost midnight. The soldiers had been on duty since the afternoon. They hadn't stopped to rest, and they had not eaten. As flames continued to destroy more and more of the city, the British, French, and Greek soldiers were doing what they could. The British had stopped the fire near the White Tower, and the French had saved the customs building in the city. There were, however, some disturbing reports about some French soldiers. A number of reports were surfacing that revealed that rather than assisting in the firefighting and helping victims of the fire, many French soldiers were preventing homeowners from rescuing their valuables and belongings and were looting those things for themselves. Yannelli had heard such reports about some of the French soldiers even as he and others were desperately trying to save lives and property. Upon hearing these latest reports he told his friend Phillipos, "Those French bastards. How low can you get? Now I know why I hated studying French in school in Constantinople. They ought to be shot." The day after the fire had been brought under control, Yannelli's wish was carried out on the order of French General Sarrail, who ordered the execution of two French soldiers who had been arrested for selling jewels they had stolen from fire victims.

By midnight of August 18 even the buildings at the seashore had caught fire, and the flames quickly spread from building to building. Three quarters of the structures were collapsing from white flames and were releasing hot ashes down on carts and cars, now both being turned into rubble by the intense heat of the fire. At 3:00 a.m. Yannelli and his unit were still walking the streets looking for victims, directing people to safety. He was exhausted and hungry. Sweat had soaked his uniform, and the metal helmet on his head seemed to be taking on the weight of a heavy boulder. He took it off, sat on the ground to momentarily catch his breath. Around him, the flames continued to devour house after house. He had never seen or experienced anything like this. He was in the middle of a disaster of epic proportions. He got up and continued his patrol. Passing a house where flames had just begun to burn, he once again heard cries for help. Once again he did not understand the language, but he had heard it many times before as a schoolchild in Constantinople—it was Turkish. Phillipos was now with him, and Yannelli motioned to him saying, "Let's go in there, someone needs help." As he spoke, the flames now seemed to spread more quickly; part of one of the walls collapsed, and Yannelli saw that within seconds the entrance might be blocked with flames preventing anyone from entering the house.

"Yannelli, don't do anything crazy! We can't get in there! We can't save everybody, and besides they're Turks!" yelled Phillipos.

Yannelli turned, grabbed Phillipos tightly by the collar of his uniform, and looked directly in his eyes saying, "Don't talk like an idiot! There are people in there! Don't act like a pig, you're a soldier, remember, you're a soldier!" Pulling Phillipos along with him, both entered the building. They knew they had only two or three minutes to evacuate whoever was in the building since the falling walls and intense heat signaled to them that the entire structure would soon fall to the ground. As they forcibly knocked down a locked door behind which they heard voices, they discovered three veiled women, screaming and sobbing as they frantically sought help. The husband had fled, leaving his wives behind to die while he had run to safety somewhere outside the house. Yannelli and Phillipos led the women out of the house through the door they had broken and into the safety of the street. "Thank God, we got to them in time," said Yannelli, as he attempted to catch his breath. Phillipos wanted to say something, but just nodded, thinking to himself, "So we saved a harem so that some other Turkish pig could have them and abandon them when he needed to save his own ass." Both men then continued on their patrol.

The fire died out on the evening of August 19. Yannelli and the others had not slept in more than thirty hours. They had sipped water when they could, and pieces of bread had been their only food. They were given orders to stop their patrols, sleep for a few hours, and begin a new assignment in the morning. As Yannelli awoke the next morning, he looked out at a devastated city. The flames had stopped, but hot ashes and smoke filled the sky, the aftermath of a burnt out city. Almost a thousand buildings had been destroyed. More than seventy thousand people had lost their homes. The fire had destroyed virtually all of the Jewish community, and more than thirty synagogues had been destroyed as well as schools, libraries, and business establishments. Mosques had also been destroyed by the fire, and the Greek Orthodox Church of St. Demetrios was also partially destroyed. The task now for the troops of all three nations was to find or create shelter for the thousands of homeless people. Thousands of Jews chose to leave the city, emigrating to Paris, Palestine, and America.

Yannelli and other Greek, British, and French units were now assigned to set up tents and build temporary huts to house people. Soup kitchens were established, and more than thirty thousand people came there, grateful for even the most meager of meals they might have. Yannelli had never experienced such devastation and suffering in his entire life. The hopelessness and needs of the people erased in his mind the ethnic and religious differences of the people he assisted. Passing through the soup kitchens were Jews with yamalkas on their heads, Turks wearing fezzes, Greek men and women, and veiled Muslim women. All were suffering, he thought. All must have prayed to God that they would survive, and yet, when all this was over and then forgotten, he knew that it was likely that old prejudices, stereotypes, and historic hatreds would again take hold. Another reason to be skeptical of organized religions, he thought. Wasn't religion the cause of all this hatred and conflict between Christians, Muslims, and Jews? He was depressed at the thought as he forcibly smiled, nodded a greeting, and passed out the limited rations of food to people who had been standing in lines waiting for two or three hours. Eventually, although it would be long after Yannelli had left Salonika, the city, guided by a master plan authorized by Venizelos, would rise again, this time a more modern and more beautiful urban community than it had been on that fateful afternoon of August 18.

The days that followed were essentially doing the same kinds of tasks, cleaning up the debris and caring for the homeless. Greece was now a full partner with the Triple Entente. Rumors were rampant that the Greek troops would soon be ordered to stop the growing Bulgarian movements into Macedonia, but nothing happened and no orders were issued. Yannelli wrote letters home to his mother and to Alexandra, never knowing whether they would ever reach their destination. He wrote to his mother assuring her that he was safe and inquiring about his brothers and sisters. He did not know when he would be returning, he wrote, but he was sending home part of the meager compensation he was receiving as a soldier. He told his mother he missed and loved her, but as he wrote he wasn't sure he missed his life in Agios Andreas. He wondered, could he go back and live his whole life there? He wasn't sure. He fully understood that what he had experienced in Salonika was tragic and the conditions terrible, but it did give him a sense of purpose and there was, he admitted to himself, an excitement to it all. His letters to Alexandra also conveyed stories of what he had seen and done. He told her that he missed her very much and that she was on his mind often, mostly when things were quiet and he allowed his mind to explore the past and think of the future. If there was an incentive to return to the village, that incentive was Alexandra. Yannelli believed that someday he would marry her, and perhaps, he thought, she would agree to not remain in the village and they could escape the routine, uneventful life that generations of their families before them had led. He tried to write to her at least once a month and eagerly looked forward to letters she sent to him, each one relating how much she missed him and that she prayed daily for his safety and eagerly anticipated his return home.

Since the month following the great fire proved to be routine and less eventful, troops were granted furloughs to return to their homes for a two-week block of time. Yannelli and Phillipos made their way back, first to Athens, then by car to their home village. To Yannelli the village seemed to be a world away from where he had been. For the first few nights he could not sleep, because of the almost total quiet of the nights, uninterrupted by gunfire, fire trucks, and thousands of human voices. He was happy to see his family, and they were excited to see him. He spoke with his mother, brothers, and sisters, catching up on what was happening in each of their lives and fascinating them with tales of Salonika and his assignments. His mother seemed to have lost weight, and she reported that she had not been feeling well over the previous six months. Yannelli offered to take her to see a physician in Nafplio, but she was not eager to go, saying that some rest and seeing him home safe was all the medicine she needed. Now that she had seen her son, she assured Yannelli, she would be feeling better soon.

And, of course, he saw Alexandra. Meeting as privately as they could, Yannelli told her how much she had been on his mind and how he longed to see her and be with her again.

"Have you really been thinking about me, Yannelli?" she asked. "I worry that you have met some other girl in Salonika and that I have been erased from your mind."

Yannelli assured her that he had met no one and, more importantly, he desired to meet no one. "I haven't forgotten you, Alexandra, I will never forget you. I love you, I truly do, but we must be patient. When my time in the army is over, then we can talk to our parents, then we can make our plans." Alexandra was comforted by Yannelli's assurances. She looked into his eyes, reached out for his hand, and he held it in his. He then held her close to him as he gently brought his lips to hers. "I love you, Alexandra," he said, 'I will always love you." The two weeks passed by quickly, and soon Yannelli joined his friend Phillipos as they made their way back to Athens and then, within two days, returned to Salonika.

Yannelli's next letter to Alexandra informed her that she would most likely not be hearing from him for a while. Greek troops had been ordered to join British, French, and Serbian troops in a major assault against Bulgaria. The Allied troops were to be under the command of the French general, Francet D'Esperey. On September 14, 1918, the order for which the troops had long awaited was issued. The combined British, Greek, French, and Serbian forces were to launch an offensive attack against the Bulgarian army. The evening before the Greek army was to move into position, Yannelli, Phillipos, and ten others sat in the barracks they were calling home. Most of the men seemed to be experiencing an emotion combining excitement and fear. Most had never before been in combat situations. They found it hard to think of sleeping when the uncertainty of what awaited them pressed against their minds. Phillipos, always seeking conversation, took the lead in trying to break the tension.

"I have a test for everyone," he announced, "a test I'm willing to bet none of you will pass." Yannelli and the others looked at Phillipos thinking, here comes more nonsense, but since there was nothing better to do, they let Phillipos talk on. Phillipos continued, "I want you all to think of three to five contributions Bulgarians have made to Western Civilization, just three to five! I will give as a prize to the first one of you who answers correctly all my cigarettes for the next two weeks. Remember only three to five contributions! I will wait for your answers but not for too long." The group said nothing, thinking through how they might respond, but none spoke up. "I'm waiting," said Phillipos, "I'll give you one more minute." Still there was silence. Finally Phillipos offered his answer, "You are all correct, you are correct because Bulgarians have contributed absolutely nothing to Western Civilization. Nothing! Nothing! For this, they deserve to die." He smiled as the others began smiling as well. "Let's face it," he continued, "even the stupid Turks created an empire, even the Romans were smart enough to steal our gods, our literature, and our architecture. But the Bulgarians? Tell me the equivalents of Sophocles, Euripides, Socrates, and Aristotle? I won't wait for an answer, because there is none. As I said, any people who have contributed absolutely nothing for thousands of years deserve to die. And now they want Macedonia? Will they claim that Alexander the Great was Bulgarian? I doubt it, because Alexander was too smart to be Bulgarian; he was a Greek, through and through." The assembled soldiers knew Phillipos was performing, putting on a show to take everyone's mind off their orders for the following morning.

"But remember," Yannelli joined in, hoping to encourage Phillipos to continue his act even further, "the Bulgarians are Eastern Orthodox Christians, just as we are. We are religious brothers."

Phillipos responded to the challenge. "What kind of Orthodox Christians fight alongside Muslim Turks? They are so stupid as to ally themselves with the same people who kept them in virtual slavery for hundreds of years. More proof, I tell you, they deserve to die! And one more thing, if Alexander the Great was all, or even part, Bulgarian, then I am part jackass!"

"I have a question for you, Phillipos," said a tall, muscular soldier. "Which would you rather be if you had to make a choice—a jackass or a Bulgarian?"

Phillipos pretended that he needed a moment to decide on an answer, smiled, and then burst out, "He haw, he haw, the Bulgarians must die." When Phillipos' performance had ended, all went to their beds, attempting to have at least a few hours of sleep before morning. The jokes were over now. Tomorrow would be no joke, and it was likely that only some would return for the next session of laughter and camaraderie.

On September 14, 1918, the joint Allied offensive against Bulgaria, which had been long awaited, began. British troops and Yannelli's unit, which had been placed with Greek soldiers from Crete, moved to the Vardar Valley and engaged the Bulgarians near Lake Dorian, close to the Greek border. On the eastern edge of the fighting, the French and Serbian troops were finding success, advancing an average of ten miles per day and taking large numbers of Bulgarian prisoners. The Italian forces in the west were meeting with similar success and had totally cut off the Bulgarian army from supply lines and further reinforcements. The British and Greek troops met heavy resistance, particularly from the fortifications and positions the Bulgarians had established in the mountains. Under orders from the British commander, Sir George Milne, Greek troops, Yannelli among them, were ordered to dislodge the mountainside Bulgarian entrenchments. With direct orders from his Greek captain, Yannelli and two others began a steep climb up the mountain to seek out the Bulgarian position. The weather was hot and the humidity high. Slowly and carefully ascending the mountain, the Greeks were coming closer and closer to within visible range of the enemy fortification. As they approached a spot where they had a clear view of the Bulgarians, they saw three enemy soldiers standing ready, searching for Allied soldiers. Two of the men were armed with rifles, a third manned a German issue machine gun. The movement of Yannelli and his two comrades became visible to the Bulgarian soldiers, and they began firing, first the riflemen and then the machine-gunner in a seemingly random untargeted manner. Yannelli fell to the ground, secure behind a large boulder as a spray of bullets hit trees, stones, any object within the range of the shooters. Yannelli stayed down, crawling low to the ground. His two colleagues had also found protection behind large rocks and were unharmed by the Bulgarian rapid fire. Rejoining them, Yanneli asked them both to move two hundred feet from where they were located, count to fifty, and begin firing at the Bulgarians. He told them that as the enemy would turn to return fire, he would, from his angle, fire at them and attempt to take all three soldiers out. The two Greek soldiers moved to their positions, did the required count, and began rapidly firing at the enemy site. As the Bulgarians began returning fire, Yannelli focused his aim on the machine-gunner, fired, and hit the soldier directly in the head. The machine gun was now silent. As the machine-gunner's comrades moved to attempt to help their fellow soldier who had been hit and utilize the now silent machine-gun, Yanneli now fired two successive shots, one hitting one of the Bulgarians in the chest, the second shot striking the other in the neck. Both men fell to the ground, and Yannelli and his comrades now quickly ran to the fortification, their rifles poised to finish the three soldiers off if, in fact, they were still alive. The machine-gunner had been killed instantly, and the man hit in the chest died within seconds of the Greeks reaching the enemy encampment. The third Bulgarian soldier, hit in the neck, was bleeding profusely; the bullet had hit a key vein. Yannelli and his comrades tried to stop the bleeding and take the man prisoner, but he, too, died within the following ten minutes.

"That was quite an exhibition of shooting, Yannelli," the one Greek soldier said to him as they prepared to locate the next Bulgarian fortification.

"I guess starting to use a rifle and hunt at age eight has its advantages," responded Yannelli.

For the next four hours the three men patrolled other parts of the mountain for additional Bulgarian offensive sites. Two more were located, and once again the three Greeks successfully eliminated the site. Yannelli again targeted and killed two more Bulgarians soldiers, and his colleagues also successfully shot two additional enemy soldiers. Two Bulgarians surrendered, and Yannelli and his colleagues brought them to the prisoner holding area at the base of the mountain. Joining a large contingent of British and Greek forces the following day, Yannelli joined the battle that was now clearly breaking the Bulgarian army. As each day passed, the enemy army was retreating farther and farther from the front. Chaos was taking hold in their ranks, and in their retreat they were deserting by the thousands, as others surrendered. Some retreating Bulgarian units were initiating a scorched earth policy, burning supplies, destroying ammunition dumps, burning railway stations, and ravaging villages. On September 26 it was announced that the Bulgarian front had been destroyed, as their army had been dissected by various Allied troops. On Friday, September 27, Bulgaria asked the Allied forces for an armistice of forty-eight hours, with the intent of asking for peace. On the evening of September 29 an armistice was signed, and at twelve o'clock noon on September 30 all hostilities ceased. It was a quick and total victory for the Allied troops. The Germans had offered no real support to the Bulgarians, and the defeat meant that the World War I front in the Balkans would no longer see fighting. The terms of the armistice read:

Bulgaria agrees to evacuate all the territory she now occupies in Greece and Serbia; to demobilize their army immediately and surrender all means of transport to the Allies.... All Bulgarian arms and ammunition are to be stored under control of the Allies to whom it is conceded the right to occupy all strategic points. The military occupation of Bulgaria will be entrusted to British, French, and Italian forces and evacuated portions of Greece and Serbia respectively, to Greek and Serbian troops."

The engagement had been a total success for the Allies and a high price in lives and humiliation for Bulgaria. The country had lost ninety thousand troops during World War I, and its hopes of an expanded nation were demolished. For the Greeks the results were land and glory. The Bulgarian encroachment into Macedonia was stopped, and the reputation of the Greek army greatly enhanced. As the Greek army returned to their base, they were read three statements from key leaders. Writing just prior to the armistice the British commander Sir George Milne had written, " I wish on this first occasion on which Greeks troops have fought by the side of the English to express to you my admiration for the way in which you have fulfilled the mission entrusted to you. You have attacked with incomparable dash naturally strong positions rendered almost impenetrable by a stubborn army...I thank you for your gallantry and tenacity, which are above all praise. I am proud to have had you under my command."

The overall commander of the Allied forces, General Frances D'Esperey, also commended the, "brilliant conduct of the Greek units." At the conclusion of the hostilities, Greek Prime Minister

Venizelos congratulated the Greek troops as well, saying in a written statement, "The signing of the military convention with the enemy crowns the battles of the National Army. The Government desires to congratulate the National Army and to express the gratitude of the nation for the work which it has completed....Glory and honor to the National Army."

For Yannelli the battles had been a sobering experience. Days after the armistice he was proud to have been part of such a successful campaign and happy that the Greek army had shown the world its skill, toughness, and tenacity. But he could not erase from his mind the four or five men he had killed. Were there others he asked himself? Who really knew where a spray of bullets actually landed? He had been lucky and survived, but he had also seen Greek soldiers wounded and some who died before his eyes. And he wondered about the men he knew he had killed. Who were they? Somebody knew them as a son, brother, or husband. Did these men have wives? Children? What would happen to them? Was all this fighting and killing really justified? For what, pieces of property? The more questions that came to his mind, the more he became troubled. But this was war, he rationalized. Those same men were trying to kill him. The questions, the thoughts, the regrets, the rationalizations kept running through his head. He loved the military, he said to himself, but this was not why.

As October arrived Greek and British troops, again under the command of General Milne, were ordered to move east against the Turks. The thought of Greek soldiers once again entering victoriously into Constantinople for the first time since 1453 excited Yannelli. But such a scene was not to be. The Greek and British forces were ordered to stop their advance at Alexandroupolis, because news came that the Turks had signed an armistice taking them out of hostilities in World War I. For Greece, her active involvement in the hostilities of the World War was over as well, almost as quickly as it had begun. Prime Minister Venizelos now headed to the Paris Peace Conference to further his vision of the Great Idea and secure as much Greek populated territory as his diplomatic skills could achieve. Within a short time Yannelli and the other Greek forces were ordered to another front of a different kind in the Asia Minor city of Symrna. But in Symrna, there would be no celebrations of Greek honor and glory.

Smyrna, 1919–1922

FROM THE JOURNAL, 1922

TODAY WE ARE LEAVING SMYRNA. IT HAS BEEN VERY DIFFICULT. ALL SEEMS LOST. WE ARE COMING HOME, BUT TO WHAT I AM NOT SURE.

With the signing of the armistice in November 1918 ending hostilities in World War I, the focus of the world was on the Paris Peace Conference, which began in January 1919. It was at this conference that decisions were to be made by the victorious Allied powers as to how the defeated Ottoman Empire was to be divided. Prior to the beginning of the peace conference Greek Prime Minister Venizelos toured European capitals to make the case to heads of state for Greece's claims to pieces of lands that had for centuries been occupied by the Turks. It was now, believed the Greek leader, that the time and opportunity had finally come when the Great Idea might actually be realized. Venizelos was encouraged by the ongoing support he was receiving from British Prime Minister Lloyd George and by American President Woodrow Wilson's call for the self-determination of all peoples. Venizelos argued that there should be Greek sovereignty over northern Epirus, the area that had been Bulgarian, Turkish Thrace, the Turkish islands in the Aegean, the Dodecanese Islands, and virtually the whole western coast of Asia Minor where there were large populations of ethnic Greeks. Greeks had lived in Asia Minor since ancient times, and it was estimated that two and one-half million Greeks lived in the Ottoman Empire at the outbreak of the World War I. Eventually, at some future date, Venizelos believed that Constantinople itself would once again be a Greek city. The Prime Minister also made the argument to the Allied powers that the Greek population living in the former Ottoman Empire was in physical danger from the Turks, since in 1915 they had enacted what were considered genocidal policies against Greeks and Armenians. Venizelos was also concerned about other nations, primarily Italy, for making claims to some of the same geographic areas that the Greeks believed were rightfully theirs. Through the force of his eloquence, personality, and diplomatic skills, Venizelos persuaded the powers at the peace conference to allow him to order Greek troops to land in Smyrna to protect the substantial Greek population that lived there.

Yannelli, his friend Phillipos, and many others who had been inducted into the army in 1917 and were scheduled to return to civilian life in 1919 were offered financial incentives to reenlist for an additional three-year period. Yannelli, Phillipos, and others from their unit accepted the opportunity and were immediately given orders to leave for Smyrna. They left where they had been stationed in Thrace, and on May 15, 1919, before any formal agreement had been reached between Greece and the Allied powers, Yannelli joined the other Greek troops as they disembarked at the port of Smyrna.

The city of Smyrna was the center of Greek life and culture in Asia Minor. The Greek population had risen from less than one third in 1800 to about one-half at the start of the Balkan wars. It was a center of commerce, and by the end of the nineteenth century the city's exports surpassed those of any other Turkish port including that of Constantinople. The community was composed of peasant farmers, middle-class clerks and shopkeepers, as well as an educated class of Greeks composed of lawyers, doctors, teachers, and wealthy traders.

The Greek community had, for years, operated with relative freedom from interference from the Ottoman Turks. The Greeks had their own system of internal governance that dealt smoothly with the Turkish government officials. Smyrna was a cosmopolitan city, and travelers reported that in addition to Greek, many inhabitants spoke French, Italian, Dutch, or English. The city was known for its large numbers of marriageable-age European ladies, and few cities exceeded Smyrna's reputation for hospitality toward European men. The citizens of Smyrna were known for their passion for cards and gambling as well for their enthusiasm to join clubs of various kinds. There was another side of the city as well, where houses of prostitution openly operated as did the often seedy hashish-saturated clubs frequented mostly by men but often by women who were offering their companionship and services for money.

The overall comfortable position of the Greek population in Smyrna changed dramatically by the end of World War I. Turkey, forced by international pressure, signed the Treaty of Sevres, which gave Greece not only Smyrna but also a large area surrounding the city for five years at which time an election would be held to determine the permanent ownership of the city. The population of the city virtually ensured that Smyrna would then become a permanent Greek holding. Venizelos, now seeing that the long desired Great Idea could actually become reality, pressed for even more parts of Asia Minor to be under Greek control. His chief of staff, Colonel Metaxas, urged caution, arguing that such an enlarged area would be difficult to control and could not be adequately defended, but his arguments fell on deaf ears. It was this enlarged Greek presence in Asia Minor and Greece's demand for even more territory that ignited a new intense nationalism in Turkey. The young Turkish officer, Mustafa Kemal, later known as Kemal Ataturk, rejected the Ottoman Sultan's acceptance of foreign domination and called for a modern Turkish national state. In January 1920 the new Turkish parliament proclaimed a new Turkish nation. This new nation, hostile to foreign encroachment in their land, now became a major threat to Greek claims in Asia Minor.

Only a year earlier, in May 1919, the reception Yannelli and his comrades had received when they landed in Smyrna had been vastly different. At eight o'clock in the morning the Greek battleship Kilkis moved into Smyrna harbor. As Yannelli and his fellow soldiers disembarked, they were met with sustained applause and loud cheers. Most of the welcoming citizens were Greeks, but there were also large numbers of Jews and Armenians in the crowd as well. The Turks who were present offered no welcome cheers and stood silently as Greek soldiers left their ship. The Greek Metropolitan, Chrysostomos, dressed in his official religious attire, greeted the troops and offered his blessing. A small group of soldiers performed a national Greek dance, to the delight of some onlookers and to the disgust of others. As the Greek soldiers moved on toward barracks that housed several hundred Turkish soldiers, a shot was heard, and panic ensued. Civilians ran for cover, and some Greek soldiers began firing randomly. Yannelli held back and in the midst of growing chaos yelled out to his comrades, "Don't fire! Don't fire! There are women and children here!" Amid the panic a number of civilians were killed and wounded. In other parts of the city violence broke out as Greeks entered Turkish quarters and robbed, raped, and killed Turkish citizens. When the outbreak finally subsided, two to three hundred Turks had died, and more one hundred Greeks had been killed. There were no accurate numbers of both Turks and Greeks who had been molested or injured.

Yannelli thought the Greek entrance to Smyrna had been a fiasco. The Orthodox ceremony at the dock had offended the Muslims, the Greek troops dancing had offended the Turkish inhabitants, and a final stupid act, Yannelli thought, had been when the Greek commanding officer had forced his troops to shout, "Long live Greece! Long live Venizelos!" as they marched toward the Turkish quarter.

Within a short three days of the Greek landing, the Greek authorities attempted to calm the situation by ordering the restitution of stolen Turkish property and by arresting and putting on trial fifty-four people, mostly Greeks, who had participated in the rampage. These individuals were sentenced to military court, and three were sentenced to death and the others to various lengths of hard labor. The tensions between Turks and Greeks continued, however, both in the city of Smyrna as well as in outlying villages. Each day it became clearer that what was perceived as the Greek "occupation" had the potential for even greater disaster.

"I don't like the feel of things here," Yannelli told Phillipos as he sat on the edge of the hard surface that was considered his bed in the headquarters of the Greek army. "I think Metaxas is correct. I don't see how we can control the ever expanding area we are taking. I know Smyrna is really a Greek city, but I think we should stop here. We are causing resentment with each mile we advance into the interior."

"Well, General," Phillipos mockingly replied, "I think you should quit planning Greek strategy and just follow orders. Maybe when you become prime minister or a general you can reverse things, but until then I think I'll just follow our commanding officer and enjoy this city when we can. Have you noticed all the young women here, Yannelli? You should pay more attention to them and leave the strategy to the real generals. We need to go out and see the town, Yannelli. You need some relaxation."

"We'll do that, Phillipos, when the time is right. We'll go out. When the time is right."

By the summer of 1920 the Greek army was successful in occupying extensive land surrounding Smyrna. The purpose of the offensive was to provide strategic depth to the defense of the city. What was alarming, however, was that these operations were met by increasing Turkish resistance. By October 1920 the Greek army had advanced farther east into Anatolia in an attempt to defeat the nationalist Turks and force Kemal to sue for peace. The Turkish leader had no intention of making peace with the Greeks, and the Greek military advance only strengthened his determination to rid the foreigners from his land. Once again Yannelli saw signs of trouble as he and the other infantrymen moved farther and farther away from their base in Smyrna. To Yannelli the growing distance from their supply lines and reinforcements could only lead to trouble. In January 1921 Yanneli's division encountered Turkish forces at the first battle of Inonu. Yannelli was in the thick of the fighting and knew that he had hit and probably killed two Turks as the enemy had attempted to capture an entrenched Greek position. But, in fact, the battle ultimately proved to be negative for the Greeks, as the Turks for the first time now halted the Greek advance into the interior areas. With the Greek advance temporarily halted, Yannelli's unit was ordered to return to Smyrna.

The next four months Yanneli's unit was assigned general patrol duties within the city of Smyrna. For the most part it was routine and uneventful duty that allowed Yannelli and the others to fully explore every corner of the city itself. On some days virtually nothing happened, and on other days disagreements between Greeks and Turks and even between Greeks and other Greeks had to be settled before they could possibly lead to violence, rioting, and even killing. Yannelli spent most nights eating and talking with fellow soldiers and writing letters home to Alexandra, to his mother and siblings, and periodically to his older brother Mihali in Chicago. He had last heard from Mihali months earlier and was somewhat surprised to receive a letter from the brother he had not seen for almost four years. Mihali had written,

Dear Yannelli,

When I last wrote to our mother, she informed me that you are now stationed in Smyrna. I have never been there, but I hear it is a lively hub of Greek commerce and culture. I hope you are well and are protecting yourself from danger. Things are going well for me here, and I think when your enlistment is up we should talk seriously about what you intend to do in the future. The economy is booming here in the United States and particularly here in Chicago. I think you should seriously think about coming here. I know I can help you find a good job, and you will be much better off than if you return to our village.

There is no future there or anywhere else in Greece. I realize you have never really thought about this and that you and Alexandra may have other plans, but I urge you to not make any concrete plans until you and I can communicate more in depth about what I am saying. You know I would not be writing this if I did not really believe that joining me in America would be the best for you. Your brother,

Mihali

When Yannelli received his brother's letter, it was somewhat of a shock to him. He had never given any thought to leaving Greece for America. All he knew about the country and the city of Chicago was what Mihali had told him and the small amount of information he had gathered by reading a story in the newspapers. He wrote to his brother expressing his appreciation for Mihali's concern about his future and said that he would not automatically dismiss the idea, but at this point, he wrote, he wanted to make the military his career, perhaps even applying for the military academy that, upon graduation, would give him an officer's rank. He ended his letter to Mihali saying, "But I promise you we will communicate with each other before I make any final, long-range decision."

The letters between Yannelli and Alexandra were more frequent, and Yannelli looked forward to receiving every letter from the young girl he had left behind in Agios Andreas. Her letters were filled with news and gossip of events and people in the village, and his were accounts of his routine duties, his battle engagements, and his observations of people and life in Smyrna. Each professed a yearning to see the other and lamented as to how much they missed one another and longed to be together again. But as the months and years passed the sentiments were real but less frequently expressed. Both Alexandra and Yannelli had evolved from teenage boy and girl to mature man and woman. Yannelli's reenlistment had troubled Alexandra greatly. She had expected he would be leaving the army and coming home, and they could jointly look forward to plans for some kind of future together. She knew she still loved Yannelli, and he knew his feelings had not changed about her, but time and distance were taking their toll. It was not that Alexandra had an interest in someone else; she did not. And as her mother and father increasingly raised the issue of marriage to Alexandra, her reply was always the same, "I know the one I want. I will wait for Yannelli." For Yannelli, the sense of loyalty and commitment was equally strong. Certainly there had been opportunities to meet other women. He was young, handsome, and presented a striking figure in his carefully tailored uniform. There were women in Salonika he had met, but none had been pursued any further than as casual acquaintances, people with whom he could converse, persons other than his fellow soldiers. And he quickly discovered that the reports of eligible young women in Smyrna had not been exaggerated. The various Greek organizations regularly extended invitations to the Greek soldiers to attend their dinners and dances and, of course, have the opportunity to meet the many young women who were present. Yannelli went to these functions along with his soldier friends, but once again none of the women he met, even those more sophisticated and more glamorous than Alexandra, made him doubt that there was indeed something very good and very real between him and the village girl from Agios Andreas. But he was young; he needed to socialize in some way, and he certainly didn't want his colleagues whom he had fought beside, to think that he didn't want or enjoy their company. So when they suggested that on one of their free nights they go to one of the clubs near the sea-coast of the city, Yannelli told the group, "Sure, let's go, I'm ready."

It had been one of those dark and gloomy days. Throughout the day clouds had hidden the sun, and rain, which began falling in the morning, increased in intensity as the day wore on. By nightfall it was raining heavily, and thunder and lightning broke the silence of the evening hours. The weather, however, did not deter Yannelli, Phillipos, and the others from their plans. All five men had been given time for rest and recreation, and they had jointly agreed to go to one of the local *rembetika* clubs. The *rembetika* clubs of Smyrna were places unlike what Yannelli had ever seen. These clubs played a particular kind of music that was both Greek and Turkish in origin. The songs were those of loss, betrayal, longing, and suffering; the closest, but by no means an exact comparison, might be the blues music of America. These clubs were frequented by the Greek urban sub-proletariat, almost an underclass. The cafes were centers of drugs and vice. Those who were regular devoted attendees were called, *rembetes* or *manges*, words that have imprecise English equivalents but generally describe men who were part of a subculture on the fringes of society. Some, but not all, were actually criminals and the clubs were, except for a particular class of women who were there to offer pleasure for a fee, exclusively male establishments. These men would sit for hours, sipping first on a thick cup of Turkish coffee and then drawing on a *narghile* or water pipe that brought hashish deep into their lungs. Others sat twirling their worry beads and observing the succession of men who would go to the center of the floor and perform a solo dance known as the *zeibekiko*. The cafes were dark, and smoke filled the air in thick cloud-like formations. The women present, some young and some not so young, moved throughout the room, talking, teasing, flirting, and openly soliciting men, many of them in no condition to even know where they were or what they were doing. The clubs had first appeared toward the end of the nineteenth century in urban centers such as Athens, Piraeus, Larissa, Salonika, and Symrna. These cafes were often called the Café Aman, where singers improvised verses often in the form of a dialogue and used the words, *aman, aman* as fillers, which allowed them time to improvise new words. The music used various instruments such as a zither-like instrument called the *santouri*, a flute, violin, a kind of lute called the *laouto*, and the *oud*. But the two key instruments were the *bouzouki* and the *baglama*, a three–stringed instrument named after the Turkish word meaning bond or knot. The songs played in these instruments were often songs that had originated in prisons and then found their way out to the *rembetika* subculture. What was common to all of these cafes was the smoking of hashish. In Greece laws had been passed against the sale and smoking of hashish in 1890 but were seldom enforced. In towns and villages in Turkey, including Smyrna, hashish smoking was legal and widely practiced. The hashish was smoked through a *narghile,* which the Greeks called *tekes,* and the smoking of the substance also became one of the main themes of the songs played and sung in the Cafe Amans. It was such a café that Yannelli and his friends entered, determined that this would be a night when they could forget war and killing and simply have a good time.

As Yannelli, Phillipos, and the others entered the room, the customers already there stopped to stare at the young soldiers, all fully dressed in their uniforms. The smoke and the smell of hashish were thick and strong. Some men with dazed looks on their faces simply stared ahead, others' eyes were closing and opening in an almost rhythmic fashion. Two men, each oblivious to the other's presence, were doing their own interpretive *zeibekiko* dance, bending, swirling, hands held high in the air with fingers snapping to the slow beat of stone-faced musicians sitting on the small stage while they played their songs.

The *zeibekiko* dance is said to have originated with the Zeybek warriors of Anatolia. The dance is a very personal one in which the individual, dancing by himself, interprets the music as he hears it and through his steps expresses his individuality. Usually only one man at a time dances to the particular song, and sometimes, if another individual takes to the floor to dance as well, it could be a cause of conflict and even violence. These men were high on drugs, and few could predict what might happen on a given night. As Yannelli's group secured a table and took their seats, the singer, accompanied by the musicians began singing his song,

"Ah, if I die, what will they say?
Some fellow died,
A fellow who loved life and enjoyed himself,

226

Aman! Aman!
Ah, if I die on the boat, throw me into the sea
So that the black fish and the salt water can
Eat me.
Aman! Aman!"

Phillipos turned to his companions as the singer concluded, "Guess we're in for some happy times, boys. Aman. Aman!" Two of his friends humored him by laughing, while the others continued to survey the individuals smoking drugs and the women who were approaching their table. On the stage the musicians and the singer began another song,

"Without a heart, I didn't believe
You could be without a heart
You melted me like a candle
Bitch, you burnt me,
And you are not sorry.
Why do you poison my heart
With so much cruelty
And take away my soul?"

The rhythmic beat of the music inspired Phillipos to get up from his chair, remove his military jacket, and go to the floor to offer his own personal *rembetika* interpretation of the song being played. "Not great, but really not bad either," said Yannelli. "He almost looks like he knows what he's doing."

"He might look even better if we tried some of that stuff," said one of the soldiers, pointing to the *narghile.* "Let's give it a try, Yannelli."

"I don't think so," Yannelli answered, "we can just enjoy watching everyone else get high."

Phillipos completed his solo dance, returned to the table, and overheard the conversation taking place. "I think it's a really good idea, Yannelli. Loosen up. Don't worry, I'll never tell Alexandra a thing," he said as he motioned to the man nearby who was the guardian of the water pipes to bring some over to their table. As the music continued and the singer went on with his rendition of another song of heartbreak and disappointment, the Café Aman employee brought the *narghile* to the table and prepared it for use by the young soldiers. Yannelli was silent. He had been in situations like this before during his deployment in Salonika but had refrained from trying the hashish he had been offered many times before. This time, his companions were more insistent, as they each took their turns at the drug-filled water pipe, deeply drawing into their bodies the substance that would, in their minds, bring forth a new euphoria. As the *narghile* was passed to Yannelli, he hesitated.

"Go ahead, soldier boy," said the soft voice of the attractive girl who approached their table, "it won't hurt you, handsome. Here, let me show you how." The young girl, probably barely twenty years old, showed Yannelli the technique, slowly and deliberately inhaling the hashish. "Your turn," she said, as she stroked Yannelli's face and seductively fixed her eyes directly into his. "Spend the next half-hour here," she said, "and I'll be back and we can spend some time alone together."

Yannelli watched the girl as she walked from the table. She was not just attractive, he thought, she was an incredibly sexy, stunningly beautiful girl. He wondered who she was and why she was working here and then quickly decided it really didn't matter. After tonight, he would never see her again anyway. He took the water pipe, and inhaled slowly, only a few times at first, and passed it on to Phillipos who was sitting to his right.

"You see, Yannelli, it didn't kill you, and within the next half hour you will really feel good."

The five young soldiers spent the next half hour passing the drug dispenser between them, each drawing more deeply as the substance entered their bodies and slowly began to have its predictable effect. Within a short time Yannelli began to feel the effects of the experience. He felt relaxed, a dryness came to his mouth and throat, his pupils began to dilate, his perception of the details of the room in which they were sitting became more sensitive, colors became brighter and more vivid. He felt that all stress he might have had was gone, and his normal reluctance to talk too much also disappeared as he now seemed to want to know everything about everybody. Within about an hour the girl who had approached them earlier returned to Yannelli's table.

"Feel good, soldier?" she playfully asked.

Yannelli smiled, reached out for the girl's hand and began an uncharacteristically long statement about how beautiful the girl was, how her eyes were magnetic, how her flowing brown hair was the most beautiful he had ever seen, and how her full red lips had hypnotized him. Phillipos looked at Yannelli, not believing what he was hearing. This was not the Yannelli he had known his entire life. No, this was a different person. Funny what a little hashish will do, he thought to himself. Yannelli seemed to be unable to stop talking until the girl, still in the grip of Yannelli's hand, gently pulled him off his chair, kissed him on the cheek, and led him away from the table, through the smoke-filled room to the stairs that led to the upper floor. As his colleagues looked on in amazement, Yannelli and the girl climbed the stairs, vanishing from view.

It was late the following morning when Phillipos finally spoke to Yannelli who had just moments before awakened from what had been an almost thirteen-hour sleep. "So, Mr. handsome soldier boy, how was it?" Phillipos asked as Yannelli rubbed his hands through his hair and over his eyes.

"How was what?" Yannelli replied, conveying a clear message that he was not interested in talking to anyone about anything.

"Come on, you know, how was she?" Phillipos asked again, eagerly awaiting a report from his friend.

"I don't know what you're talking about, Phillipos. She was a nice girl. Everything about last night was like a fog. Nothing seems clear today. I'm tired of talking. Let's get going. We have orders for today, you know."

Phillipos knew Yannelli well; he had known him since they were four or five years old, and he knew that nothing more would come from his friend's mouth about the events of the previous night. He realized that the Yannelli of the last night was an aberration. The real Yannelli, the military soldier, had now returned. He knew that when his friend had said, "We have orders for today, you know," it was time to stop asking questions.

The orders that Yannelli had mentioned were for their unit to be prepared to once again move deeper into the interior of Asia Minor to secure even more territory for the Greek government. The Greek army had achieved some success as Turkish forces had retreated after the battle of Kutahya-Eskisehir. The Turkish parliament, unhappy with their military leader, Ismet Inonu, now asked Mustafa Kemal and Chief of General Staff, Fevzi Cakmak to lead the Turkish forces. Yannelli's unit and the other Greek forces now met fierce resistance from the Turks and engaged them in a twenty-one day battle at Sakarya. The Turks were positioned on a series of heights, and the Greeks had to storm the positions and occupy them. The Greek forces had the numerical advantage, but their losses were heavy. Yannelli and his comrades had successfully secured two of the Turkish positions, but had lost five men in the assault. What was becoming clear was that the Greek advance had lengthened their supply lines, cut off communication, and was exhausting their ammunition supply. The length of the battle had exhausted everyone, and slowly the Greeks withdrew to lines they had held months before. It was not a good sign, felt Yannelli. The Greeks had more men but still could not achieve their objective. His concerns about the overextension of supply lines seemed now to be warranted.

"I think you're right," Phillipos said to Yannelli as they sat in the ragged tent that served as their shelter during the almost month-long battle. "I don't know how much longer we can do this." What both Phillipos and Yannelli did not know was that at virtually the same moment as the Greek forces were withdrawing to previous lines, the Turkish parliament was bestowing a five-star designation on both Mustafa Kemal and Fevri Cakmak for what they had done to check the Greek advance in this long battle. But for the Greeks, the worst was yet to come.

The Greek position in Asia Minor continued to deteriorate. Changes and conflicts in the political situation in Greece created a climate of uncertain leadership, and international support for Greece's claims for territory in Asia Minor became increasingly weaker. By late August 1922 the Greek front in Asia Minor had collapsed, and the Turkish nationalists led by Mustafa Kemal had clearly taken the initiative. On September 1, 1922, news arrived in Smyrna that the Greek forces had abandoned Ushak, a site one hundred forty miles east of Smyrna. As the news found its way to the troops stationed in the city, a sense of foreboding developed. Upon hearing the news Yannelli wrote to his family not knowing whether he or the letter would ever reach the village in the future. He wrote,

> Dear Mother,
> Things are not going well here. Our forces have fought with courage and distinction, but we have suffered some serious defeats. We have just gotten word that our position at Ushak has been lost. This is not good news. Ushak is a commercial and strategic center. Until now, it was considered impossible for us to lose. We hear that the British consulate is telling its citizens to leave and return to England. My sense is that all of us, if we survive, will be coming home soon.
> Your son, with love,
> Yannelli

In the first weeks of September Greek wounded soldiers began arriving in Smyrna. They came in tightly packed train loads, so overcrowded that some men were sitting on the roofs of the cabs. Soon other soldiers, not wounded but who had retreated back to Smyrna from the interior, began streaming into the city. They came in trucks, on camels, horses, and mules. Many thousands were coming by foot, some men holding up comrades who had been wounded. Soon civilian refugees from the interior areas also began flooding the city. They walked with their children, draft animals, and whatever household goods they could carry. Some went to the homes of relatives; others were taken in by strangers. The streets and roads became almost impassable as the crowds became larger each day. Yannelli and his unit were assigned to help with the temporary location of those rushing into the city in an increasingly chaotic situation. Yannelli helped direct people to places where they could stay until something more permanent could be decided by the higher authorities. He directed women, children, and old people to churchyards, cemeteries, and schools, anywhere the refugees could make temporary makeshift homes. Everything Yannelli had feared and repeatedly talked to Phillipos and others about was coming to pass. The Greek four-hundred-mile front had been too long. The Turkish offensive had required a rapid deployment of Greek forces from one area to another, which could not be done because of the distance between various points on the front. Because of this extremely long front, there were too few troops in reserve, and communication between various points was ineffective. And finally, the shortage of materials, such as ammunition, and the time required to get supplies from one point to another had affected the morale of the troops. And now, thought Yannelli, catastrophe was imminent.

The onset of this catastrophe came on September 8, 1922, when the Greek command received the order that the Greek retreat should continue and that the defense of Smyrna should be abandoned. As the word spread that the Greek forces would not defend the city, the Christian population also began to move in more toward the coast, hoping somehow and in some way to be able to find refuge on some boat and be moved to safety. By September 9 it was clear to all that the Turks would soon be entering the city. Within hours they did come, at first some four hundred cavalry riding into the city with their swords drawn. On that same day looting became widespread, and the killings increased. The Turkish commander rounded up Greeks and Armenians who had been leaders during the Greek occupation, court-martialed them, and quickly carried out their sentences as they were executed by gunfire. Chaos now took hold of the entire city. The Greek Orthodox Archbishop Chysostomos had been working tirelessly to help refugees find safety in the Cathedral Church and had been trying, with little success, to persuade foreign representatives of European powers to provide protection to the Christian population. On the evening of September 9 Turkish soldiers took the Greek cleric to the home of the Turkish commander, Nureddin Pasha. When the Orthodox Christian leader left the building, Nureddin walked on the balcony of the home and told the assembled crowd to do whatever they saw fit to do with Chysostomos. The crowd seized the Archbishop, took off his religious attire, and dressed him in the outfit of a local barber. Then the crowd used their knives to stab and mutilate him. As the Archbishop fell to the ground, bleeding and battered, one man whom Chrysostomos had once helped, put an end to the religious leader's suffering with four shots to his body.

Through the next week the collapse of the Greek presence continued. Yannelli continued to help refugees and worked to try to stop looting and atrocities, but it was clear to him that for the

Greeks all would soon come to an end. On Wednesday September 13 a fire broke out in the Armenian quarter. Witnesses had seen Turks moving from home to home with cans of gasoline prior to the start of the fire, which now began to spread far beyond its point of origin. As the fire spread, so too did the panic of those in the city, and thousands began moving to what they perceived was safety at the waterfront. Now Yannelli and the others were ordered to the seashore to attempt to control the crowds rushing there to find safety. The fire continued to spread. Warehouses, business establishments, and homes were consumed, block after block, by the raging flames. There were frequent loud noises as buildings crashed into the ground and ammunition storage areas exploded. The smells of burning buildings, smoke, and oil filled the air that was constantly also filled with sparks of fire from the massive burning that was taking place. When the fire finally died, the European, Greek, and Armenian sections were totally destroyed, and only the Jewish and Turkish sections of the city remained, scarcely touched by flames. On September 14, 1922, the order was received by all Greek troops. Evacuate immediately.

"It's over," Yannelli said to Phillipos, "it's all over." As he embarked on the ship that was to take them all back to Greece and an uncertain future, Yannelli stared at the city they were abandoning. It was not only the city they had lost, he thought, it was much more. The Great Idea, the dream that Greece would encompass Greek settlements in Asia Minor and recapture Constantinople was also lost. And a sense of personally being lost with an uncertain future took hold of Yannelli as well.

Michael and Jenny, 1980

As Mr. Alfearis finished telling Michael and Jenny the story of Yannelli's time in the army, he had a faraway pensive look on his face. "That was all so very long ago," he said. "We were young men then, and now I am an old man, and my friend Yannelli is gone."

"But it sounds like my father and you had an incredible time," Michael interrupted. "It was a combination of excitement, danger, triumph, defeat, and, finally, great tragedy."

"It was all that," responded Phillipos. "But I think your father really liked the whole experience more than I did. He just liked the whole discipline of it all, and, although he never really told me this, there was something about the danger and excitement of combat that I always believed got his juices going. Now don't misunderstand me, I'm not saying he enjoyed shooting at people and killing some, even if they were Turks and Bulgarians, but he did believe in the Greek cause and at times I really thought he was fearless in battle situations."

Michael was eager to find out more about what Phillipos had told them about the night at the *rembetiko* club, the Café Aman. "Mr. Alfearis, that night you told us about—the night you all went to the Club Aman—was that the only time you and my father went to places like that?"

"No, no," Phillipos said, "all of us went to a number of places like that many times. Your father liked the music and the singing, and he loved to watch the men, most of them high on hashish, do their personal interpretation dances. The only reason I told you about the Club Aman was because it was the one time Yannelli really acted in a way that surprised us all, although I have to admit, we did put a lot of pressure on him to try the hashish. It was the one and only time I ever saw him use the *naghile* and take in the hashish. I think that one time taught him a lesson, and he decided it wasn't for him."

"But what about the girl you told us about? Did he finally tell you what happened that night?" asked Michael.

"No, he never did, and we had an almost unwritten agreement that when it came to women, we just wouldn't pry into each other's business. All I can tell you was that your father was a handsome figure in his army uniform, and there were many young girls who wanted to meet him. Other than that, Michael, I think enough has been said."

It was clear to Michael that he would be receiving no further information from Phillipos about his father's relationships with women. He sensed that there was more to tell, but he also respected the bond of secrecy, friendship, and silence that Phillipos and his father had forged so many years before. He then changed the subject, wanting to know how they felt as they left Smyrna and what they talked about on the ship that was bringing them back to Greece. "That must have been one of the saddest and most depressing journeys home you all ever took," offered Michael. "What was it like?"

"It was very depressing," said Phillipos. "None of us could erase from our minds the scenes we had just left behind—the burning city, the thousands of refugees clamoring for positions on boats that would allow them to escape and the realization that we, the Greek army, were leaving in humiliation and defeat. Your father thought we should have stayed there and fought the Turks to the end, but he was the first to respect orders and commands so, of course, he left with the rest of us. On the short voyage home, we all did very little talking. For many of us, including your father and me, our enlistment time was over, and we needed to think about what we would do now with ourselves."

"What did you want to do?" asked Jenny.

"It was never a big problem for me. I was content to return here to the village, find a wife, have children, and make a living raising sheep and selling olives, the same way my father, grandfather, and generations before had done. I don't regret my decision. I have had a good life. I will die a contented man."

"And what did my father have in mind for himself? Did he tell you anything about what he wanted to do?" Michael asked,

"Yannelli told me when we were sailing home that his commanding officer had told him that he should consider going to officer's training school, and if he did apply, the officer would call some people to recommend him. He seemed very excited about the possibility. When I suggested to him that it would be a hard life, being sent from place to place, he said that he thought he would enjoy such an experience. And when I told him that the chances of being killed in some future conflict would increase the longer a person stayed in the army, he merely smiled, shrugged his shoulders, and pulled from his pocket a small square item and a small crocheted cross his mother had given him when he had first left for the army. The small square object, his mother had said, contained a splinter from the cross upon which Jesus had been crucified. 'These have watched over me so far,' he told me, 'and they will keep me safe in the future.' Your father then smiled again and put the items back in his pocket."

Michael smiled too, remembering that he had found both items when he and George had looked through their father's belongings after he had died.

Phillipos went on to explain that when they both returned to their village, he quickly adjusted to the daily routines of village life, but Yannelli had a more difficult time. "Your father," Phillipos started, "found conditions at home very different from what he had expected. Suddenly he was forced to rethink everything he had planned and take a course he had never seriously thought about. Let me tell you what I know and what I can remember..."

Agios Andreas, 1922

FROM THE JOURNAL, 1922

I AM BACK IN OUR VILLAGE NOW. IT SEEMS STRANGE, I HAVE
BEEN AWAY SO LONG. THINGS ARE NOT THE WAY I EXPECTED
THEM TO BE. THE HOPES AND PLANS I HAD NOW SEEM IMPOSSIBLE
TO BE REALIZED. I AM TORN IN SO MANY DIRECTIONS—WITH MY
FAMILY, WITH ALEXANDRA, AND WITH MY RESPONSIBILITIES.

When Yannelli's enlistment was over he spent a few days in Athens and then left to return to his home and family in Agios Andreas. Getting off the new bus that now made the route through the Peloponnesus, he experienced a strange, unsettling feeling. As he walked through the village, it seemed as though nothing had changed, and yet, in his mind, everything had changed. He had been away for a number of years, leaving the village while still really a boy but now returning a grown man. He had traveled from this location and these people to places far away and had met and fought alongside Englishmen, Frenchmen, Serbs, and Italians. He had seen urban centers like Salonika and Smyrna peopled by individuals of various nationalities, speaking a variety of languages, and praying to God not only as

Greek Orthodox Christians but also as Roman Catholics, Anglicans, Jews, and Muslims. He had been witness to glorious moments of victory as well as the depths of humiliation and defeat. He had fought bravely in combat, and he knew that in those battles he had taken the lives of other men. Yes, they were the enemy, Bulgarians and Turks, but he continued to dwell on the fact that they were still men who had mothers, fathers, sisters, brothers, wives, and probably their own children as well. These events had made him think deeply about life itself, and the thoughts were never far from his mind. The experiences had matured him faster than any passing of years could have done. And yet he also knew that there was something about army life, the bond with other men, the constant exposure to new places, the order, discipline, the sense of pride in serving his country that he would now miss. And, when he was completely honest with himself, he acknowledged that he would even miss the thrill of combat, the strategy, the excitement, the rush of adrenaline that he experienced in each encounter. This is why, when his commander told him that he would recommend him for officers' training school to pursue a career in the army, Yannelli was thrilled and returned to Agios Andreas prepared to rest, catch up on family issues, and then announce his plans for the future.

Yannelli's two youngest sisters were growing; Maria was now twelve, and Erini was ten. Yannelli's mother, Despina, was in good health but was struggling to survive economically. Yannelli could not help but see the worry and sadness in his mother's eyes.

"Mama," he said as he sat with her at the old wooden table in the house, "you seem sad, you're not happy. Tell me how you are doing. What's on your mind?"

Despina looked at her son, reached out to hold his hand, and did her best to hold back any evidence of tears in her eyes. "It's been hard Yannelli, it's been hard. Since your father died, I have been trying to do everything for our family alone. Thank God for what you did while you were away. The money you sent allowed us to survive, but it's been very hard."

"Haven't the others helped Mama?" Yannelli asked. "What about Manoli, Christos, and even Mihali in America? Hasn't anyone helped?"

Yannelli's tone of voice was rising in exasperation. What about his brothers, he thought. Why haven't they done something?

Despina hesitated again. She was reluctant to complain about any of her children. She loved all of them, but they were all different and none of them were like Yannelli. "Christos," she said, "seems to have trouble working steadily at anything. He starts, then stops. He stays to himself and says virtually nothing to any of us. He seems depressed, seldom laughs or even smiles. I worry about him."

Yannelli rubbed his forehead and took a deep breath that signaled a sense of frustration. "And what about Manoli or Mihali?" he asked.

"As you know Manoli married too young, I think, but he hoped that the dowry he received would help him start a family and give some relief to us as well. The dowry really wasn't very much, and I think he may have gotten even less than was promised by his wife's family. I'm really not sure, but Manoli is in no position to help. We seldom hear from Mihali. He hasn't been home in years and is married to some woman in Chicago. He seems to have forgotten that he is the oldest child and that he has a family in Greece, I really don't know. There are some things I just don't understand, Yannelli."

"Mama, you know I'll do what I can, but I have an opportunity to do something I really want and I want to tell you about it." Yannelli told his mother about the possibility of going to officers' training school and that he hoped he could have a career in the army. Despina listened, focusing on every word her son was relating.

"Yannelli," she said, " that would be a great opportunity for you, but I ask you to think carefully before you do anything. We have little, my son. We are poor people. Your father is gone, your brothers, for all the reasons we have discussed, are of little help. Your sister is married and faring not much better in her own life. Maria and Erini are still at home and in eight or ten tears they should marry, but who will marry them? What kind of life can they live in this village with no husband? Yannelli, Yannelli, you are our only hope, my son. Only you can help us and help your sisters." Despina's voice was now pleading, and a sense of desperation was in her words to her son. She never said it directly, but Yannelli knew clearly what her message was. Despina was telling Yannelli that she knew he wanted a military career but was asking him to forgo that dream because his family needed him. He was the only one she could count on. Yannelli slowly rose from the chair, walked over to his mother, gently cradled her head in his hands, and kissed her forehead.

"Don't worry, Mama, don't worry. I will think of something, but don't worry."

"Thank you, Yannelli, thank you. I love you son, I love you."

"I love you, too, Mama," responded Yannelli as he walked out the door into the path that led him to the seashore. He needed to think. Suddenly the road he thought he would travel for his future faced an obstacle. Was it a temporary setback? A detour? Or would he now have to embark on a road he had not forseen and did not want? He needed to think.

The seashore had always had a calming, clearing effect on him. As a child he had gone there to swim, and when he had been troubled about anything, simply sitting on the rocks and looking out at the deep blue water seemed to clear his mind, remove doubts, and allowed him to analyze things rationally and walk back to the village with a plan to resolve any problem. Yannelli sat on the large rock on which, five years before he had scratched out the first letters of his name and that of Alexandra. Alexandra came to his mind immediately. What about Alexandra? He would see her that evening, and they could talk. But what would they talk about? He had left for the army telling her that he loved her, and she had said that she loved him as well. The unspoken assumption was that after the army, perhaps not immediately, but fairly soon, they would marry. But much had happened while he was away. He was more mature, he had seen much, and he had done much. He believed his feelings for Alexandra were no different, but he wasn't sure. And what about her, he wondered? Were her feelings the same, or had she some doubts? After all, she was older, too. Yannelli knew he would have to answer all these questions. And if their feelings had not changed and they decided to marry, what would that mean? Could he still have his dream of a military career? And if they did marry and decide to live the life of villagers, how would that help his mother and sisters when he would have his own responsibilities for his wife, children, and home? Thoughts kept streaming through his mind, as he looked first at one scenario, then another. He was confused and there were no easy or clear answers, but one thing did seem to become clear. The dream of a military career seemed to be slipping away.

In the evening he met Alexandra, and they sat together sipping coffee and eating pastries in the village square. The fact that they were there, sitting in full view of others who were present, was an indication as to how things were changing in the village. There were still rules, restrictions, and taboos to be sure, but the years of war in the Balkans, the World War, and the turmoil of the Venizelos years had created cracks in some of the old ways. Arranged marriages and the existence of the dowry were still the rule and not the exception, but the absolute taboo of a young man simply talking to a young woman had fallen away. It was difficult to maintain such a practice when so many young men, like Yannelli, had gone to war, seen violence, bloodshed, and experienced ideas from English and French fellow soldiers. To treat such men as children who could not be trusted was simply impossible and would not be accepted or tolerated by them.

"I'm glad you're home, Yannelli," Alexandra said softly. "I prayed every night that God would watch over you and protect you from harm. And thank God, He did."

"You look beautiful, Alexandra. Your letters meant so much to me, kept me going, and I virtually ran to our mailman whenever they announced that the latest delivery had come. But I come home to some problems, Alexandra, and we have to talk about them."

Alexandra sat silently, waiting for Yannelli to continue, not knowing what he would say. Her hair was now longer than she had worn it before, and the summer sun had lightened even more her already blond hair. She wore no makeup and wore the standard blouse and skirt that were a virtual uniform among the village women. But she still was beautiful, Yannelli thought, as he paused to think of how to go on with what he needed to say. Village children were running through the town square, and their playful screams sometimes made it difficult to carry on a normal conversation.

"I wish we had some privacy," said Yannelli, "where did all these little ones come from? People must have been active while I was away." He smiled.

"There's not much else to do here, Yannelli. Have you forgotten?"

Yannelli finally went on to tell Alexandra about the problems his mother was having, the lack of money, the lack of support from his brothers, and the worries about his younger sisters. Alexandra could see that Yanneli was uncomfortable, not really addressing any issues that pertained to both of them.

"And what about us, Yannelli? What does all this mean for you and me?"

"I'm not sure," he answered, "I just don't know. I'm confused, and there are so many things I have to sort out."

"What aren't you sure about, Yannelli?" Alexandra leaned forward and with a lower voice asked, "Do you still love me? Do you still want to marry me? Be honest, Yannelli. Please, tell me the truth."

Whatever doubts Yannelli might have had were now quickly gone. He realized the time away had changed nothing. He did love her, and he did want her for his wife, but how could this happen? How could he resolve all these conflicts? "Yes, Alexandra, I love you, I still love you, and I will always love you. Has anything changed with you? Am I the one you still want to marry?"

"Of course, Yannelli, I love you deeply. You don't know how much I have missed you, you just don't know."

The two young people continued their conversation for another hour. Soon the crowd that had gathered at the village center began to thin. The children left with their parents for their homes. Only a few old men, widowers, remained, not wanting to leave their conversation companions and return to the silence and loneliness of their empty homes. Alexandra and Yannelli also left, and they walked the short distance to Alexandra's family home. There was no one around and the village streets were empty. Yannelli boldly took Alexandra in his arms, kissed her, and simply and reassuringly said, "Don't worry. We'll work it all out. I love you, and we will be together."

In the days that followed Yannelli spent time catching up with his siblings and getting to know his youngest sisters who had grown so much during the time he had been gone. His visited Manoli and his young wife and was glad to see that despite what had happened in the past, Manoli seemed to be functioning well. He was living the life of a typical villager, trying to make a living with olive trees and sheep. It was clear to Yannelli that Manoli would most likely live and die in the village, content to live a life similar to what generations of their family had lived before them. Maybe that was all right, Yannelli thought. Maybe he should do the same. But upon deeper reflection he really knew he could not live such a life. He needed and wanted something more. Christos was another story. Yannelli worried about him, and he knew that something was wrong with this brother. When Yannelli spoke to him, he seldom engaged in real conversation. He would be in his house for days at a time, never venturing out and often not completing the work he was required to do. Yannelli wondered, had something happened to his brain after the episode with the girl from Argos? Had something snapped in him? Yannelli had no answers, but it was clear to him that his mother had been right: Christos could not be counted on to help her in any way. His sister Stamatina was doing well, and he was happy to see that she had seemingly survived her ordeal with her first husband, Yorgos. Her son. Tassos, was growing into a handsome young man, and when Yannelli visited his home, the boy ran to him and hugged him with a strong, tight embrace. "I want to be like you, Yannelli," the boy said, "and I want to be a soldier like you. Tell me about the army. Tell me about the war. Did you really kill any Turks? How many?"

Yannelli patiently sat with the boy and told him select things about his army experiences, which the boy absorbed with his eyes wide open and his attention focused on Yannelli's description of the battles against the Bulgarians and the Turks.

"Someday I'll be in the army, too," the boy confidently announced, " and I'll be just like you."

"I know you will, Tassos, and I'm sure you will be a good, brave soldier." Yannelli kissed his young nephew and left Stamatina's house happy that she, her sons, and her new husband had found some peace and happiness. He had not heard from his brother Mihali for a while, from the time he left Smyrna, and he now thought about Mihali's words about coming to America. That evening he sat down to write to Mihali, telling him about the situation in the family and the dilemmas with which he was confronted now that he had returned home,

> *Dear Mihali,*
>
> *I am out of the army now and back in our village. Overall, things are well except that our mother is having financial troubles and is concerned that unless we can secure an adequate dowry for our young sisters over the next few years they will never marry. Alexandra and I want to marry, but this does not seem like the right time now with so many problems to be settled. I have been recommended for officer training school and I want very much to go, but that seems unlikely now. In your last letter you spoke about me coming to America. You must tell me more. What would I do there? How could I help our family here if I came? Could I bring Alexandra with me as my wife?...*

Yannelli's letter went on for pages with question after question about America. He had never thought about that option, but he had not anticipated the situation he now faced at home. Within weeks Mihali responded to Yannelli's letter. America was different, he wrote. There were, he said, tremendous opportunities available, since the economy was very good and America had emerged from the war as a major military and economic power. Mihali continued,

> *The future is here, Yannelli. It is not in the village picking olives and herding sheep. Forget this idea of a military career. Join me in starting a new business and we can both prosper. I would not bring Alexandra here for at least the first year or two, until you make the transition to a new country and a new life. After that,*

you can send for her, marry, and raise your family here. The worst
that can happen is that you come here and decide America is not
for you and then you can go back home. Thousands of Greeks have
done just that, but I believe you are making a big mistake if you
don't at least take a chance.

"Take a chance." Yannelli read Mihali's words and thought about
them over and over. Maybe his brother was right. No one said he
would have to stay in America forever. Maybe he could go, make
some money, return to Greece and marry Alexandra, and also care
for his mother and his sisters. Maybe that was the best answer.
Clearly there was nothing in his village, or in all of Greece for that
matter, that could solve his problems. Yannelli was slowly coming
to terms with the fact that he would not have the military career
he so passionately wanted, but he was young and maybe there were
opportunities in America he knew nothing about. Others who had
left Greece were constantly sending money back to their villages,
providing dowries for their sisters and daughters, and even sending
enough money to build schools, hospitals, and new churches. Sure-
ly, he thought, there really must be many opportunities in America.
As he continued to ponder his options, the thought of going to
America was one Yannelli could not dismiss from his mind.

As he sat at the kitchen table, his two young sisters, Maria and
Erini, joined him. "When are you going to marry Alexandra?" Maria asked, smiling as she posed the question.

"I don't know," answered Yannelli, "but when we do marry, you
will be the first to know. Maybe you both can be bridesmaids or
flower girls."

"We would like that," said Erini.

Yannelli loved his young sisters. They were both developing into attractive young girls. Both were very smart and were doing well in school. But as he spoke with them, he knew that in his village their looks and intelligence alone would not guarantee that they would someday marry and have a good life. A dowry would be required for each girl, and Yannelli knew that the burden of providing the dowry was now his, and his alone, to bear. "And girls," he told his sisters with as serious a tone as he could, "don't worry, when the time comes I will make sure you will have a choice of many young men to marry, unless you decide to become nuns—that will save us a lot of money."

"Nuns!" screamed the girls, "we're not going to become nuns! Yannelli, please, we don't want to be nuns!"

Yannelli kissed the girls and assured them that he was joking and that he would be there for them when the proper time came. Or would he be in America? The thought would not leave him. He knew that he would have to make some decision soon. For the following weeks he helped his mother in any way that he could, he met with his old friend Phillipos, and continued talking about the future with Alexandra. He reviewed his options over and over and finally his head seemed to clear, and he made his decision. He would go to America, but only for a while to earn some necessary money for the family. Unable to sleep, he sat at the table and wrote to his brother,

Dear Mihali,
I have decided to come to America. I want to come and find work which will allow me to earn enough money to help our mother

and then I will return home to marry Alexandra. I have thought about this decision for a very long time and I believe it is the right one. I will admit to you that I am nervous. I love Greece and really don't want to leave. The uncertainty of what I will do in America and how and where I will live concerns me.

I know nothing about the country and I cannot speak or read the language. When I come, Mihali, I am counting on you to help me find work. I have been through war and seen much death destruction, but I must admit this move to America scares me more than anything I have experienced. I plan to leave as soon as I can take care of the necessary immigration papers. Please let me know how I will get to Chicago and where I will live and what work I will have.

Your brother,

Yannelli

Within weeks Mihali responded to Yannelli's letter. He said that Yannelli had made the right decision and that his concerns were normal ones and he should not worry. He told his younger brother that he could live, at least temporarily, with him and his wife and that it would be easy for him to find work in Chicago. The economy was good and in America, he said, they were calling the 1920s a time when everyone would do well and many would get rich. He gave Yannelli the name of a Greek individual to contact in New York after he landed at Ellis Island and said that person would provide a train ticket for him to come to Chicago. "I'm very happy you are coming, Yannelli," Mihali wrote, "it will be good to see you and have you close by. We can do great things together, so don't worry.

I have never let you down in the past, have I? And I won't this time either."

Yannelli worked in the weeks ahead to deal with the Greek bureaucracy that handled immigration issues, papers, and documents. Like so many things in Greece, it was who you knew that could expedite things. Fortunately, one of Yannelli's former army colleagues worked in the government department that dealt with immigration issues, so his arrangements went smoothly. Finally the paperwork was completed, the ship on which he would sail was determined, and the date was set. He would leave in exactly one month, November 18, 1922. Two things remained to be done. He wanted to see all of his family together before he left, and he needed to see Alexandra alone.

Yannelli's mother invited all of her sons and daughters and their children to her home for dinner to wish her son good luck and to say, what they all hoped would be a temporary goodbye. It was a good and joyful evening. The entire family had not gathered together in one place for a very long time. As Yannelli sat at the table and enjoyed his mother's meal of lamb, potatoes, bread, cheese, olives, and salad, he could not help but think of the events that had transpired in the years that had passed. Katerina and his father were gone, and his thoughts raced to the events that had surrounded their lives. Mihali had left home so long ago but had returned to deal, in ways that Yannelli had tried to erase from his mind, with problems Stamatina and Manoli had encountered. At the table he looked at Manoli, who seemed well, but who really knew what thoughts or demons he might privately face. Stamatina seemed better, but he wondered if she really knew what had actually happened to her husband, Yorgos. He suspected she did, but the topic had never been raised by her or by anyone else. Certainly, Yannelli thought, some in the family, like him, must have connected the events of that terrible night and Mihali's abrupt leaving of the country. But whatever anyone might have thought, no one had ever asked questions or spoke of those events. Many things, thought Yannelli as he sat with his family, went unspoken, and he went back and forth in his thinking as to whether that silence was a good or bad thing. This evening, however, seemed like some of the old happier times of his childhood when they all were happy and laughed, and he cherished the companionship of all his brothers and sisters.

"We will miss you, Yannelli," said his brother Manoli , "and we will anxiously await your coming home again."

"Good luck in America, Yannelli," said his young sister Erini, "please write home and tell us what it is like there."

"God bless you and keep you safe, my son," his mother said, "We all love you."

When the evening dinner was over, everyone returned to their homes. Yannelli and his mother walked outside the house and sat on the old benches his father had often used on hot summer nights when he would seek the comfort of cooler air and rest from a day of work. "Yannelli," his mother said, "I know you are doing this for me and for your sisters." She reached out for her son's hand and held it gently. "I love you very much, and I will miss you." Despina's voice began to crack and tears filled her eyes. "Please come back, Yannelli, please don't leave our lives and your family like your brother Mihali did, please!"

"Mama," Yannelli said softly, "don't worry. I'll be back. I want to come back. This is only a temporary thing. I'll make some money, help you, and send money home for the girls' dowries and then I'll be back."

Despina sat silently listening to her son's efforts to ease the pain of separation. She believed her son but in her mind wondered if he really would come back. Would she ever see him again? America was so very far away. Would he change? Would this be another child she would lose? The tears in her eyes now came streaming down over her face, and Yannelli took her in his arms. "Don't worry, Mama, I promise you, I will be back as soon as I can." He took his mother's hand and together they slowly and silently walked back into the house.

With his immigration documents now in order, Yannelli prepared to leave his home and go to Athens and then to the port at Piraeus to leave for America within a matter of days. He was nervous, and he had one more goodbye to say—to Alexandra. Once again Yannelli wanted to be with her by the seashore, away from the prying eyes and ears of the villagers who were always eager to know everyone's business, particularly that of two unmarried people. The night was cool, and Yannelli wore one of the army jackets he had been issued and was allowed to keep. Alexandra wore a dark blue sweater that she had knitted herself, and her long blond hair was pushed back with a head band to keep her hair in place as the wind came off the water. A week before Yannelli had told her of his decision, but she had said little, telling him that he must do what he believed he must do. But tonight was different. Yannelli would be leaving in the morning to board a ship that would take him thousands of miles away. He had, of course, gone away before to Salonika and to Smyrna, but this was not the same. This time it was America.

"Alexandra," Yannelli said as he reached to take her hand, "you know why I am leaving. It's the only chance my mother can survive, the only chance my sisters will have a future. I love you, and I want to marry you. After one year I will either come back, or I will send for you to come to America. This is what I want, and I hope you do too."

Alexandra listened, showing little emotion. Finally she said, "Yannelli, I have waited for you since we were very young. I prayed and waited for you for all those years you were away. I love you, too, and I want to be with you, but…." Alexandra stopped, wiped a tear from her eye, "but I want you to come home. I don't want to go to America, Yannelli. I want you to come home! We are Greeks, this is our country, our place, not America." The tears were now flowing from her eyes. "Please. Please, Yannelli. Come home to me, and let us start our life together."

Yannelli pulled her close, wrapped his arms around her shoulders, and cradled her head against his chest. He said nothing, not sure of what he should say as Alexandra continued to cry. He lifted her head, wiped the tears from her face, and gently kissed her and kissed her again and again. "Alexandra," he finally said, "I want you, and I want what you want. Let me go and see what happens. Hopefully, I can earn enough in one year to come home. I love you, Alexandra, I want you to be my wife. I promise you, we will be together."

Yannelli and Alexandra walked back the short distance to the village center and then walked her to her house. It was not yet dark, and individuals were still walking in the village streets, but Yannelli did not care or worry about what the village gossips would say. He took Alexandra in his arms, held her close, and kissed her. "That was not for goodbye," he said, "it was for both of us to remember—for just one year." Alexandra was now crying uncontrollably.

The next morning Yannelli had his one suitcase packed. He had slept little the night before. He could not stop thinking about Alexandra, his mother, his brothers and sisters, his village, his country. On this day he would begin a journey he had not wanted. He wondered if he would come back again? He wanted to. He thought he would, but what if he did not return? How could anyone who had not experienced what he was about to do really understand what it means to leave everyone and everything you have ever known to go to a distant place where you know nothing and nobody? He was nervous. No, he was, for one of the few times in his life, truly scared. The bus to Athens was to leave at 9:00 a.m., and as he sat at the table with his mother sipping coffee and eating bread and cheese, mother and son said little. It was as if everything that needed to be said had been said. He had heard his mother crying the previous night, and he could see the pain and sadness in her eyes this morning. Finally, it was time. Yannelli went to his mother; now both mother and son were in tears.

"Don't worry, Mama, please don't worry. I will write to you, and in one year I will be back. And don't worry about the money. I will send it to you. I love you, Mama."

Despina could barely speak, the tears seemed unstoppable as the son she had held in her arms now tried to comfort her in his embrace.

"God bless you, my son. May God watch over you and bring you home. I love you, Yannelli. Remember always, your mother loves you." Yannelli held his mother a moment longer, kissed her on the forehead, and walked through the door to the bus. As the bus pulled away, he looked through the window at his home, not sure if he would ever see it again.

The next morning Yannelli, along with hundreds of others, boarded the ship, the *Byron/Vasilefs Constantinos*, at the port of Piraeus. He had one small suitcase and the equivalent of thirty-eight American dollars in his pocket. Within the hour the ship was to leave the port for New York, for America. And Yannelli would leave behind everything he had known and what his life had been about. It was a destination to a new land. And a new beginning.

Michael and Jenny, 1980

That must have been one of the most difficult decisions of his life," Michael said. "It's hard for me to imagine making that kind of move, leaving everyone and everything you have known all your life, for some strange place where you know virtually no one."

"It was difficult," said Phillipos, "and I know I couldn't have done it, but Yannelli felt strongly that he had to do it for his family. They really were struggling. They were poor, there's no other way to say it."

"But didn't he find it hard to leave Alexandra? After all, she had waited so long for my father while he was away in the army."

Phillipos nodded his head. "Leaving Alexandra was probably the most difficult thing Yannelli had to do, even more difficult than leaving his family. But Alexandra did not want to go and believed Yannelli would be returning fairly soon. I think your father thought the same thing or believed that Alexandra would change her mind and eventually follow him to America."

"But I'm still not clear about what happened between Alexandra and my father. He did not go back, and she never came to America and eventually married someone else."

"A lot of things happened when your father went to Chicago, none of which he could have foreseen. Months, and then years, went by, and

I guess they went their separate ways. He only gave me a sketch of what happened in his letters to me."

Michael had always wondered what his father's life had been like in America when he finally got to Chicago. He asked Phillipos, "Mr. Alfearis, you just mentioned letters from my father. Did you regularly keep in touch with him? Did he talk about what he was doing? How he was feeling? Did he talk about coming back to Greece? Had he met someone new that he cared about before he met my mother, and is that why things with Alexandra didn't work out?"

"Your father and I did write to one another for many years after he went to America. I did find it somewhat strange that he never once talked about coming back to Greece, but I guess everything changed when Alexandra told him that she was to be married. All I know is what he told me in the letters he wrote, but our correspondence pretty much stopped after he met and married you mother. But I can tell you the little that I do know..."

America, 1923–1941

T he voyage from Greece to New York was long and tiresome. The sleeping quarters were small and uncomfortable, and Yannelli never had a full night's sleep during the entire time. There were so many fellow Greeks on the ship that Yannelli wondered what would happen to his country if this rate of emigration continued. They were all going to different destinations in the United States—some to Michigan, Ohio, New York, California and some, like him, to Chicago. The arrival at Ellis Island in New York was an experience he would never forget. Thousands of people from various ports in Europe crowded in long lines into the immigration processing center in New York Harbor. There were old people, families with children, and young, single individuals like Yannelli. The faces and the polyglot of languages created a virtual picture and map of Europe, although the majority seemed to be Italians, Poles, Russians, Serbs, and Greeks. In what seemed to be endless lines, individual's papers were checked for authenticity, and each person was given a physical examination. Yannelli passed the document and physical checks, but many did not and were sent to a separate area, there to be processed for deportation back to their home country, their dreams of a new future in America shattered.

Arriving in New York City, Yannelli immediately attempted to contact the person his brother Mihali had told him would assist in arranging the train trip to Chicago. But even this small, basic task was difficult. Yannelli could not read, speak, or understand English. He recalled a few words he had learned from the British troops he had encountered in Salonika, but these were hardly enough to allow him to function in a city as large as New York. Every sign he saw, every word his ears heard meant nothing to him. Somehow, he managed to reach his New York contact who provided lodging and food for the night and then took him to the train station where he spent a portion of the thirty-eight dollars he carried for the ticket to Chicago. On the train Yannelli thought about what direction his life was about to take. He wondered how he would function in this new and strange environment and whether the decision to come to America was really the right decision. The uncertainty of everything troubled him. What would or could he do here? Where would he live? How could he work and earn money to send home when he had little education; had no trade; and could not speak, write, or understand the language? He was sure about one thing, however; he was now twenty-five years old, starting a new life in a new land. His name, Yannelli, was fine for his youth in Greece and for those who knew him in his family and in his village, but all that was now behind him. In America, he would, he decided, not be known as Yannelli but rather as Yianni, or John, as the Americans would say.

The meeting with his brother Mihali was both emotional and somewhat strange. It had been some years since they had seen one another. Mihali, now married to his second wife after divorcing the nurse who had cared for him after his motorcycle accident, seemed very American. He could read, write, and speak English well, and his new wife, Mabel, was of Swedish ancestry. They did not socialize in the world of the Greek Orthodox Church and the Greek immigrant community. His brother was working for a company, the Chicago Pie Company, that delivered pies to Chicago restaurants, and he told Yannelli that he could, within a short time, find him a job there once he learned how to drive one of the delivery trucks and secured his driver's license.

The physical appearance of the brothers was also changing. Mihali now had a neatly trimmed mustache, wore glasses, and had hair that was thinning even more than it had been when the two brothers had last met. Yannelli, too, was experiencing a premature loss of his already fine, light-brown hair. The brothers were almost the same height, but Yannelli always seemed taller because of the longer legs that characterized his body structure as well as because of the military bearing that he never seemed to have lost from his army days. After Yannelli informed his brother that he thought it was now the time and place for people to stop calling him by his childhood name—that he was now "Yianni" to other Greeks and "John" to Americans, Mihali told his younger brother that in the presence of the many non-Greeks with whom he associated, including his wife, he wanted to be addressed not as "Mihali" but rather as "Mike." The discussion of their names, as trivial as it was, had an impact on Yannelli. From Mihali and Yannelli to Mike and John. The thought gave him a strange feeling; it seemed as if part of their identities had been altered, and this was part of a price they had to pay to be accepted in America.

For about six months Yannelli lived with his brother and sister-in-law and worked in a restaurant as a kitchen helper and dishwasher. He attempted to formally learn English by enrolling in a night class but quickly abandoned the idea as he sat next to immigrants from around the world and saw the teacher struggle to communicate to a class in which ten or twelve different languages were spoken. He decided he would learn on his own. After six months he had earned enough money to rent a small apartment and live by himself. He had been grateful for his brother's help but never felt comfortable living in his house. By the end of the year he had learned how to drive, he had secured his license, and Mihali was able to get him a job as a truck driver for the Chicago Pie Company. It was a good job, paid well, and allowed Yannelli to move throughout the city and meet new people. He now began to earn enough to send some portion of his pay back to Greece, which he sent to his brothers so that they could help their mother and begin saving for the two younger daughters' dowries. Besides his brother, Yannelli made a few friends, fellow Greek immigrants like himself, but the nights and weekends were lonely. He would often go to the shore of Lake Michigan and sit alone for hours at a time, simply starring out at the water. His thoughts were always about another body of water, the sea that touched the shore of his home in Greece, and about his mother, brothers, sisters, friends, and always Alexandra. The first year in America went by quickly, and it soon became clear that the promise he had made to come back to Greece in a year could not and would not be kept. He could not afford either the time from his job or the money to make the trip, and he had not earned enough money to take care of all his family's financial needs. He wrote to Alexandra, explained the situation, and was troubled by her return letter. To Yannelli, the letter's tone seemed distant and remote. She wrote that she was disappointed that he had not returned, and she was beginning to think that the situation would remain the same even next year and perhaps the year after. She spoke of the fact that she was getting older and that her parents were concerned about her future. Over the next months she wrote less frequently, and Yannelli knew that something was changing. As the second year of his arrival in America quickly passed, he received Alexandra's final letter:

Dear Yannelli,

I am writing to you because I told you that I would always be honest with you. Over the past two years it has become clear to me that it is unlikely you will ever return home. I'm afraid the time for me to wait has ended. My parents have agreed to allow me to marry a man who has been coming to Agios Andreas to visit his cousin but lives on the island of Hydra. I hope that you will find what you seek in America and that you can find happiness as well. You know that, in some way, I will always love you.

With love,

Alexandra

Yannelli was saddened by the news, but in many ways it was something he had expected. Two years in America had changed him as well. Increasingly, as he learned the language, made a decent salary, and became familiar with American life, he liked his new home. This really was a different and unique country, he thought. It would be a good place to marry, start a family, and educate one's children to take advantage of the opportunities the country offered. These opportunities for him in America were limited—he only barely knew the language, and his years of formal schooling were very few. But for the children he might someday have, the opportunities were limitless. And besides, he thought, Alexandra had made it clear, over and over, that she would not leave Greece and come to America. Once again, Yannelli thought, he would have to start again, this time in the personal side of his life.

Finding the woman he would want as his wife was not easy. In the years that followed many of the restaurant owners he met through his pie delivery route had wanted him to meet their daughters and other available relatives, but none of these women had interested him. This was still not an era of "dating," at least not in the Greek-American community. Introductions and courtship were certainly more free than in Greece, but one did not just date for the sake of dating. The ongoing relationship with a woman meant something more serious, most likely probable marriage, and thus far Yannelli had not met anyone who, in his mind, would fit into that category. He, unlike his brother Mihali, wanted to marry a woman from a Greek family who would understand his background, language, culture, and religion.

Yannelli did not lead a monastic life however. There were woman in his life in the years after Alexandra—just not Greek or Greek-American women. He met women, mostly Polish, German, or Irish women, and had brief relationships with them. However, these were temporary, fleeting connections that gave him some semblance of a social life and responded to his needs but that he always knew would never be permanent.

Like many Greeks in Chicago a major avenue for socializing with other people of Greek ancestry were the picnics sponsored by the various organizations whose members were immigrants from a particular region of Greece. Thus, in Yannelli's case, the Chicago organization was the Pan-Arcadian Society, an organization whose membership include Greeks in Chicago who were born, or whose parents were born, in the Arcadia region of Greece. These picnics were not casual outings in some park or forest preserve but rather functions held in various outdoor locations within Chicago itself. They were almost formal occasions, where women came in their finest dresses and men wore white shirts, ties, and suit jackets. These events were held throughout the summer months, and the formal dress code was never relaxed even on days and evenings of blistering heat. The only concession to the heat at a time when nothing was air-conditioned was that men might temporarily shed their jackets as they participated in the various Greek folk dances to the accompaniment of the Greek band composed of clarinets, violins, a bouzouki, and an occasional guitar or drums. These were important venues for Greeks to socialize and meet old and new friends. They also allowed parents to bring their marriageable-age sons and daughters to meet one another and perhaps start some connection that could lead to marriage.

It was at the Pan-Arcadian picnic in Chicago in the summer of 1930 that Yannelli first saw a young girl who caught his unwavering attention. She was a small woman, probably not much taller than five feet. She had short black hair, so black it was as if she had just stepped out from an underground coal mine. She looked young, probably twenty, or at best, twenty-two. He was clearly interested in the girl and wanted to know about her. Who is she, he asked himself? Is she from Chicago? He wondered who her parents were and where they were from. He began asking questions of individuals who then led him to other individuals until he found someone he knew and could trust. He was told the girl was Panayiota Sikokis, although for some reason she was known as Blanche, a name Yannelli had never heard associated with anyone Greek. Her mother and father, George and Venetta Sikokis, had been among the earliest Greek immigrants to Chicago, her father arriving in the city in 1894, when he was twenty-one. Her mother, an orphan, had arrived in 1902, at age seventeen to live with an aunt. Years later they had married and had two sons and two daughters. The mother and father, Yannelli learned, had come from the villages of Paleohori and Leonidion, two communities in the same general area of Yannelli's village of Agios Andreas in Arcadia. Yannelli also discovered that the daughter was still single and was indeed young, in fact younger than he had guessed. She was only eighteen years old. Eighteen, thought Yannelli, as an immediate sense of disappointment came over him. Eighteen! What would an eighteen-year-old girl want with a thirty-two-year-old man, he thought? He quickly made a mental self-assessment. His hair was thinning even more now, and he would probably lose it all soon; and he was beginning to add some weight to what had been his lean, military years body frame. I'm thirty-two, she's eighteen, he thought to himself. I'm losing my hair and I've gained a few pounds, I'm an immigrant from the old country, and this girl was born in Chicago and went to school here. Would she even know the Greek language? His command of English had certainly improved in the seven years he had been in Chicago, but he still did not feel confident when engaged in conversations that were totally in English. And what about the age difference, he wondered. In Greece a fourteen-year difference would have meant nothing; it was common. In fact, age differences there between a man and woman could be as high as twenty-five or thirty years. But this was America, he reminded himself. At this, Yannelli stopped thinking and speculating; he decided he would forget about this girl—it just wouldn't work, he thought.

The years that followed were ones of an established routine. Yannelli continued to work for the Chicago Pie Company, socialize with fellow Greek-Americans, and keep company for short periods of time with women who were not part of the Greek-American community. Throughout the difficult years of the Great Depression Yannelli hardly felt its impact. His salary was good, he lived alone in a small apartment, he spent little on entertainment or on himself, and even with the constant flow of money he sent to his family, he was doing well financially and living a life better than many Americans who had lost their jobs and their savings. The money sent to Greece was, of course, for his mother and particularly for dowries for his two younger sisters who were still unmarried. Yannelli's mother died in 1932, and he was deeply saddened by the event. He was particularly distressed by the fact that his job prohibited him from making the long voyage home for the funeral. With his mother's death, he continued sending funds home to his brothers, Christos and Manoli, to act as guardians of the dowry money until such time as an engagement or marriage was to take place. But in 1933 he received a letter from his brothers asking for money for the dowries for the two sisters who were about to be engaged. Yannelli was confused. For ten years he had regularly sent money home for that very purpose—to provide dowry money for his sisters, and now his brothers were asking for money for dowries for the girls. What was going on? he asked himself. What about the thousands of dollars he had already sent home? Finally an answer arrived in a letter from his brothers:

Dear Yannelli,

We write to you to humbly ask for your help and forgiveness. In the past you have done so much for us, and we can never forget those things or thank you enough. We know that what we about to tell you will anger you, and, if so, you will be justified in feeling such anger. While our mother was alive, she knew that you had entrusted us with the safekeeping of the funds you had sent for the dowries for Maria and Erini. But we have, we are ashamed to say, violated that trust. Each of our economic needs were so dire, so great, that we used the money to support ourselves and our families. We had every intention of replenishing the dowry funds when things got better for us—but they have not gotten better. We cannot replenish the funds, and our sisters will not marry without the dowries, and we ask, we beg, that you provide the necessary funds so that they can marry. Please, please, forgive us and help our sisters.

Your brothers,
Manoli and Christos

Yannelli held the letter in his hand and read it over and over. He could not believe what he was reading. For more than ten years he had not missed a month when he did not send money home. He lived frugally and deliberately did not seek a wife for himself for all those years so that his sisters could find a husband and lead a decent life. And now his brothers had squandered the money, all of it! He was angry, in fact, very angry. All that money, he thought, all those years, and now—nothing! But as his initial anger subsided, he knew that he could not abandon his obligation to his sisters and his promise to his mother. He went to the bank, withdrew almost all of his savings, and sent the money directly to his two sisters with the explicit instructions that the funds were to be used exclusively for each of their dowries. After explaining to his sisters what he had been doing for them over the past decade, he told them he could do no more. If this money, he said, was used for anything other than the required dowry, he could provide no further assistance. And if they did not use it for the purpose of the dowry, there would obviously be no marriage for either woman. He did not bother to answer the letter from his brothers, and he never wrote to them again.

Yannelli's connection to his homeland was now becoming weaker and weaker. His parents were gone, his brothers had betrayed and deceived him, Alexandra was married, although not totally forgotten, and his sisters, whom he did not know as adult women, were about to be married and lead their own lives. His task now, as he saw it, was to work to replenish his own now diminished finances and seriously begin searching for a wife of his own.

The various delivery routes followed by the drivers at the Chicago Pie Company were periodically changed to accommodate new customers in the expansion of the company. Yiannelli's original route had taken him to the South side of Chicago and into the nearby suburban towns of Berwyn and Cicero. In 1936 he was assigned a new route, this one taking him through the Chicago downtown district and extending west to just past Western Avenue. The customers were essentially the same as before, restaurants that bought pies to serve to their customers. On this new route, one of Yannelli's stops was to a restaurant on Western Avenue just immediately north of Harrison Street located next to an ice cream and candy store. Both stores were owned by immigrants from Greece, and both were examples of how Greek-owned businesses had developed in Chicago. While there were some Greek immigrants who worked in factories in nearby Indiana steel mills, the average Greek immigrant aspired to be his own boss and control his own destiny. Intense individualism and independence in the Greek character found expression in the open opportunity of America, and that aspect of their character very often was realized through Greek entrepreneurship. Given a small chance, the Greek immigrant wanted to work for no one else, and that desire translated into starting one's own business. That entrepreneurial spirit, in Chicago, most often resulted in Greek-owned restaurants, confectionary shops, and small grocery stores. The two stores Yannelli encountered on the corner of Harrison and Western streets were examples of this often-repeated scenario. Delivering his pies to the restaurant, Yannelli would inevitably look into the confectionary store window to see who the individuals were who owned it, knowing that they, like him, were Greek immigrants.

One afternoon after making a stop at the restaurant next door, he looked into the confectionery store and saw a young woman working behind the counter. She seemed somewhat familiar to him, but he could not place exactly why she did so. He decided to walk in, and when he did, things suddenly came together in his mind. That girl, he thought! The girl behind the counter! She was the same girl he had seen at that Pan-Arcadian festival more than six years before. She was obviously older now, but there was no mistake about it—it was the same girl! Yiannelli quickly introduced himself to the young woman and then to her father who had been working in the back making his chocolates. He told them about his job, where he was from in Greece, and proceeded to order coffee and a small cup of vanilla ice cream. And so began a regular routine Yannelli would follow: after delivering his pies to the next door restaurant he would, without fail, go next door, order something, and talk to with the proprietor and his daughter when she was working. The conversations with the owner, George, were enjoyable, and soon Yannelli met the owner's wife, Venetta, as well. But his real reason for the frequent visits was to see and speak with the daughter, Panayiota, the girl known to the neighborhood customers as Blanche. As months passed Yannelli knew that finally he had met someone he believed could be his wife. He spoke to her father, George, and asked permission to pursue his interest and see if Blanche might have similar interests. Although neither Yannelli nor Blanche would consider it dating, with full knowledge of Blanche's parents the couple went to dinners alone, and periodically to the movies. By the winter of 1936 Yannelli and Blanche were engaged. A casual conversation had grown into friendship and love, and they made the decision to spend their lives together.

• • •

In June 1937 at the Annunciation Greek Orthodox Church on La Salle Street in Chicago, they were married. He was thirty-nine years old, she was twenty-four, but the age difference now seemed irrelevant. The newlywed couple honeymooned driving along the shore of Lake Michigan and crossing over into Minnesota. Driving south from Duluth they drove through Wisconsin and approached a small resort community named Baraboo. The town's main tourist attraction was a small, clear body of water called Devil's Lake, which was situated between tall bluffs that had been created generations before during the Earth's Ice Age. Upon seeing the lake, Yannelli's eyes filled with tears. There was something strangely familiar with what he saw. It was not exactly the same, of course, but it immediately conjured up images of his village in Greece. The bluffs were not mountains, the lake was not the sea, but the configuration of water and land looked very much like what he had experienced as a boy on those summer days so long ago when he had gone hunting with his sister Katerina. He began to cry. But these were tears of happiness. He was at a new and good place in his life now. He never let memories of Greece slip far from his mind, but he loved everything about America and had found a woman to love as well as a friend and companion to spend his life with. The many years of lonely days and nights were now over. He wanted a family, and at thirty-nine years old, he could waste little time. He knew his purpose now: it would be to love his wife, provide for her, and have their children. He was in America now, and with every ounce of energy and hard work, he would strive to give those children opportunities he never could have had. In March 1938 Blanche and Yianni—he would never again in America be known as Yannelli—had their first child, Michael, named after Yianni's brother. In December 1941 a second son was born, George, named after Blanche's father. John Bakalis was now an American, and he would see to it that this ideal they talked about in his adopted land, "The American Dream," would be a reality for his two young boys.

Michael and George, 1981

ichael's journey was now complete. After thanking Philipos and Jenny for their help and saying goodbye, he headed home for Chicago. The search for his father, Yannelli, had ended. He had found answers to questions that had troubled him as well as answers to questions he had never known to ask. He had discovered much about his family's history and the origins and history of the Greek people whose blood still flowed in his veins. He had discovered noble deeds and good people as well as tragic events and deeply flawed people in his family's past.

The journey had not altered Michael's view of his father but only enhanced it. He was still the finest man he had ever known, but now he understood the origins of those admirable character traits. He was saddened knowing how much his father had given up, how his dreams and aspirations had been detoured and stopped by obstacles that were not of his making. He had previously known his father as a good and quiet man, one who said little but often displayed aspects of how he felt about many things—his family in Greece, his wife and children in America, and the country and village that had been his home and shaped him as a man. And now, as he reflected on his own childhood and upbringing, Michael realized what a powerful role model his father had been. As a child Michael had witnessed true love and respect between his mother and father. He had never heard or witnessed a negative word from his father or mother about each other; in fact, he had never witnessed anything that could even remotely be considered an argument or disagreement between them. He had never heard his father speak negatively about anyone or utter any word of prejudice toward any race, religion, or ethnicity in what must have been to him a strange multi-ethnic place like Chicago. And he had never heard even the mildest of profane words from his father's mouth. Yes, he had been a role model for what a real man should be, Michael thought.

And somehow, in his quiet way he along with Michael's mother had conveyed to their sons a strong drive, an intense work ethic, and a desire to succeed by being the best that they could be in whatever endeavor they were involved. So it was with a deep sense of pride and satisfaction that Yannelli, or John Bakalis as he was known in America, sat in the chambers of the Illinois House of Representatives in 1971 as his son, Michael, was inaugurated as the elected State Superintendent of Public Instruction for the State of Illinois, the first American of Greek ancestry to be elected to a statewide constitutional office. As Michael looked down into the seats from the platform where he was seated, he wondered what his father was thinking at that moment, this man with such a limited opportunity for an education watching his son with a PhD degree being sworn in as the head of all of Illinois education. And he wondered again what went through his father's mind when, just a few years later, he watched his younger son, George, being sworn in as a judge after having received his law degree and established a distinguished career as an attorney. Those Michael had met in Greece had told him that at a young age Yannelli often wondered if when he became an old man, he could judge as to whether he had had a successful life. Michael wondered if, at these two public ceremonies honoring his sons, his father could feel confident that he had succeeded.

278

When Michael completed his travels to assemble the pieces to his father's story, he met with his brother George to tell him what he had discovered.

"That's really interesting stuff," said George, sitting in his office located just outside the judge's chambers where he had been presiding just an hour before.

"It really is," Michael said. "It gives me a whole new perspective of who Dad was and what made him the kind of man he became."

"I wish I had been along with you to meet all those fascinating people," said George, "especially Alexandra, Dad's first love. It must have been kind of strange to meet her."

"It was different, I must admit," said Michael, "but she was a very nice lady. I think Mom might even have liked her."

'Well, I not so sure I'd go that far!" laughed George. "So," he continued, "did you find out anything more about any other relationships Dad might have had? I can't believe there weren't others. He came to America in his early 20s and didn't marry Mom until he was almost forty. Something must have happened."

"I really don't know," responded Michael. "I think you're right, there must have been some women he cared about during those years, but I was more interested in those formative years in Dad's life in Greece when he was shaped into the person he ultimately became. I really think I know him better now and, if possible, love and admire him even more now."

"Really?" questioned George. "Why do you say that?"

Michael stopped for a moment to collect his thoughts and try to summarize for his brother those things he better understood now about his father. His thoughts were momentarily distracted by the photograph hanging on the wall behind his brother's desk in his courthouse office. "You know, George," he started, "every time I come to your office I stare at that picture and tell myself that something is wrong here. Here you are in Illinois, a judge presiding in a court of law based on United States judicial precedents and cases settled with references to the Constitution of the United States of America and you have a picture of General Robert E. Lee hanging in your office, a man who led a rebellion against the United States of America and the very Constitution that you have sworn to uphold. Remember, in his lifetime, he was considered by many to be a traitor who was lucky he was not hanged or shot by a Union firing squad."

"Come on, don't be so dramatic," said George, sitting back in his chair, still attired in the black judicial robes he had on from the previous few hours when he had presided in the courtroom. "I admire Lee, the man and the general. He was a person who was, above all, a gentleman, torn by conflicting loyalties to the United States of America and to his native Virginia. He seldom, if ever, spoke negatively of anyone, including President Abraham Lincoln, and he lived by a code of honor and duty that he took very seriously. He was devoted to his family and to the military. He was caught in unique historical times and when the war was over, he dealt with defeat with dignity and did much to bring the nation together again. He was a man of character, Mike. Remember the respect and honor General Grant showed Lee at Appomattox? Grant knew Lee and understood the code he lived by, and he respected him. That's why he's on my wall."

Michael listened to his brother's explanation and defense of his photograph of General Lee. For a few moments he said nothing, thinking as he stared at the photograph on the wall. "George, you know what? He was not a general, but if you simply substitute Dad's name for Lee, almost everything you just said would be a description of all the things I discovered about Dad. The only difference is that Lee had the opportunity to fulfill his dream of a military career and Dad didn't."

George turned his swivel chair around almost full circle to once again view the picture that had hung on his wall for years. "Really?" he said. "Is that what you discovered about Dad?"

"Absolutely," said Michael. "I honestly believe he could have been a general if he had had the opportunity to make the military his career, but things, all family things, intervened, and he felt it his duty to deal with those things. All of the life experiences I discovered shaped him and his values, and it was those things that you and I, consciously and unconsciously, absorbed from him. He was truly a good and decent and honorable man. In Greece, I never once heard anyone say anything negative about him, and the same is true of anyone I ever met here at home. You know, I doubt you or I could pass that test. He was respected by people because he showed respect for them. He was liked and admired by people because, just as you and I experienced, no one ever heard him speak negatively about anybody or anything. Think about it, did we ever hear him once say anything negative against the Turks, like most other Greeks from Greece do? And that respect and attitude was evident toward women as well. For a man from rural Greece in his time, he was a clear exception who treated all women as he always treated men, with respect as equals. I think his experience with his sisters had a lot to do with that."

"I guess you're right," said George, thoughtfully considering what his brother was saying. "And you know, Mike, he never seemed to complain or regret, at least verbally, about having to leave his country and aspirations behind when he came here."

"Considering all he had been through and all he had experienced," said Michael, "he probably would have been justified to express some regret. Who knows? Maybe he did feel it sometimes to himself, but you are right, he never publicly said anything. What drove him, I discovered, and made him who he was were the exact same things you just said about General Lee: honor and duty. It was, to him, an honor and duty to serve his country. It was honor and duty that made him take on the troubles members of his family faced that I told you about. And it was honor and duty to his family that made him leave his home and family and his dreams and come to America. That's what he was all about George, that's what I discovered in Greece."

George listened, understanding for the first time aspects of his father that he, too, like his brother, had never really bothered to ask or think about while his father lived. "Mike, do you think in his older years he believed he had lived a successful life?"

Michael pondered George's question. A successful life? It was a concept that meant so many different things to different people. In America, he thought, people might make that judgment on the basis of wealth, fame, position, or status. Then, after thinking, he answered his brother.

"You know, George, he was probably the most successful man I ever met. I just hope you and I can be at least half the success he was. When it's all said and done, what really counts in life? Dad knew the answer, he understood. He was a devoted husband, a very good father, and he put his family, both in Greece and here, above anything and everything. You and I have been lucky; we have achieved a great deal in terms of education, respect, and recognition, but none of that would have been possible without how he lived, what he valued, what he sacrificed, and what he taught us by his example. So, yes, I know Dad could look back and feel that he had lived am successful life. Absolutely."

George nodded his head. Michael's journey had given him answers about his father as well, answers both had asked on that day of their father's funeral. But then, smiling and looking at his brother, he said, "But, Mike, you know you have gotten only half of the story."

"Half? What do you mean, half?" asked Michael.

"Well," said George, "now we know all about Dad's family, but what about Mom's side?"

About the Author

MICHAEL J. BAKALIS has had a career as an educator and government official. He served as State Superintendent of Education in Illinois as well as Illinois State Comptroller. He also served as Deputy Undersecretary of Education in the United States Department of Education and taught for many years at Northern Illinois University, Loyola University, and Northwestern University. He was the founder and current president of the American Quality Schools Corporation, a not-for-profit organization that manages charter schools in the Midwest. Mr. Bakalis received his Bachelor's, Master's, and PhD degrees from Northwestern University and has published widely in the fields of education, history, and public policy.